The Day Australia Fell

The Unforeseen Series Book One

Keith McArdle

National Library of Australia Cataloguing-in-Publication data:

McArdle, Keith, 1978- author.
 The Reckoning : The Day Australia Fell
 Unforeseen Series ; v. 1.
 978 0 9925657 0 1 (pbk.)
 1. War Stories. 2. Alternate History. 3.   Adventure Stories.
A823.3

Cover design by Adrijus Guscia, Rocking Book Covers

Connect with Keith online:
Website: http://www.keithmcardle.com
Facebook: https://www.facebook.com/KeithAuthor
Twitter: https://twitter.com/KeithAuthor

TABLE OF CONTENTS

ACKNOWLEDGEMENTS

My wife, Simone, you are my driving force. Thanks honey for supporting and always believing in me. Thanks also for giving me a kick in the pants when I needed it.

Many thanks to my proof readers Cameron Evers, Natalie & Pete Massicks and Anthony Crompton, your help and advice has been invaluable.

DEDICATION

This is dedicated to all the men and women who have served or are currently serving in the Australian or New Zealand Defence Force. You keep us safe and make us proud.

Kane was unconscious. He came to with a groan, groggily opened his eyes and stared up at the dark grey sky. His confused mind attempted to make sense of the muffled thuds and whip-like cracks near his head. Lethargically, he brushed mud from his face, licked dry lips with a parched tongue and tasted blood. With ears ringing, he rolled onto his side and looked at the crater at his feet. Amazing what one mortar round could do. On the other side of the crater lay two Australian soldiers. They had been cut to pieces by the explosion. Both were dead. The mortar round had landed almost on top of him, Christ knew how he survived. A sense of dread filled Kane as he focused across the open ground to the tree line from where the enemy soldiers were advancing. This was meant to be a live fire exercise and when the fire-fight began, Kane thought two Australian platoons had accidentally engaged each other. It had happened before. He yelled for a cease-fire and turned to his signaller, but before he could issue a command, saw the opposing force. Not only was his platoon vastly outnumbered, this was an enemy force. A real enemy force. Not some war game. They were hell bent on killing Kane and his entire platoon. He had seen the amphibious vehicles first. They had been advancing in a convoy, but upon seeing Kane's platoon, the first five vehicles had quickly moved out into extended line, stopped, and began deploying troops.

The high pitched ringing slowly faded to be replaced with shouts, semi-automatic rifle fire, explosions, and in the distance, the loud crackle of a machine gun. The ground shook with an explosion, the shock wave reverberating through his body as another mortar round landed in the near distance, violently throwing mud and grass skyward. Grabbing his rifle, Kane climbed to his feet and sprinted back towards a large tree behind which he went to ground. Rounds slammed into the ground nearby with powerful thuds.

"You alright, sir?" shouted a distant voice behind him.

"Yeah," Kane roared in reply, fired several shots and sprinted back to another firing position. After several short bounds he was with his soldiers again. Within minutes, Kane's platoon had withdrawn from the firefight and their weapons fell silent. They continued to take short bounds before going to ground behind trees and logs. Distant pops could still be heard from the advancing enemy, but this too stopped after a short time. The Australian bush was silent, not a bird cried or an insect buzzed. Branches creaked softly in the gentle breeze and the leaf litter crackled quietly as light rain began to fall. All was silent except for thudding boots on wet ground and sharp, rasping breathing as Kane and his men continued to withdraw into the scrub. The Indonesian force would not be far behind them.

SYDNEY AIRPORT - 0930 HRS

typical day. The sky was a bright blue, the sun beating down lending warmth to the people scurrying to or from the passenger jets. The airport, like a well-oiled machine, seemed to operate flawlessly.

Grant Bridge had been a security guard at the airport for almost thirteen years and he had seen some weird and wonderful sights. He stopped as the gate in front of him opened, allowing the passengers to depart the Boeing 737-800, a sleek looking aircraft accommodating 156 passengers. He loved aircraft. It belonged to the Indonesian Garuda Airlines fleet.

Grant glanced at the tail number and mentally noted that he had not seen this particular plane before. He waited as the passengers moved through the gate towards the baggage collection area. He paused and noticed they were all men, all aged in their early twenties, with only a few notable exceptions being older, but no older than forty. Every one of them were clean shaven with neat haircuts and, strangely enough, they all carried identical bags over their shoulder. Grant frowned. Following them, he unclipped the radio from his shoulder.

"Control, this is Golf 8," he spoke into the handset.

Moments later a crackled female voice responded, "This is control. Go ahead 8."

"We've got about a hundred and fifty people who have departed an Indonesian aircraft. They all look the same." He sighed as he realised how stupid he sounded.

"8, is this a joke?"

"Control, no, what I mean is they are all men, all fairly young, fit looking, all carrying similar bags. Just seems odd."

"8, monitor the situation and report back if anything looks suspect. Control out."

That was that he decided. His suspicion was probably misplaced, and the way he had made the report made him sound like some red neck country hick. He chuckled and shook his head.

Two of the men sat and placed their bags down chatting to one another. The others carried on, following the signs to the baggage carousels. Grant followed the large group, and as he passed the two seated men, he glanced at them. One of them had unzipped his bag, still chatting to the other.

Grant's heart stopped as he saw the man's hand curl around the pistol grip of a small weapon. From where he stood, it looked like an MP-10, a small machine gun capable of firing 9mm rounds. These bullets were lethal at close range.

The Indonesian looked up at that moment and his eyes locked onto Grant's. Determination washed over the man's face and he pulled the gun out, bringing it round to bear. What happened next seemed to take place in slow motion. As Grant reached for his own piece, a Glock 17, an image of his wife's face appeared in his mind, clear as crystal. She had a beautiful smile, then as quickly as her face had appeared, it vanished. His hand gripped the weapon and brought it clear. He fired twice into the man's face, which disappeared in pink mist as his body slumped to the side.

The second man was on his feet and had thrown the bag from his weapon. He fired a short burst towards Grant, who stood rooted to the spot. Something which sounded like an angry bee, buzzed past his face. The muffled sound of screaming and panic echoed around him as he brought the Glock around to point at the second attacker. He could issue a warning, but given the situation, that would be useless. He fired three times, the first round ripping through the man's bicep, the second and third taking him in the centre of his chest. The corpse hit the floor with a dull thud.

"That way," he roared at the screaming, panic filled throng of civilians behind him, pointing away from where the gunfight had taken place.

They turned and fled, pushing and shoving each other, trying to get away from the danger. One Chinese man, however, ran towards him. Christ! There was always one. The man was elderly, and as unbelievable as it might seem, maybe he had not heard the guns and was confused as to what was happening. He stopped the man who yelled a sentence at him in Mandarin.

"That way!" he yelled, pointing behind the elderly man. Glancing over Grant's shoulder, the man's eyes widened in fear and he ran away.

Whirling, Grant watched as the group of Indonesians all now with weapons in their hands, had taken up positions. One stood and took aim at him.

"You've got to be kidding me," yelled Grant to no one in particular as he sprinted for the closest door to him, which was the female toilet. He barged through the door as he heard the weapons firing outside. He smashed into the next door, bounced off and fell onto his arse.

Grant looked up and saw the word 'Pull' clearly marked under the handle. He cursed savagely, scrambled to his feet and pulled the door hard, stepping through. Nervously fumbling the set of master keys attached to his belt, he locked the door behind him. Grant sat against the wall with a sigh. Fear gripped him as he realised he would probably die here. In a toilet block. In a fucking toilet block.

He tightly squeezed the transmission button on his radio and spoke, his voice wavering with nervous tension. "Control, this is Golf 8! We are under attack! I repeat! We are under attack! Shots fired! Almost two hundred armed men! Near Gate 76!"

The several seconds of radio silence that followed felt like an eternity before an equally worried voice emanated from the receiver, "Golf 8, roger that."

Grant shook his head and checked his Glock. Pulling the magazine clear he emptied the rounds onto his palm. Six rounds, one up the spout. He pushed the bullets back into the magazine and slapped the magazine into the weapon. Not much good against almost two hundred soldiers.

He thought of the old Chinese man and hoped he had survived. Hearing the squeak of hinges, he knew the first door to the female toilets had been pushed open. A rattle followed as they tried to open the locked door. He could hear Indonesian voices whispering outside the door. Then they fell silent. The hinges squeaked again as they left, but not before he heard a dull metallic thud right outside his door.

What the fuck was that? His brain instantly began analysing the sound. He had never heard it before, but fear washed over him as he realised it was probably a grenade or some other kind of explosive device. He stood and dived through a toilet door, landing near the bowl. Grant wrapped his arms around the toilet with all his strength and hoped for the best.

The explosion that followed, rocked him to the core, but that was the only damage it did. To him anyway. As for the door, it was a ruin. Unknown to Grant, in the immediate aftermath of the detonation, an Indonesian soldier had stepped through. He held his breath as he heard booted feet slowly crush the shards of ceramic, concrete, and wood on the tiles of the toilet block.

Glancing around the toilet behind which he was taking cover he could see a man's legs from the knees down. Slowly raising the Glock, he took careful aim and fired a shot. The round slammed into the man's left knee, his weapon dropped to the floor with a clatter and he fell to the tiles, screaming with pain and holding his knee. Taking a breath, Grant aimed again and fired a shot into his enemy's head. The screaming stopped abruptly and Grant was on his feet. Barging through the door he ran forward and scooped up the small machine gun. Holstering his Glock, he pulled the MP-10 into his shoulder, aimed towards the doorway and walked backwards towards his original position.

He blinked as a small round object was hurled into the toilet block, it bounced off a wall with a metallic clink and came to rest at Grant's feet.

"Fuck!" Grant shouted as he looked down at the grenade. Acting without thinking, he picked up the grenade, ran forward and tossed it back out the door. He heard a string of incomprehensible Indonesian words, but the urgency in the voice was clear in any language. Grant ran from the doorway and squatted in a corner as the explosion reverberated through his feet.

Standing, he pulled the MP-10 into his shoulder again. He could hear his heart beat thundering in his ears as he felt the adrenalin pumping through his body. Glancing at the body on the floor, he noticed that another grenade was attached to his belt. Keeping the weapon pointed at the doorway, he knelt beside the corpse and with one hand managed to detach the grenade.

Holding the weapon between his upper arm and his chest, with trembling hands he pulled the pin out of the grenade and with two long strides was at the shattered doorway. As he glanced around the corner he could see that the external door was in numerous pieces, partly hanging off its hinges with the rest scattered in small pieces on either side of the threshold. Grant could see out into the airport. He saw nothing but clean carpet and some empty seats in the distance. There was no noise and no movement. With a sharp breath he stepped forward, threw the grenade out and ran back into the toilet block, taking cover. There were no shouts this time. The explosion thundered, but again no shouting, no movement, no noise.

After almost ten minutes of gathering the little that remained of his courage, Grant edged toward the internal doorway. He stepped through, the weapon pulled into his shoulder. At the external doorway he carefully looked around, but could see no one. On the carpet, there was a large, fake pot plant lying on its side. The clay pot had smashed. Stepping out into the airport itself, he looked both ways but could see no one. He flinched as the noise of distant gunfire and screaming broke the silence. This was like an alien landscape. Usually people were scurrying back and forth chatting and laughing, the public address system was almost constant as announcements called for late passengers, reported flight arrivals, departures, delays, cancellations. Now? Silence. Utter silence. Although a faint smell of fresh coffee still lingered in the air.

A neon light flickered softly nearby and a half full Coke Zero bottle lay on the carpet beside a bench seat. He could see a dark patch of liquid on the carpet and as he knelt by it, he realised it was blood. He was not sure whether one of the Indonesians had been injured, or if an unfortunate passenger had been in the wrong place. Standing, he moved slowly down the deserted airport lounge towards the exit. Another long crackle of distant gunfire shattered the silence. Grant made sure he watched behind him as he moved. He had no idea where the Indonesian soldiers were. He did know, however, that they would think nothing of killing him.

Another crackle of gunfire erupted in the distance, and with it more screams, shouting and a noise he knew all too well. It was a popping sound, many in quick succession; the unmistakeable noise of a Glock-17 handgun. Grant now knew that other security guards had joined the fight. Automatic gunfire bellowed out again. This time it was sustained, the constant chattering never falling quiet. Dispersed between the gunfire however, was that all too familiar popping. Grant began to run, holding the MP-10 sub machine gun with both hands. The gunfight became louder as his breathing became more ragged and strained. He noticed as he passed that one of the viewing platforms was riddled with bullet holes, and there sat an elderly couple slumped against each other in their final embrace. They had each taken a bullet to the head.

A woman lay face down on the floor outside Gate 48, the carpet dark and wet around her, blood covered her top. He continued to run, his chest burning and his legs growing weaker with each minute. The gunfire was very loud now. More bodies. At a glance he counted nearly ten in the group. Grant never thought he would live to witness this. Not in his lifetime.

"Control, this is Golf 8," he gasped into the radio. No response. He tried to make radio contact again. Nothing.

Darting around a corner near Gate 26, the air around him came to life with the frightening and very powerful noise of bullets passing by at close range. Running to a wall, he took cover behind a concrete pillar. He had never experienced this before, and never wanted to again.

He flinched as tiny chips of concrete were ripped from the pillar by ricocheting bullets. With fear washing over him, Grant crept towards the edge of the pillar and glanced around it. He could see at least six guards in the near distance taking cover behind similar pillars. One was slumped with his back to the wall, cradling his arm. The guard was not moving and very pale. The uniform near his shoulder was soaking wet with bright red blood. The guard's foot jumped as a bullet slammed into his lower leg, but the man did not move. He was dead.

"Christ," muttered Grant. He licked his lips, hands shaking with adrenalin mixed with a deep-pitted terror. "Christ," he repeated, took a deep breath and ran from cover. Grant sprinted as fast as he was able, taking up a position behind a pillar closer to his comrades where he waited for the enemy fire to find interest elsewhere. He realised he was screaming at the top of his voice. Breathing hard he peeked around the corner, brought his MP-10 up and stared down the sights. He could see part of a leg sticking out from a pillar in the distance, the man was kneeling. Grant released a long burst. A spray of pink mist exploded from the leg and the Indonesian fell sideways, gritting his teeth, his face contorted in agony. Grant fired again, this time bullets stitched the man's chest and throat. The Indonesian went still. Instead of feeling triumph and anger, he felt sick. Holding the vomit at bay, he tried to gain the attention of his comrades, but they were all facing away from him, in their own personal battle against the Indonesians. One of them turned from the pillar behind which she was taking cover and began reloading a magazine. She glanced up, met Grant's gaze and nodded, her face full of terror. She knew she would probably die today.

Movement caught Grant's eye and he brought his gun up, firing another long burst at an Indonesian who had run from cover away from him. A round hammered into the man's right butt cheek. If it weren't so serious, it would be funny. He pulled the trigger again, but the MP-10 was out of ammunition. The Indonesian hopped away, but not before a bullet hit him in the square of his back. One of the guards was up and running forward. He took cover, fired three quick shots and then ducked out of sight. The Indonesian was writhing on the floor, trying to crawl away.

Grant swore loudly and sprinted from cover again, moving quickly forward and diving to the ground behind another pillar. Pushing himself into a kneeling position, he slung the MP-10 and drew his Glock. The Indonesian who he had shot so recently was now still. Enemy gunfire was not so incessant, as the Indonesians had mostly withdrawn from the fight, leaving several to fight a rear guard action. Realising this, Grant was content to stay behind the pillar to wait for the remaining enemy to move away as well.

In the distance, a thundering noise grew steadily into a crescendo. He knew that sound. It was the familiar roar of helicopters. Not just one or two, but a lot of them. He could hear the whup-whup of their blades and feel the vibration through his feet. They must have been very low. Then he saw them through the glass of the nearest viewing platform. Blackhawks. There were ten of them, maybe more, in close formation and flying fast. The aircraft must have been pushing more than 250 kilometres per hour. Within moments they were gone.

Looking at his watch, Grant dared to breathe again. "Thank God," he exhaled, knowing the Army had arrived. "Oh thank God."

In less than a minute, a distant firefight began, although he could not hear individual weapons. It was more a wall of sound, interrupted by the thundering roar of grenades, and less powerful, muffled crumps. He knew the latter noise was probably tear gas being deployed. The intense fight seemed to stop within moments of it starting. Grant looked at his watch again. Less than three minutes had passed.

"Clear!" a voice distant voice shouted. This same word he heard over and over again, only it was slowly growing louder.

"Guys!" shouted one of the security guards. He recognised Shorty's voice. "Come here, now!"

On legs of jelly, their hands shaking, the guards gathered around Shorty. There were five of them all up. He knew that in section D of Sydney Airport, on any given shift, there should have been twelve guards on duty. They had taken heavy losses.

"It's over," Shorty said. "Now everyone drop your weapons and put your hands on your head. It's important we don't look like a threat. These guys don't fuck about. If they think you're a threat, they will kill you!" he spoke the last four words slowly, to emphasise the importance of that point.

Grant remembered Shorty had been a soldier. He probably knew what he was talking about. They dropped their Glocks in a small pile. Grant dropped the MP-10 on top of the pile and stepped away.

Shorty's eyes lit up and a grin opened up on his face when he saw the sub-machinegun. "Well done mate!"

The guards stood in an extended line, hands on head, and waited. Grant was replaying the events in his head over and over. His legs shook and his heart thundered in his chest. Only now did he begin to smell the strong aroma of cordite in the air. One of the guards bent over and vomited on the floor. He groaned and vomited again. Muttering a string of profanities, he moved away and dry retched. As the sickly smell of warm vomit drifted over them, the guards moved away from the area several metres.

Grant could still hear the shouts of "clear!" They were loud, and he knew the Australian soldiers, probably TAG East were almost on top of them. He had read about TAG East in the Sydney Daily Telegraph only weeks before. Tactical Assault Group East. The group was made up predominantly of Commandos, with members of the SAS and Navy Clearance Divers dispersed throughout the unit.

He flinched as he saw them come around the corner. They moved quickly and with purpose. He had the overwhelming feeling that they missed nothing as they scanned the scene before them. The soldiers were dressed completely in black, their faces hidden by black gasmasks, which gave them an almost inhuman quality.

Thirty or forty brushed passed the motionless guards without a word or a sideways glance. Five of them remained in the near distance, their weapons now pointed towards the ground.

"You five, get over here!" a muffled voice yelled.

The guards needed no encouragement. With a sigh of relief, they moved as one.

"Hurry up!" the muffled voice shouted.

"Am I glad to see you boys," said Shorty. "I thought…"

"Shut up and move," growled one, grabbing Shorty by the collar and pushing him forward. "Faster!"

The guards ran at a trot, with several black-garbed soldiers in front of them and a couple behind. It was not long before they came upon the scene of the fire-fight. Dead Indonesians littered the carpet everywhere. One of the guards began dry retching again.

"Get moving!" barked a soldier, pushing him forward.

The brass casings of spent cartridges also littered the floor and the smell of cordite that enveloped the area was so strong Grant could almost taste it. He coughed and spluttered, his eyes watering and throat constricting as the lingering trace of tear gas assaulted his senses. He was rewarded with a shove in the back as he slowed down to cough. After some time, the dead Indonesians became fewer in number, and the corrosive scent of tear gas dissipated.

Within minutes they had been taken downstairs towards the baggage carousels and were being ushered into a large crowd. There must have been several hundred people gathered in the area, chatting softly, crying quietly or simply silent, staring like stunned mullets. Grant thought there would be dozens of these groups throughout Sydney Airport. He noticed another group of guards nearby and after gesturing to his colleagues, the group made their way over.

"What the hell just happened?" asked one, his voice shaking.

No one replied.

"Nasty bastards," muttered the female guard as she eyed the departing backs of the black clad soldiers.

"They've got a job to do. We need to be secured and kept out of their way, simple as that," replied another. It made sense.

After what seemed an age, the helicopters returned and more soldiers were delivered, this time dressed in normal camouflage uniforms. There were medics carrying backpacks of equipment, general infantrymen carrying boxes of food and water, as well as three Army chaplains. The chaplains would be busy today, reassuring the living and praying over the dead. Today would go down as a black day in Australia's history. But as the crowd stood together in silence, listening to one of the chaplains as he told them what was going on and how they would proceed from here, none of them knew just how bad it really was. Every airport in each capital city of Australia had been attacked in the same way at exactly the same time.

It would be only a matter of hours before the Australian government would realise the attacks on their major airports, which had tied up all of Australia's anti-terrorist capability, had been nothing but a decoy…

Hay Point Coal Terminal
1030 hrs - Day of assault on all major Australian airports

"**Bill?**"

Bill grunted in partial acknowledgement as he flicked through The Daily Mercury, chuckling at a Garfield cartoon. Mackay, situated on the central coast of Queensland, Australia, about twelve hour's drive north of Brisbane, was a great place to live. The weather was beautiful all year round. It was great fishing weather and Bill knew where he would rather be, but today he was at work in the operations room of the Hay Point Coal Terminal. The operations room was situated on the land side of the one kilometre long conveyor belt that fed coal to the bulk carriers waiting out at sea.

Bill glanced up. "Yeah," he finally replied.

"What's this dickhead doing?" John muttered holding a pair of binoculars to his eyes.

Bill picked up his binoculars and altered them until he was focused on a bulk carrier that had broken clear of the queue. Coal carriers could wait anchored in line at Hay Point for days, sometimes weeks at a time as ships in front of them were filled with coal. Today, there were no less than twelve in line, each patiently awaiting their turn. But Bill was focused on the Indonesian flagged bulk carrier that had raised its anchor and was steaming towards the coast away from the others.

"Raise him," Bill said.

Using the intricate, not to mention, very expensive radio system they had in place, John tried several times to speak to the captain of the ship in question. There was no reply.

While he kept the binoculars to his face, Bill picked up a nearby phone, dialled a memorised number and as soon as it was answered said, "Activate the chopper."

"Yeah, ahead of ya mate. Already done," came the reply.

Bill replaced the handset and put the binoculars down, a frown of confusion on his face.

"What the hell's he doing?" Bill asked.

"No idea, but in another half click he's going to run aground."

Bill grunted again and turned to watch the helicopter as it flew slowly out towards the Indonesian bulk carrier. The helicopter stationed at Hay Point was used to fly out specialists, and sometimes interpreters to land on the ships to talk to the captain. Sometimes wires were crossed or a captain did not understand exactly how the process worked. In these situations it was easier to land on deck and approach the ship's captain face-to-face.

"Keep an eye on 'im," Bill said gesturing towards the Indonesian bulk carrier that was still powering towards the coast. "I'm getting a coffee, want one?"

"Yeah, righto," muttered John, staring through the binoculars.

He had worked coffee making into a fine art and within minutes Bill had returned with two steaming cups. He put them down and remained on his feet, hands on hips, watching the bulk carrier. It had slowed somewhat, but was still heading towards the coast. The chopper had almost arrived. It slowed to a hover and began to descend towards the deck of the ship.

Bill sat with a grunt and picked up his coffee. As he was bringing the cup to his lips, he saw a bright flash from the deck of the ship and a dark object streaked through the sky, slamming into the helicopter in a ball of flame. The chopper began to spin out of control.

The pilot had barely commenced his mayday transmission before the helicopter hammered into the ocean, a plume of seawater erupting into the air. Then the noise of the distant explosion rolled over the operations room. It sounded like a mighty bass drum had been struck.

Bill lowered his coffee carefully back onto the desk, his mouth open, and his eyes never leaving the small area of sea into which the chopper had disappeared.

"Jesus Christ!" yelled John, "Did you just fucking see that?" his chair went flying back into the wall as he leapt to his feet.

Despite the shock of what they had just witnessed, Bill quickly gathered his thoughts and in moments began to hit his stride. The emergency procedure. He jumped into action, picked up the phone and dialled a number he had never had to use before. It was listed neatly on a piece of paper attached to the far wall. After he punched in the numbers he waited quietly as it began to ring.

"Christ," shouted John, still on his feet, his hands clasped over his head. "They shot the bloody chopper down!"

"Quiet!" shouted Bill, "I know!"

He cleared his throat as the phone was picked up on the other end.

"Bill Hues here, calling from Hay Point Coal Terminal. We just lost a chopper." Bill blurted the words out. "An Indonesian bulk carrier shot it down. We need you here now!" A long pause was accompanied by an incredulous look. "What do you mean you're too bloody busy? Bullshit! We need you!"

As Bill continued his now strained conversation with the Australian Federal Police, he watched as the bulk carrier slowed to a stop and dropped anchor. Within minutes, a vertical crack began to appear in the centre of the hull. The crack became wider. Bill fumbled with his binoculars before bringing them to his face with a shaking hand. The front of the ship was opening up slowly, and with a sinking heart he saw the deck within the ship. It was filled with a mighty hovercraft that took up the width of the ship. But that was not what filled Bill with abject fear. As the great doors swung fully open and the hovercraft left the bulk carrier to begin its journey towards the shore, his eyes moved back to the ship. He saw the deck was lined with military vehicles, four abreast and as far back as the light streaming in would allow. Finally the amphibious vehicles moved forward one after the other. They drove into the ocean and made their way under speed towards the coast of Queensland.

"It gets worse," Bill muttered into the phone.

The amphibious assault vessels stopped short of the coast, their daunting hulks bobbing gently in the calm ocean. The hovercraft had moved up onto the beach and was offloading steel slabs one after the other. A huge team of soldiers quickly worked together to piece the makeshift road straight up the beach and onto the bitumen road on the other side. Within twenty minutes they had finished. The convoy of amphibious assault vehicles, perhaps fifty in total, accelerated onto the road of steel, up the beach and onto the bitumen road. At the highway, they turned ominously towards Mackay, one after the other like clockwork. Cars that were in the way were either rammed off the road, or shot to pieces. After twenty minutes the convoy set up a defensive perimeter in Mackay airport, killed or captured the staff and made ready for the numerous C-130 Hercules aircraft that were already airborne from Indonesia. The aircraft were filled with soldiers and military hardware.

THE RECKONING

One hour after Australia's entire anti-terrorist capability was committed in every airport of each capital city, Indonesia's Marines made landfall in remote locations like Mackay to secure the airports. Remote airports in every state of Australia were captured and within hours, Indonesian military aircraft began touching down.

Five hundred Indonesian paratroopers jumped over the Riverina region of Southwest, New South Wales. In less than three hours they had secured one hundred and thirty thousand hectares of rice.

Ben, a twenty-seven year old computer builder, grabbed cans of baked beans, spaghetti, tuna, in fact every can of food he had in the pantry. He shoved them all in a bag, ran for the car, threw it all in and started the vehicle. Swearing, he climbed back out of the car and marched to the front door before realising it was locked. Running back to the car, he switched it off, took out the keys and returned to unlock the front door. Striding past the television still showing muted vision of the attacks on Australia's airports, he went out into the backyard to the garden shed. It was padlocked. He swore loudly. The key was inside but time was of the essence so he kicked the door hard. It buckled, but still held. Kicking it again the door buckled at an impossible angle but remained shut. A curtain flickered in the window of the next door neighbour's house and the face of an elderly woman appeared. She scowled at him.

"Wanna take a bloody photo?" Ben shouted, kicking the shed door a third time. The door gave way and he fell to the ground with a curse. The old lady was laughing now.

Picking himself up, he brushed himself off and pushed his way into the garden shed. He grabbed the ten litre petrol container. It was full. Retreating from the shed, he stumbled back out onto the lawn and looked triumphantly back at the neighbour's house. The old lady was scowling again. He grinned, gave her the finger and ran back inside.

Climbing back into the car he turned the key. Nothing. The vehicle could be a temperamental piece of crap sometimes, but persistence usually won the day. Turning the key again the engine roared to life, blue smoke wafting into view in his rear vision mirror. He crunched it into reverse, flattened the accelerator and backed out onto the road, the nose of his vehicle scraping the driveway loudly. Slamming it into first gear he dropped the clutch and stalled.

As he turned the key he noticed that the old lady was back, this time at the front door of her house. She was still scowling. Ben turned the key, the engine once again roared to life. The old lady shook her head as Ben accelerated away, giving his neighbour a couple of friendly beeps.

He roared around the corner, heading for his parent's house on the south side of town. They lived near the airport, so although they purchased the house at a very decent price, they were forced to put up with the noise of the airport for most of the year. Ben screamed to a stop behind a car at a set of red lights. He revved the engine a couple of times and within seconds the lights turned green. The car in front remained stationary.

Ben cursed. "For fuck sake. Go!"

It was then that he noticed the driver of the car in front, an elderly gentleman, was staring at Ben in his rear vision mirror.

"Don't bloody stare! Drive! What is it with you bloody geriatrics?"

The old man shook his head and slowly moved off across the intersection. When Ben had just entered the intersection, the traffic lights turned amber. With a curse he flattened the accelerator and roared around the outside of the old man's car, coming to a violent halt at the next red light. The elderly man rolled to a gentle stop behind him. Ben stared at him in the rear view mirror. The old man was shaking his head with a frown creasing his already lined face. Then he started beeping at Ben.

"Settle down pops," Ben said to the rear view mirror, watching as the old man leant on the horn.

"Senile old prick." Looking away from the rear view and noticing the lights had gone green, Ben dropped the clutch and stalled. He turned the key. Nothing.

"You piece of shit!" shouted Ben, slamming his hand onto the steering wheel. Again he turned the key, which produced several clicks, but the engine remained silent. The old man behind him slowly pulled out, and drove sedately around him. As he passed, he caught Ben's eye and flipped him the bird, before carrying on down the road. Ben couldn't help but see the funny side of the moment. He chuckled and turned the key once more. The engine roared into life just as the lights turned red.

Eventually, he reached the south side of town. During the last several kilometres of his drive, he had noticed thick smoke turning the sky dark. As he looked upon the airport, he pulled over and stopped. Applying the handbrake, he opened his door and got out, looking out over the devastation in quiet horror. Half of the homes of the south side were alight, and many had already burned to the ground. Judging where his parents lived, he looked down at the area. It was well alight, flames towering over the houses, black smoke spewing into the sky.

"Bloody hell," Ben said, fumbling in his pocket and taking out his phone.

Dialling his father's mobile number it rang out to voice mail. He tried four more times, each with the same result. Leaving a brief voice message, he ended the call. Staring out at the airport, he noticed military vehicles had overrun the area.

Climbing back into the car, he accelerated away from the curb and down towards his parent's house. As he drove, the smoke became thicker, to the point where he could only see twenty metres in front of him. He had not seen a soul, not a person or a vehicle. What the hell was going on?

Suddenly out of the smoke appeared a woman carrying a little girl. They were running down the middle of the road. He slammed on the brake and came to an abrupt halt. Both the woman and the girl had the neck of their shirts up over their nose and mouth.

"Help us!" screamed the woman.

Ben opened his door and coughed as the thick smoke invaded the car. He climbed out and ran around to them. The woman had shoulder length, light brown hair and piercing blue eyes.

"Are you alright?"

"Yes," she replied, but tears cut through the dark soot that stained her face.

"Get in, I've gotta find my parents," said Ben.

The mother and daughter climbed into the car. As Ben was about to move off, the woman grasped the handbrake.

"Don't go down there," she pleaded. "My God don't go down there."

"I've gotta find my parents!"

"They're either dead or prisoners! For Christ sake, don't go down there! Just drive, I'll explain."

"Where the hell do we go?" Ben asked.

"My father's place, he lives out of town. Out west. Get on the road leading out past the old sugar mill, I'll tell you where to turn off."

"What's happened?" asked Ben.

"It's a terrorist attack. We're under attack!"

Ben had been driving for almost three hours now. He looked across at Katie. She was still awake, but was staring out the window at the passing terrain. She looked sad and terrified all at once. Jade was fast asleep on the backseat. She was only five years old and the day had taken a terrible toll on her both mentally and physically. There was a good chance that their way of life was gone forever. Katie had introduced herself and her daughter, but had not spoken much after that. Ben just drove and did not try to force conversation. Apart from the one or two other cars they had overtaken, the road was deserted. The only other signs of life were a goanna, that scuttled into the bush before the car reached it, several kangaroos, and a large brown snake sunbaking on the opposite side of the road.

"Take your next left," Katie spoke quietly, gesturing at a small road in the distance. The road was dirt, and Ben was forced to slow down to a more sedate pace. His tyres were almost bald, so he knew it would only take a little oversteer to be amongst the thick bushland either side of them. It would not end happily.

"Jesus, how much further?" Ben asked.

"A long way yet," replied Katie as she resumed gazing out the window. "Dad lives on a cattle property. This is all his property, but the house is still another forty or fifty k's yet."

Ben whistled, slowing as the road dipped down to a creek crossing. It was as dry as a bone.

"That's a lot of land!"

"Not really," Katie said, "stations up in the Territory can be tens of millions of acres in size. Dad's is only tiny compared to those ones." She managed a weak smile.

After almost another hour of driving, Ben drove over a cattle grid, guarded by two large hardwood posts either side of the road. The posts were at least 6 metres in height and between them hung a large slab of hardwood carved into which were the words "Bent Wood Cullen Bone". A narrow dirt track that served as the driveway wound around a small hillock, down through a shallow creek and through a pine plantation. The two kilometre driveway opened out at last, giving way to a huge single story brick house. There was a black Nissan Navara parked out front.

The house was surrounded by a wide deck and sitting on a chair watching them, a rifle leaning against the wall nearby was a large man in his sixties. He was not fat, but neither lean. It was easy to see that he had been very well built at one time.

"Grandad!" shrieked Jade, stretching in the back seat. She pushed her foot into the back of Ben's seat as she stretched.

Katie smiled and waved. By this time the man was on his feet and walking towards them.

Katie introduced the two men as they climbed out of their seats. "Ben, this is my father, Mick."

Mick looked Ben up and down, grunted, and held out his hand. Ben winced as Mick's strong handshake strangled his fingers. The older man was bloody strong!

"And where are you from?" asked Mick, kneeling down to pick up his granddaughter.

"Originally from Sydney. Had to get away from the big smoke though. Was driving me crazy."

Mick nodded. "Pansy city boy, eh?" he said turning away.

"Dad!" admonished Katie, looking at Ben and rolling her eyes. "Sorry, he's a bit abrupt."

Ben shrugged. "That's alright."

Later that evening they sat around the dinner table talking. Mick had been listening to the radio throughout the day. He hated television and refused to own one. Mick had heard about the attacks on the major airports in the capital cities, however, the assault on the airport in town was disturbing news to him. Whilst Jade lay curled up under a blanket on a mattress in the corner, the adults talked in hushed whispers as they listened to the radio. It became evident that Australia was currently being invaded by Indonesia on all coastlines and in every state. If only it were a terrorist attack as Katie had originally thought. If only.

The news on the radio was a running commentary on what was taking place around the country. For the time being, Darwin had been the only capital city to come under sustained attack by the Indonesians and prevail against the onslaught. A combined force of Australian infantry, an Australian armoured battalion and United States Marines had fought the Indonesians to a stand still, eventually overrunning them. The Northern Territory was well geared for an onslaught from the North and their training had paid off. However, it was only a slim victory in the coming war. Indonesia simply went around Darwin.

As they tried to remain awake, they listened as town after town came under Indonesian martial law. Rumours began about concentration camps, where Australian citizens who had not been killed were being held prisoner in seemingly appalling conditions. The death toll climbed as the hours ground on, and then some time just before 3:00 AM the sobering voice of the radio news presenter stated that Sydney had fallen. The Australian Defence Force had fought a hard, well planned action, which began on the coast and finished on the streets of inner Sydney. The ADF, however, had been badly outnumbered and were eventually overrun. Sydney was isolated, the first capital city to fall into the hands of hostile forces. As mass panic ensued, Sydney's populace began fleeing. Thousands were killed in cold blood. Some tried to fight back against the newcomers, but the uprising was put down with extreme and rapid violence.

Feeling that she could take no more, Katie rushed out of the room in tears. Mick simply sat back in his chair, arms folded, staring at the ceiling, occasionally shaking his head. Ben simply stared out the window at the blackness outside. Neither man could believe what he was hearing.

The emotion was evident in the radio presenter's voice as he continued the commentary. The host fielded a telephone call from a listener who suggested that Indonesia were using large 12-wheeled armoured vehicles upon which were mounted 50-foot antennas. These vehicles were dotted around the country to create a secure communication network for the command and control element of the Indonesian force. Within thirty minutes, a defence spokesman confirmed on air that the 12-wheeled vehicles were a reality and were definitely communication vehicles. If anyone were to see one, they were advised to immediately call the crisis hotline number the government had established in the hours after the attacks began. Mick wrote the number down on a piece of scrap paper and stuck it to the wall beside the radio.

Mick dozed in his chair and Ben lay on the floor nearby, snoring softly. Neither man heard the news that following a hard fight, Melbourne had also fallen to the invaders. At 4:58 AM, as the household slept, the radio presenter's voice was replaced with quiet static. His voice never returned. They were cut off and alone.

CHAPTER THREE

*"*__B__*ritish Prime Minister Martin Hughes joins US President Andrew Baker in condemning Indonesian invasion of Australia. United Nations summit to be held tomorrow."* The Sun newspaper, London.

Williamtown Airbase, New South Wales

With the start-up procedure complete, Jase taxied his FA-18 Super Hornet to the end of the runway, turned and was immediately given permission to take off. Jase and his wingman, Mack, throttled up to full afterburner and took off together in a tight formation. One hour before, Mackay had been attacked by an enemy force and their mission was not only to scout the area, but to wreak havoc amongst the attackers.

Jason had been a fighter pilot now for twelve years, and had only seen a smattering of real missions over war torn Iraq, and several 'hush-hush' missions over Afghanistan. But aside from that, most of his career had been consumed with training. He had never expected to use his skill-set against foreign troops in Australia. The loud, deep rumble of the runway went silent as the wheels lifted. The landing gear tucked itself smoothly away and the fighters banked north, climbing and accelerating. The 1,600 km journey would take less than 90 minutes.

They levelled off at 15,000 feet and had crossed over the border into Queensland almost 40 minutes into the flight. Although they rocketed over Brisbane, Jase had enough time to cast a glance over the tiny city below him. He thought it odd that so many coal carriers were so close to the city's port.

When they were still 200km south of Mackay they began seeing the black smoke spewing into the sky. It must have been coming from the burning city. As they flew north, the smoke became darker until it eventually blotted the ground from view completely. With 50 km to fly before they descended to scout the airport, Mack's voice boomed into his earpiece.

"Bandits, bandits, bandits, bearing one-niner-zero, closing fast."

Jase instinctively flicked the safety off, spotted the pair of black dots climbing towards them. He changed radar with his thumb, checked the Identify Friend or Foe (IFF) and saw the approaching aircraft were no friends. The Australian fighters flew past the approaching enemy aircraft beneath them, rolled inverted, pulled back and descended into the dogfight.

Within 15 seconds Jase was 2km behind one of the bandits. Mack had made a hard turn as he chased the second bandit, but at this point in time, Jase was concentrated on the enemy aircraft in front of him. The FA-18's main-gun belched a second long burst and the bandit went into a break turn to the right, laying down a string of flares. Jase entered the break turn chasing his opponent and commenced the G strain. The G strain was a manoeuvre to help maintain the blood in the pilot's head, and thus keep him conscious. It consisted of tensing the lower body and concentrating on heavy, rhythmic breathing all whilst being aware of what the opponent was doing.

Behind the bandit again, Jase fired another short burst from the fighter's Gatling gun and watched as the enemy rolled inverted, pulled back and dived towards the ground far below them. Once again flares burst from the aircraft, which would have defeated any missile that might have fired. Jase took a breath, rolled on his back and pulled back hard. He lost sight of the bandit. Continuing to pull back and conducting the G strain, Jase looked straight up though the canopy and saw his opponent rocketing away beneath him. The noise made by the FA-18 as pilots conducted this inverted turn was affectionately called "under the waterfall" because that is exactly what it sounded like.

The bandit was level now and conducting a break turn to the left, but there was nothing Jase could do about it. He was still pulling back to avoid the ground, which was not as distant as it had been seconds before. Now level, he entered another break turn as he continued to chase. He was less than 500 metres behind. The bandit began a series of jinks, which were random flight patterns, rolls, sharp descents and ascents. He knew that the bandit had exhausted all of his defensive tactics. Then he saw an opening for a shot. It would last less than 2 seconds, he knew. With a dull thump, the heat seeking missile rocketed from Jase's plane. The bandit began a break turn and deployed flares, but too late. The missile ignored the nearby flares and turned the bandit into a fireball.

"Splash," muttered Jase. He could feel the sweat on his brow. The dogfight had lasted about 25 seconds and the Super Hornet had burned almost 200 pounds of fuel. He had also descended to 3,000 feet. Glancing up through the canopy, he saw Mack darting and weaving far above him as he chased the bandit. The chase lasted less than a minute before the bandit was shot down. The FA-18s rejoined formation and continued towards Mackay's airport, wary of any other enemy aircraft on combat air patrol in the area.

They flew low, called map of the earth, to help reduce the chance of radar detection. Flying well below the smoke cloud, within minutes houses were zipping by beneath them. Banking sharply, they turned towards the airport. The place was like an ant's nest, aircraft were landing one after the other. Two C-130 heavy lift aircraft were waiting at the end of the tarmac for the signal to take off. Attack helicopters were parked neatly side by side on the flight line. Then they had flown by.

"Christ," said Jase.

"Yeah, quite," agreed Mack. "Let's take another look and see if we can't do some damage."

The FA-18s turned back towards the airport. The main gun belched a long, loud burst and Jase watched as a stream of trace rounds ripped through one of the C-130s. Mack opened up and laced bullets along the parked attack helicopters. Slamming on the airbrake, Jase descended violently, levelled out and opened up with another long burst which tore into one of the landing aircraft. The aircraft lost control and smashed into the runway, its landing gear collapsing. Sparks exploded from the flanks as the plane slid along the tarmac on its belly. He was about to line up another aircraft when he heard a familiar high pitched rhythmic beeping which sent a wave of dread through him. Someone on the ground had locked onto him and was about to fire a heat seeker. The beeping quickened until it became one long sound. Jase broke to the left, rapid muffled thudding meant his flares had deployed. He felt a shudder and heard a muted explosion behind him. The missile must have hit one of the flares.

"Time to leave," Mack's voice crackled over the radio.

"Roger," said Jase coming out of the turn, relieved the lock on warning had fallen silent.

They would have enough fuel to fly home, but they both knew there was no spare fuel for another dogfight. The FA-18s had given the Indonesians pause, but that was about the full extent of their attack. Within the hour, the invading force was running Mackay airport again as if nothing had happened.

"There's nothing," Mick said as he twisted the radio's tuning knob. "Every station's off air."

The others remained silent as the older man persisted with the radio.

With a sigh of frustration he gave up and rubbed his face.

"Jesus, what the hell's going on out there?" asked Ben.

"I hate to think," whispered Katie.

"We're going for a look," said Mick, grabbing the car keys.

"No we're not Dad! We're safer here!" said Katie. Jade looked on with wide innocent eyes.

"No, me and him," said Mick, gesturing towards Ben. "I want you to stay here, but we're going out there to have a look."

Ben shrugged and nodded, "yeah alright."

"Good," Mick picked up a rifle and slung it over his shoulder. He walked to the gun cabinet, unlocked it, pulled out a second rifle and a box of ammunition.

"You ever shot a rifle before?"

"No," said Ben honestly.

"You've never shot a rifle before?"

"Never."

"Bloody hell! I taught my daughter to shoot when she was ten!" said Mick shaking his head.

"Good for you," said Ben, taking a step back as Mick whirled on him.

"Bloody pretty boy, you were probably too busy rubbing gel into your hair and picking out your next pink shirt to do things like shoot a rifle or ride a motorbike."

"Stop it!" Katie reprimanded them both as she stepped in between the two men.

Ben had his fists clenched and his jaw set. Mick was not backing away either, he glared at Ben, but nodded and reluctantly handed the younger man the second rifle.

"I'll give you some shooting tips on the way in," he grumbled.

The men were silent during the drive into town. Mick was not talking because he did not like Ben, whilst Ben was quiet because he was terrified for his life. Mick had hammered down the dirt driveway and after sliding sideways onto the bitumen of the main road, he accelerated up to almost 180 km/h. The Navara's engine was screaming as they rocketed down the highway. As soon as they had turned onto the main road they could see the smoke thickening the sky in the distance.

"Wanna slow down?" Ben asked.

"Newsflash city boy, Australia just got invaded! You think the bloody cops will be out running speed cameras and RBTs? I reckon they might have more serious matters to deal with!" he said shaking his head. "Fair dinkum," he said quietly.

About 20 km out of town was a small Foodworks, petrol station and bakery. Mick intended to stop there for supplies. Travelling into the centre of town was just asking for trouble. They would end up captured or worse.

As they drove, Mick spoke about weapon safety, how to aim and how to pull the trigger. Snatching the trigger resulted in the barrel being jerked slightly upwards and increased the risk of missing the target. Gently squeezing the trigger worked effectively. The weapon should be aimed at the centre of seen mass, which Mick explained was the chest. One bullet could do a lot of damage in that area of the body, all but guaranteeing a kill.

"So how many people have you shot?" asked Ben chuckling.

Mick shrugged, "it's been a long time, but a few."

"You serious?" Ben asked, his good humour long gone, to be replaced with fear. He could be sitting next to a serial killer he realised.

"Relax pretty boy, I'm a Vietnam Vet," Mick said, keeping his eyes on the road. "We got into a few scraps over there and yeah I shot and killed a few of the enemy."

"What was it like?" Ben asked.

Mick was silent, it was obvious he did not want to talk about it. As they tore past a large open paddock, cattle stood close to the fence chewing slowly on pasture and looking stupidly at them. They did not pass any other vehicles on the road. It was usually a quiet road, Mick knew, but he expected to pass at least two or three other cars.

They arrived at the small shopping centre in good time. Apart from one other car, it was deserted. The front window of the bakery was smashed. All of the bread, pastry and cakes had been taken. The till had even been smashed open on the floor.

Mick parked the Navara, passed a rifle to Ben and climbed out of the vehicle. Both men cocked the rifles, flicked the safety off and slowly approached the Foodworks. The sliding doors had been wedged open. As they walked into the store, the men could hear talking and laughing from the back of one of the aisles.

"Friendlies coming in," called Mick loudly.

The voices went silent. Two young men strode into view, chests puffed out, but when they saw the weapons they took a step back.

"We don't want any trouble," said Mick, "but have no fear, if you fuck with us, we'll shoot you, ok son?"

"We're outta here man," said one of the youths. The pair disappeared and reappeared moments later carrying a box each full of food.

Mick reversed the vehicle up to the doors of the Foodworks and they started loading in food. Most of the food was non perishable goods like cans, freeze dried packets, dried fruit, dried noodles, toiletries, bottles of water. Mick also spent a lengthy period of time in the laundry aisle picking out items, placing them in a box and passing it to Ben. He then moved quickly to the automotive aisle and stacked bottles of brake fluid and other items into a box. With the Navara packed, they drove over to the petrol station with a squeal of tyres.

The owner of the station, who had long departed, seemed to have unlocked the bowsers controller as the pump started immediately. Nice of them. Mick filled the Navara with diesel, then filled a 20 litre jerry can with petrol. As Mick was walking around the vehicle to the driver's side he heard the engines and watched several Indonesian military vehicles pull into the drive way. They stopped in the middle of the road blocking the exit. Watching in horror, he watched as the rear ramps of the vehicles opened and soldiers began running into view.

"Ben, shift over to the driver's seat!" roared Mick.

Mick ran to the passenger side, climbed in, reached back and pulled the rifles onto his lap. Flicking the safety off, winding the window down he took aim and fired. The round took the closest soldier in the chest and he fell to the concrete like a rag doll.

"Fuck! Go! Go!" he shouted at Ben.

"They're blocking the road, I can't get out!"

"It's a fuck'n four wheel drive you galah! Now bloody go!" yelled Mick.

Ben revved the engine, dropped the clutch and stalled.

Mick fired a second shot. Another Indonesian soldier died. But then the return fire started.

Another Indonesian died. "If you don't get this moving, you're fuck'n next!" Mick shouted. A staccato of metallic thuds exploded in the cabin as return fire peppered the vehicle.

The engine roared to life and the vehicle accelerated away violently. They bounced across the shallow ditch and out onto the bitumen. Mick leaned out the window as far as he dared, before taking another shot. The bullet missed its target, ricocheting off the concrete with a loud whine.

"What the fuck was that back there?" Mick whirled on Ben.

"I dunno, I panicked!" he stammered.

"You bloody panicked? Your panic almost got us killed! You need to relax and think clearly!" Mick growled.

The rifle had one round up the spout, but the magazine was now empty. Mick ejected the magazine from the weapon's breach and began refilling it. They drove in silence for several minutes before Ben made a small noise, half way between a grunt and a squeak. Mick looked at the younger man, a deep frown etched into his forehead.

"Shit, behind us!" Ben stammered.

Shifting in his seat, Mick glanced back, his heart sinking as he watched the Indonesian vehicle closing on them fast. They were giving chase! Mick leaned over and looked at the speedometer.

"Ninety k's an hour! Are you bloody serious?" yelled Mick slamming his hand onto the dashboard. "You bloody nancy boy, push your accelerator down until it can't go any further. Put it through the bloody floor if you can!"

With a roar the Navara picked up speed, a mob of kangaroos looked up from their grazing, watching the vehicle tear past them. Mick leaned out the window and fired an un-aimed shot at the animals that scared them into movement. One bounded away into the underbrush, but three others leapt out onto the road straight in front of the chasing Indonesians. Just as Mick had hoped. The enemy vehicle swerved dangerously, missed the Kangaroos, but almost lost control in the process. The rear end started to skid round, but the driver somehow managed to regain control and continued the pursuit.

Cursing, Mick leaned across and looked at the speedometer. 160 km/h. Better. Unbuckling his seat belt, the older man pushed himself out of the window, bracing himself against the seat as the roar of wind hit him, threatening to tear him clean out of the vehicle. He pulled the rifle into his shoulder and took careful aim. He fired the first shot with no effect. The round seemed to have missed the target altogether. Pulling the bolt back he reloaded, aimed and fired another shot, which smacked into the bitumen just in front of the chasing vehicle.

The rifle bucked against Mick's shoulder. This time the bullet sparked against the armoured plating of the Indonesian vehicle. At least now they were pulling away from their enemy. Another sharp report and the bullet hit exactly where Mick had been aiming. The front right tyre. With a loud explosion of escaping air, the tyre disintegrated into large pieces of rubber and the vehicle pulled sharply to the side of the road. The driver attempted to regain control but oversteered. The rear end slid around so the vehicle was skidding sideways for a moment before it began to flip. At that speed the Indonesian vehicle flipped at least thirty times, large sections of metal tearing away. The bonnet flew through the air like a piece of corrugated iron in a cyclone.

The enemy was growing smaller as the Nissan pulled away, but Mick thought he saw a human body being flung out to land heavily by the side of the road. The Indonesian vehicle came to rest on its roof, steam hissing out of the engine compartment.

"You think its going to explode?" asked Ben glancing in the rear view mirror.

"You've watched too many Hollywood movies, boy," muttered Mick. He flicked the safety catch on, put the rifle down and fastened his seat belt.

The Navara handled surprisingly well at speed, Ben found. They passed another mob of Kangaroos, but this time they bounded away into the forest. Within ten minutes the forest had given way to open fields of pasture. Herds of cattle lay on the ground together in the shade of trees. But occasionally several were out together munching contently on the grass.

"Here! Here!" Mick said pointing to a fast approaching dirt road.

Ben braked hard, turning onto the road leading up towards Mick's house. They passed through the entrance gates labelled 'Bent Wood Cullen Bone', over a cattle grid and onwards along the narrow road that cut through the thick Australian forest.

"Grandad!" Jade shrieked as they pulled up to the house. The little girl came running from the veranda and flung herself into Mick's arms.

"Hello my girl," he said hugging her to him.

"How'd it go?" asked Katie not far behind. "Jesus are you alright?" she asked as she spotted the bullet holes peppered around the cabin.

"We're ok," said Mick, putting Jade back down. "A bit touch and go there for a bit, but nothing to worry about. I don't think we'll be going to Foodworks again though. It's crawling with Indonesians now."

Katie helped them carry the boxes of goods inside. Ben was quiet. He was obviously shaken by the encounter. As Katie began unpacking the food, Mick sat on the veranda cleaning the rifle. Ben stood nearby, leaning on the rail and staring out at the forest.

"You look worried pretty boy," said Mick absently.

"Stop calling me that!" Ben whirled around, glaring at the older man.

Mick was unfazed. He held the bolt up for inspection, and then began cleaning it again.

"I'll call you what I want, boy. There are men eight years younger than you out there fighting in places like Afghanistan, North Africa and places we probably don't even know about. Yet you act like a boy who was taken off the tit too late in life."

Ben shook his head and turned away, muttering under his breath.

"You need to get your head around what happened today. Australia's never been invaded before, but I've got my money on the fact it's going to get a lot worse than what we experienced today. It's only the beginning. Once the Indo Army has set up camp the real fun will begin. A quarter of our fighting capability are overseas and the other three quarters are probably out there right now going through sheer bloody hell."

Mick fell silent as he placed the weapon back together before looking out at the sinking sun.

"So what I'm saying is it's up to people like you and me to take the fight to the Indos. You need to get your head around that, because at the moment you're about as useful as a plastic spoon at a gunfight. I've seen your type all my life, walking around the street in your fancy clothes, gel in your hair, chests thrust out like you own the place. Just a bunch of loud mouthed weaklings is all you are."

Ben whirled around again, a dangerous glint in his eye.

Mick jumped to his feet. "That's more like it!" he said, stepping forward. "That fire in your eyes is what I want. That's what we need right now." He stopped inches from Ben. "Feel free to have a swing, boy, but you'd better knock my block off. Coz if you don't I'll use your guts for garters."

Katie appeared. "What the bloody hell is going on out here?" she asked, hands on hips.

"Oh, me and the boy," Mick said, gesturing at Ben, "we were just talking."

"I know you too well dad," said Katie. "Now stop it." She walked back inside to start preparing dinner.

Mick turned back to the younger man. "She does know me too well," he grunted, stepping away and sitting down.

Ben turned away and looked out at the darkening forest once more. The sun had turned a deep orange as it failed in the west. Australia was in real trouble, he knew. In fact it was worse. Australia was doomed.

Insects buzzed quietly throughout the forest canopy whilst crickets sang their melodious harmony. The ambush had been set up almost three hours ago. After checking the time, Kane folded the sleeve back over his watch. The new moon lent no light to the terrain, serving the purpose of the Australian soldiers. Kane lay in the centre of the ambush, his soldiers silently lying either side of him in extended line. Each soldier was separated by ten metres, making the killing ground about 130 metres in length.

The safety catches of the weapons had been disengaged long before they arrived at the ambush site. This had been done so that when the Indonesian force patrolled along the road in front of them, they would not be alerted to a possible ambush by clicks of safety catches. The road was five metres to their front and could just be seen in the blackness as a dull grey, wide strip.

Kane had a piece of 'hootchie' cord tied to his right hand and another to his left. Hootchie cord was very strong, thin cord used for tying the soldiers' hootchies (a piece of camouflaged plastic under which one man could sleep) up at night. The cords reached out to the last soldier on each flank. When the soldiers heard the enemy approaching they would give two tugs, alerting Kane to not only the presence of the enemy, but from which direction they would approach. Another piece of cord was tied to a tree at waist height leading away from the road and back into the depths of the forest. This had been placed so that when the ambush was over, the soldiers on each flank would file into the centre and then follow the cord, moving into single file to their rally point in the depths of the forest. At no point before, during or after the ambush would there be talking. Noise discipline would be maintained at all costs.

Kane would initiate the ambush by firing a Claymore mine set up closer to the road. This would signal the rest of his soldiers to open fire. The Claymore was an anti personnel weapon about the size of an A5 book inside which were 700 grams of plastic explosive. In front of the explosive were 700 ball bearings. The plastic case was moulded in a gentle curve so that when the weapon was fired, the ball bearings would spray at waist height over a wider area. A small detonator was screwed into the Claymore case. Attached to the detonator was a long length of cable. It was to this cable that the initiation device, affectionately known as the 'clacker' was attached. The 'clacker' was a similar concept to a hand gripper used by fitness fanatics to improve hand grip strength. However when the 'clacker' was depressed, it created a small electric charge which was sent down the cable into the detonator at the other end, thus causing the Claymore to explode.

After their firefight with the Indonesians several days before, Kane's platoon had lost more than half their number. A platoon normally consisted of around thirty soldiers. Now Kane had thirteen left, including himself. His platoon sergeant was dead, so too was his signaller. All but one of his section commanders had also been killed. They had dropped packs during the fight. Now equipped with only their patrol webbing, they had minimal food and only two litres of water per man, instead of six litres. They had been careful, trying to preserve both food and water, but the soldiers were almost out of both. Soon it would be time to start living off the land.

He passed through his mind the faces of each soldier he had lost, remembered their names and cursed himself silently. It would be a difficult task informing their wives, girlfriends and mothers about their loss. That is if they even made it out of this mess alive. Christ knew what was happening elsewhere in Australia. But from some of the reconnaissance patrols he had led, it was clear that the Indonesians had landed in force. He knew that the road in front of which he lay was used not only as a secondary supply route by the Indonesians, but also frequented by enemy ground troops moving through the area. It was one of these groups of soldiers moving through that he hoped to ambush and kill.

The ambush itself would not stop the Indonesian invasion. It would, however, let the enemy in the local area know that they were not invincible and that there was an Australian force of unknown number out there, willing to engage and kill them. One small seed of doubt implanted in the minds of the enemy was enough to begin making them overcautious, nervous and prone to accidents.

Placing the 'clacker' on the ground, Kane slowly moved his hand and brushed his face gently, forcing the mosquito to take flight. Picking the 'clacker' up, it fit snugly in his hand.

An effective ambush took not only patience, but the discipline to keep quiet. No unnecessary movement, no talking, or, for that matter, coughing, sneezing or farting. If, however, a cough could not be held at bay, it was best for the soldier to cough into his bush hat to help suppress the noise.

The bloody mosquito was back. Placing the 'clacker' down gently, Kane slowly rubbed his neck softly. He froze as he heard the distant noise of jet engines. They carried the distinct, powerful pitch of fighter aircraft, not the sedate sound of a passenger jet. The aircraft grew closer. They were low, very low. Within minutes they had passed over, their engines rapidly growing quieter as they departed. More than likely they were Indonesian fighters, but he had no way of knowing.

The forest was silent once more, as it had been when the soldiers had crept into position hours before. With the rumble of the jets now gone, the crickets hesitantly began chirping again, blissfully unaware of the Australian soldiers silently lying in wait. An owl hooted softly in the distance and the forest canopy rustled quietly in the gentle breeze. Still no hint of Indonesian activity. Kane decided that if there was no activity on the road in another two hours, he would move his men back into the forest for a rest and prepare a second ambush another day.

Kane knew morale was low. His soldiers, only days before, had lost more than half their brothers. This was an extended family where soldiers became acutely aware of every habit and mood of the man next to him. A single loss of life was devastating, but to lose half the platoon in one fell swoop? That was catastrophic and it had dealt a killing blow to the morale of the soldiers. In some small way, an ambush would not only have a negative effect within the Indonesian lines, it would raise morale amongst his men, he knew.

Silence again. It took Kane several seconds to realise the crickets had fallen quiet. All he could hear was the gentle rustle of wind through the leaves high above him. Then he felt two firm tugs from the cord attached to his left wrist and the adrenalin began to flow. He gripped the 'clacker' more firmly, turned his head slowly and listened. Nothing. Not a sound. A mistake may have been made, he guessed. A distant branch moving in the breeze seen by weary eyes or a strange sound. As Kane began to relax again, he heard the scuff of booted feet kicking a rock into the undergrowth. He closed his eyes, and listened intently. There it was again! The sound of booted feet walking on the dirt road. He looked intently but could see no movement.

A murmur of quiet voices and then a burst of laughter. The talking was louder now, and not a word of English was spoken. Then he saw them. They were moving slowly and with confidence, which was good. It meant they suspected nothing. In the almost non existent light, Kane could only see the faint silhouettes of the enemy as they trudged past in single file, talking and laughing. Before initiating the ambush, he wanted to make sure that the centre of the enemy line was in front of him. That way, the entire Indonesian column would be hit at the same time. He tried to count the enemy and stopped at thirty. With still many more soldiers following, he knew that all of his soldiers lying along the 130-metre length of forest would have at least one enemy in front of him.

With a snarl, Kane clamped his hand around the 'clacker' and fired the device. The Claymore exploded with a deafening roar, sending a dull shudder through the soldiers lying nearby. Ball bearings whistled through the air, tearing through flesh and shattering bone. A moment later, the Australian platoon opened up with full automatic fire. Kane threw the 'clacker' aside, took up his weapon and opened fire. There was no need to aim, at this range it was like shooting fish in a barrel.

Within seconds his magazine was empty. There was hesitant return fire on the extreme right flank where a cursory counter ambush drill was being initiated by surviving Indonesian soldiers. Merciless Australian automatic gun fire commenced again, silencing the Indonesians. The ambush was over. Untying the cord from both wrists, Kane knew that the men on each extreme flank would roll up the cord. His soldiers would now start moving into the centre before following the waist high cord into the depths of the forest behind him. He could hear the screams and groans of the enemy wounded. One of them had a consistent productive cough. He was probably bringing up blood. Not long and he would be dead.

As predicted, the cough became softer and more intermittent, until finally, it stopped altogether. The injured, however, continued to let the surrounding forest know about their pain. The Australians silently withdrew, the last man out cutting the waist high cord at the tree. It would be gathered up at the other end. Once they arrived at the rally point, the thirteen soldiers shook out into all round defence and went to ground. They would stay there for some time, in case the Indonesians chose to conduct a follow up.

Kane knew they probably would not. Well, if they knew what was good for them they would not. But as fate would have it, what was left of the Indonesian column could be heard blundering through the forest towards their position. The Australians remained silent, at this point there was no need for them to open fire. Their enemy would more than likely pass them by clueless to their presence.

Fate was a filthy bloody bitch decided Kane as his heart rate quickened again, the familiar adrenalin pouring through his body. Twenty metres in front of him, he caught sight of the dim outline of an enemy soldier as he pushed passed a tall, thick grass tree. Another appeared behind him, then another.

They were rushing straight towards the Australian position. Without any chance of the enemy passing around them, Kane cursed silently and pulled the weapon into his shoulder. Using the dimly illuminated battle sights on top of the scope, he lined up the closest Indonesian and fired. Immediately, the soldiers nearest to Kane opened fire.

"On me, extended line," roared Kane firing single shots in quick succession.

A bullet slammed into the ground nearby with a powerful thud. The Australians, who had been in all round defence, peeled back one by one in quick succession, until they were in extended line facing the enemy. The machinegun on the left flank roared into life with long bursts. Usually the machinegun never fired at night, but on the verge of being overrun, Kane knew his soldiers needed all the firepower they could muster.

"Get a flare out!" shouted Kane.

Both sides were fully engaged now, the Indonesian return fire almost as thick as the Australian attack.

"Throw a fuck'n flare!" roared Kane, unsure if his men had heard him over the noise of the gun battle.

Moments later, the forest was illuminated by a bright yellow light as the flare burst into life behind the Indonesian position. This served to silhouette the enemy, made worse by the fact that none of them had chosen to go to ground. Fighting from a prone position on the ground not only made a soldier a smaller target, but added increased protection from shrapnel, which usually exploded up and out. The Indonesians were either standing, or kneeling. The closest enemy to Kane was kneeling and leaning against a tree, firing towards the Australian position. The flare lit him up like a beacon and Kane fired two rounds in quick succession, the bullets slamming into his chest, throwing him from view.

Those Indonesians who had chosen to stand, firing from the hip, were cut down systematically. Slowly, minute by minute, the Australian soldiers regained the initiative. Had there been artillery on line, Kane would have called in a fire mission and obliterated the Indonesians from existence. Then as suddenly as it started, it was over. There was sporadic fire from the enemy as they fled back towards the road. The flare spluttered, died and the forest returned to darkness.

"Cease fire," shouted Kane.

Not a movement, not a word, not a sound. The forest was quiet as the Australians lay, perspiration beading their brows, adrenalin thumping through their veins. With ringing ears they attempted to listen for any sound that would indicate enemy movement. Apart from the now distant screaming and groaning from the wounded who lay bleeding on the road, the forest returned to relative peace. Even that noise made by the enemy slowly dissipated. Whether that was because the surviving enemy had rendered first aid on the wounded, or because the wounded had bled out, Kane did not much care.

The ambush had been a success. Never again would the enemy walk this stretch of road with such confidence. For at least the first month they would flinch at every abnormal sound. Their morale had taken a pounding. Now it was just a matter of hitting them again and again in different locations and in various ways. There was no way that what remained of Kane's platoon was capable of overpowering any large enemy force. That, however, was no longer the point. Cut off and alone, the Australian soldiers were now guerrilla fighters. They had motivation, they knew the country like the back of their hand, and as the Indonesians had found out, were not afraid to stand and fight a numerically superior enemy.

Guerrilla warfare was about morale. Fast, relentless hit and run raids regardless of season, weather or terrain wore the enemy down. One hundred soldiers with poor morale could be engaged and overrun by a determined force a quarter of their strength.

Following the ambush and the subsequent enemy pursuit, Kane knew that his soldiers would be low on ammunition. Already low on food and water, their next target would be enemy supplies. The road upon which they had initiated the ambush was the secondary supply route through the area. It was just a matter of picking a place, time and a carefully selected target, probably a truck.

Now there was utter silence. There was no hint of enemy movement through the forest. No birds, no wind, even the crickets had not summoned the courage to recommence their endless song. Still the Australians lay motionless, watching, waiting, listening. They would remain thus for the next half an hour.

Two soft clicks from Kane was all it took for the platoon to begin withdrawing from the position. They moved slowly, placing each foot down gently. If they felt a dry twig beneath their boot, they lifted their foot and placed it down elsewhere. Although slow, it was as close to silent as humanly possible. The three kilometres to their night harbour position would take them until sunrise.

Allowing his soldiers to rest throughout the day, Kane sat quietly preparing their next move. The soldiers rotated through sentry duties before retiring to sleep. They would be active at night and sleep during the day. During their previous patrols, Kane had seen a perfect area for a vehicle ambush. Some 6 km from their current position, the road took a sharp left turn. However, before the hairpin bend lay a washout, where previous heavy rain had partially destroyed the road. This, aside from the bend in the road, would force the vehicles to slow to a walking pace. Perfect for a fast, hard hitting ambush.

While the two soldiers remained on sentry, watching and listening for enemy in the area, Kane gathered his soldiers together and gave orders, which included information like the situation, mission, how the mission was to be executed, administration and command.

As the sun began to wane, the soldiers started their patrol towards the ambush site. It would take them ninety minutes to cover the 6 km. The patrol was uneventful, apart from two kangaroos, which brought the soldiers to a halt. Before the kangaroos were identified, the soldiers had gone to ground, preparing for a fight. The animals, however, moved away within minutes to graze in peace elsewhere.

Kane took ten soldiers with him and lay in wait near the road. He had chosen a well concealed site just prior to the hairpin in the road. He had selected this spot, because as the vehicles negotiated the bend, they would lose sight of the vehicle behind them. Once the ambush was underway, this alone would buy him several minutes before the other vehicles stopped to investigate. Hopefully the driver would not notice the absence of the vehicle behind him. Possible, but not likely.

His remaining two soldiers lay in wait further down the road. These men were his scouts, they would let him know how many vehicles were in the convoy. If the rear tarp was rolled up, they would also let him know if the vehicles carried troops or potential supplies.

He had thought long and hard about how this could be done, and decided once again to use the 'hootchie cord'. Tied to his right wrist by a slip knot, the cord was held by one of the seven soldiers. The number of tugs on the cord indicated the number of vehicles in the convoy. A string of erratic tugs indicated the last vehicle carried troops. They would obviously ambush the last vehicle, as long as it carried supplies.

Of course, the silent communication the hootchie cord offered was only useful during the last hour of daylight. Once darkness enveloped them, Kane would only have forewarning about the number of vehicles in the convoy. He would have to take his chances as to whether troops were on board. If they were unlucky, they would break contact and withdraw as quickly as possible.

To the west, the sky began turning hues of orange and eventually soft pink as the light began to fade. Within twenty minutes, the sky was gun metal grey and the crickets had commenced their symphony. The ten soldiers with him were bunched up close. There was no safety in distance here, they would need to move fast and as one unit, which could not be achieved if they were spread out. Once again, their safety catches had been disengaged prior to arriving at the ambush site.

It was another hour before the distant growl of engines came to them. The noise drifted into silence and recommenced a moment later with the gentle breeze. The engines grew louder and within minutes the headlights of the lead vehicle could be seen swaying down the rough dirt track. Although there were other vehicles behind the first, it was difficult to know how many. Exactly the reason for the positioning of his two soldiers further down the track. The familiar sound of the Unimogs drifted across the waiting soldiers. The Indonesians used a similar Unimog variant to what the Australian Army used.

The first vehicle passed by at about 40 km/h, but as it approached the washout, it decelerated to walking speed. Moments later the vehicle negotiated the hairpin bend and was hidden by the forest. The acrid aroma of diesel fumes wafted over the silent soldiers. The second vehicle drove by, Kane was able to see a small red dot emanating from the passenger side window where an Indonesian soldier was taking a drag on a cigarette.

The third vehicle rumbled past, but this time Kane could hear laughter and loud talking from the rear. Obviously this one carried soldiers. He felt the tug from the cord tied to his wrist. All the vehicles had obviously cleared his two scouts. The tugs stopped at ten. Ten vehicles. Unknown if the last carried soldiers. But it was worth the risk. Given what had happened to Australia in recent times, there was not much else to lose.

As the ninth vehicle drove by, Kane tapped the soldier either side of him, signalling that the next vehicle was the target. The message was passed down the line from soldier to soldier. Adrenalin, that familiar animal, began sinking its teeth into them and injecting its potent venom into their blood supply. Heart beats quickened, fear drifted away and warriors prepared to fight. He untied the cord from his wrist and threw it aside. The vehicle was almost on top of them when Kane jumped to his feet, sprinted forward and climbed onto the sidestep of the passenger side. The window was wound down. Bringing his rifle to bear, he pushed the barrel into the cabin and fired several quick bursts. Warm water splattered on his face. He reached in and felt an Indonesian soldier on the passenger side. Panicking he fired another burst into the enemy. Licking his lips, he tasted blood. The liquid sliding down his face was not water.

The Unimog slowed to an idle, grinding forward at less than 5 km/h. Now with the driver dead, it began drifting towards the trees dotted along the side of the track. Meanwhile Kane's remaining soldiers had swarmed around the rear of the vehicle and with several flashlights, had cleared the rear of the truck. No soldiers, just boxes of supplies. Bloody perfect!

One of Kane's soldiers had run to the driver's side, opened the door and climbed into the cabin. Reaching across the driver's body, he unclipped the seat belt, stepped back onto the side step and pulled the corpse out.

"Driver change," the soldier growled sadistically as the body hit the ground with a dull thud. It was the voice of Spud, Kane thought. Spud was his last remaining section commander and the next in command.

Kane pulled the deceased passenger out. The body hit the ground with equal force. He pulled himself up into the cabin. Spud regained control of the Unimog and brought the truck to a halt.

"In the back!" Kane yelled. There was no point being quiet. Shots had already been fired. Almost a minute later there were several sharp raps on the back window indicating that all the soldiers were now in the back of the vehicle.

Conducting a u-turn, Spud accelerated away until he reached a small break in the forest. At this point he steered off the road and into the forest. They continued to dodge bushes, shrubs and trees, branches scraped along the flanks of the truck. Eventually, after almost ten minutes, Spud brought the vehicle to a halt, turned off the lights and shut the engine down.

The soldiers quickly dismounted the Unimog and shook out into all round defence around the truck. Cut off and alone, Kane and his men had no idea how the rest of Australia fared. Many of their brothers in arms had already been killed. In addition, they had no idea how their families were, if they had even survived. This drove them, motivated them and angered them. But it also meant that they would continue to fight, even to the last man. If the Indonesians were successful, then it would not come easily. Kane wanted to make sure of that. He was succeeding.

'*Australian Prime Minister invokes ANZUS treaty in a desperate effort to thwart Indonesian invasion!*" Washington Post, Washington D.C.

Bent Wood Cullen Bone property

Ben was awoken by creaking floorboards. He yawned, stretched, placed his hands behind his head and stared at the ceiling. The sun was just starting to rise. After a few minutes, he climbed out of bed. Quietly making his way out onto the veranda, he saw Mick standing with his back to him, staring out at the forest.

"You hear it too?" Mick asked, turning.

"Hear what?"

"Thought I heard a couple o' gun shots," Mick said softly, turning back to the surrounding forest in the near distance.

"Dunno, I didn't hear anything."

"Keep your flam'n voice down! You'll wake the girls," hissed Mick.

"Sorry."

A burst of distant, automatic gunfire shattered the peaceful morning, followed by a long string of single shots in quick succession.

"Didn't think I was going mad," said Mick softly.

"Who is it?" asked Ben.

Mick turned to the younger man and glared at him. "What am I, a bloody psychic now? Christ boy, how the hell should I know?"

The two men fell silent for a while, listening to the forest.

"I can tell you who it's not," said Mick. "It aint any of my neighbours. Whoever it is, is shooting on my land. You wouldn't even hear a three-oh-eight gunshot if any of my neighbours were shooting on their land. My closest neighbour is at least ten kilometres away."

"Poachers maybe?"

Mick turned to the younger man with an incredulous look on his face. "Poachers? This look like an African game park to you? Christ boy, switch on! It'll be the Indo Army if it's anyone."

"I meant to say hunters," said Ben, clenching his jaw. He was starting to become tired of being talked to like an idiot. "And how do you know it's the Indonesians?"

"I don't," replied Mick. "But I'm gunna find out and you're coming with me."

"What about breakfast?" asked Ben, following the older man into the house.

"What about it? You can have your tomato with prosciutto and an egg when we get back," said Mick shaking his head. Stopping abruptly, he whirled on the young man. "Is it me, or did Australia just get invaded? There's probably people out there who haven't eaten anything for the last three days! And you're worried about breakfast?" Mick shouted. He was angry. He hated weakness, and complaining about one missed meal in the face of such overwhelming adversity was, in his opinion, complete and utter weakness.

"Sorry, I'm just hungry."

"So am I, boy! So am I! That's not the point!" Mick growled. "We have a duty greater than ourselves now. Don't you get that? We have to survive, yes, but we've got to fight these bloody bastards as well. Our diggers are out there either fighting or dead, for all I know."

Ben nodded with a sigh. "Yes I get that."

"Do you?" Mick was shouting again, his anger boiling over. "I don't think you do!"

"What the bloody hell's going on out here?" Katie appeared from her bedroom, eyes puffy and hair a mess.

"Sorry love," said Mick.

"You'll wake Jade!"

"I know," said Mick holding out his hands. "I'm sorry."

"Why were you shouting?" asked Katie.

"The boy asked a stupid question."

"His name is Ben!" hissed Katie.

Mick nodded, but said nothing.

"Someone's been shooting on Mick's land," said Ben.

"That's right. Me and the boy are going for a drive. You go back to bed love, we'll be back soon."

Katie scowled, shook her head, walked back into the bedroom and closed the door quietly behind her.

"Right," said Mick, satisfied he had taken care of the situation. "Let's go."

Once again the Nissan Navara hammered down the dirt driveway.

"You got any idea where the shots came from?" shouted Ben over the rattling of the vehicle as it thumped over potholes, washouts and uneven ground.

"Got a rough idea," replied Mick. "You remember what I told you about shooting?"

"Yeah, mostly."

"Good, you might need it today."

Ben nodded nervously and tightened his clammy hands around the rifle lying across his lap.

After five minutes, Mick pulled off the road, stopped and turned the engine off.

"We'll walk the rest of the way."

The two men moved through the forest with care. Mick walked in a half crouch, rifle pulled into his shoulder, ready to shoot. Ben tried to emulate him, but found it awkward and unnatural.

The younger man was worried about his parents. They could be dead for all he knew. He tried not to think about it, hoping instead that they had been captured and were being held prisoner. He would see them again when this was all over. If it ever ended. A hand hit him in the chest stopping him mid stride with a grunt. Looking up, he saw Mick glaring at him.

"Indos," Mick mouthed silently. Quietly turning away, Mick moved slowly to a large iron bark and knelt beside the tree.

Looking beyond the grumpy old bastard, Ben saw the forest thinning until it gave way to open pastures. In the middle of the field were several trucks and a group of Indonesian soldiers. He flinched as another burst of gunfire erupted and a nearby cow fell to the ground.

The two men crept to the outskirts of the forest and lay down, watching the proceedings. They had been shooting Mick's livestock. One of the trucks was filled with dead cattle. Probably fresh meat for the troops. When they had gathered several more carcasses, the soldiers mounted the vehicles and departed, disappearing over a small rise in the paddock.

Mick knew this particular paddock was at least three hundred and fifty acres in size. Once the older man was sure there were no more enemy in the immediate vicinity, he rose to his feet, signalled for Ben to follow and walked out to the area where the vehicles had been parked minutes before. The grass was saturated with blood and strewn around the area were spent ammunition cartridges.

"Where did they-"

Mick whirled on Ben holding an index finger to his lips, before mouthing, "shut the fuck up!"

After inspecting the area for sometime, Mick gestured that they were moving on. They walked in the tracks of crushed grass the trucks had left behind. Ben wanted to ask questions, but knew Mick wanted silence, for good reason too, he thought. At the top of the rise in the ground beyond which the trucks had disappeared, Mick stopped and slowly took a knee. Without looking around, he signalled for the younger man to do the same.

Looking over Mick's shoulder, the young city boy saw a plateau of higher ground about a kilometre in the distance. That was not what had gained their attention, though. What was significant, was the conglomerate of vehicles parked on top of the plateau. There were easily more than twenty Indonesian military trucks parked in a large ring, facing outwards. But in the middle of the circle was a large 12-wheeled armoured vehicle. Two mighty, fifty foot antennas stretched up into the sky.

Ben recalled the message broadcast over the radio when he first arrived with Katie and Jade. That had felt like a lifetime ago now. The Indonesian vehicle was obviously a communications vehicle that made up part of the invading force's secure network.

The carcasses of the cows were being dragged off the truck and butchered. Once done, the cuts of beef were placed in one of three refrigerated trucks. These trucks would probably supply hundreds of soldiers in the local area.

Whilst the men did not speak, Ben instinctively knew that Mick was angry. After all, this was his livelihood. He bred cattle to sell as meat and the enemy soldiers had slaughtered a profit. Although he had many more thousands of head grazing throughout various paddocks in the surrounding kilometres, it was only a matter of time before the Indonesians killed them all.

Mick tapped the younger man on the shoulder and jerked his thumb back the way they had approached. Time to go.

Mick disconnected the call and slammed the mobile phone down on the desk.

"The Army will be here within the week," he said.

"Just like that?" Katie asked. "I didn't think our Army would still be a fully functioning force."

"Apparently they are, or at least part of it is," said Mick, taking a sip of coffee.

They were silent, lost in their own thoughts for some time before Ben spoke.

"How is it you still have power?"

"Four kilowatt solar system. It's fed into batteries, so I'm completely off the power grid. As long as the solar panels or batteries don't fail, we'll have endless power here."

Ben nodded, impressed.

"They invade my country, they almost take my daughter and grand daughter, and then they start shooting my stock. When will it bloody end?" Mick shook his head, leaning forward.

"Are you alright Grandad?" Jade asked, padding over and placing a small hand on top of Mick's head.

"I'm okay, chicken," he looked up with a smile, lifting the girl into his arms. She squealed as he held his granddaughter close, kissing her hair.

Ben stood and walked out onto the veranda, looking out at the surrounding forest in the distance. The sun was well past midday now. There had been no more shots since the morning. He had heard the faint sound of trucks coming and going throughout the day. It was probably only a matter of time before the Indonesians discovered the house. Then what? Death? He felt a gentle hand touch his arm.

"Are you ok?" asked Katie.

Ben turned and tried to smile. He failed.

"I keep thinking about mum and dad," he said.

Katie nodded. To her credit that's all she did. She did not say that they would be alright, that he would see them sooner or later, that they would be hiding away in their home safe and comfortable. Ben respected her for that, because he knew that the truth was the first words she ever spoke to him. They were either prisoners or dead.

"Dad went out on his boat every Saturday. He'd spend more than half the day out on the water. Occasionally he'd catch something," Ben chuckled.

Katie remained silent, listening to him.

"He loved that bloody boat," Ben shook his head. "Mum loved to cook. There wasn't a day went by that she wasn't cooking up some new recipe she'd seen on TV, read in a magazine or heard from a friend." Ben's shoulders shuddered as he cried softly. "They're probably bloody dead. I hope they died quickly," he sobbed.

"I'm sorry," he said and wiped the tears away. "Crying like a big baby."

"It's okay, Ben," Katie said, rubbing his back, "I understand what you're going through. I lost my mum the year before last. She died of cancer. It's a bit different to an Indonesian invasion, but any loss, regardless of the situation, is difficult." She placed a hand on his chest and turned him towards her. "And I'm not saying your parents are dead. I'm just saying that right now, you worry for them, for their safety and well-being, and that's okay. It's nothing to be ashamed of."

"Mummy, grandad wants to know what's for lunch." Jade appeared on the veranda.

"Go and tell him to make it himself," Katie said walking towards the child.

"Grandad, mummy said-" Jade shrieked mid sentence as Katie pulled her into an embrace.

"I was joking!" said Katie, planting a kiss on Jade's cheek.

The woman looked over her shoulder at Ben, smiled and walked inside. Ben followed her departing form, watching the sway of her hips. She was not fat, nor skinny, just the way a woman should be, thought Ben. She was a good-looking woman.

Craig's long, unkempt hair was whipped away from his bearded face by the rotor downwash of the Blackhawk helicopter as the aircraft tore across the night sky at over two hundred kilometres per hour. Camouflage paint lent his face a demonic presence as he placed the helmet on, strapped it into place and clipped the night vision goggles to the socket on the helmet. He rotated the goggles down so that they were sitting over his eyes, staring out at the hazy green image of the forest far below. They must have been close to fifteen thousand feet in altitude. Leaning across to Matty beside him he tapped the man's arm.

"Two minutes!" he said into the throat microphone.

Matty nodded, pulled his helmet on and adjusted the night vision goggles.

Each man carried an M-4 carbine, capable of firing single shots or full automatic 5.56mm bullets. Both weapons were fitted with a silencer. The weapons were pointed muzzles down to the floor of the helicopter, held between their knees. The bulge of their parachute packs dug into their backs as they sat on the edge of the aircraft seat, waiting to deploy out into the cold night air. On drop lines fixed to their parachute harness were attached their backpacks, each weighing close to forty kilograms, stuffed with extra ammunition, high explosive devices and food.

The loadmaster manning the door gun beside Craig, tapped him on the arm and held one finger up.

"One minute!" said Craig, beginning to count the seconds in his head. "Let's go!"

With all the weight they were carrying, the movement of the soldiers was awkward. They crouched by the door and slowly, carefully slipped over the side of the Blackhawk, holding onto strong points of the helicopter. By this time, Craig had counted to fifty.

"Ten seconds," he said, the throat mic activating as it detected his larynx moving.

Craig looked up at the loadmaster above him, the man nodded once in farewell.

"Now!" The soldiers released their grip of the helicopter and they fell away from the thundering beast, the rotor blades slapping the night air furiously.

Their parachutes were deployed almost immediately and as he gained his bearings, Craig steered the parachute towards their destination, some fifteen kilometres to the west. At fifteen thousand feet most of their journey would be made silently as they glided through the moonless night. Being a special operations parachute, they could be steered with one hand, which left the soldier's master hand free to hold his weapon.

There was no talking between the two men as they glided towards their destination. It felt like he was on another planet, thought Craig, as he watched the distant landscape below him slide gently by. He could not see the ground very well from this altitude, but what little he could make out suggested there was no Indonesian outposts or camps setup anywhere. He hoped the Army had not been given a bum steer about the Indonesian mobile HQ rig by some local yobbo who thought it might have been a good joke.

The ground below looked so peaceful at altitude. Apart from the intermittent snap of the parachute canopy, silence reigned as they drifted slowly towards their target. It was hard to believe that Australia had been invaded when surrounded by such peaceful solace. Difficult to think that tens of thousands of people were already dead, or that almost ten million Australian citizens were starving in concentration camps dotted around the country.

The Australian Defence Force was much smaller than it had been before the surprise invasion. Entire infantry regiments, although having accounted for themselves exceptionally well, had been annihilated. The Navy had lost all of its capability. Although HMAS Newcastle was still out there somewhere. She was the only Australian Naval ship to survive the Indonesian's water borne onslaught, which had commenced 24 hours after the land invasion proper.

Craig checked the altimeter strapped to his wrist. He could see the infrared hands of the device through the night vision goggles. They were at 8,000 feet and falling nicely. At this rate they would land close to target. Craig looked down past his feet, watching a tiny, lone vehicle turn onto a road before it silently accelerated away beneath the canopy of the forest, hiding it from view. Heading north. He made a mental note.

"You got that vehicle?" Matty's voice crackled from the tiny speakers pushed into his ear cavities.

"Roger," replied Craig.

The air was warmer now than it had been aboard the Blackhawk. Craig had been itching to get amongst it, and when the call had come in specifying the location of a nearby Indonesian communications vehicle, he and Matty had been at the chopper almost five minutes before the aircrew.

Four vehicles turned out onto the same road as before, slowly accelerating and again disappearing beneath the forest canopy.

"Must be a main supply route," whispered Craig into the throat mic.

Although Matty did not reply, Craig knew that he had probably already plugged the position into his GPS. Matty was a very good soldier. The fact that his parents had been Indonesian refugees in the 70s meant nothing. He was more Aussie than most sixth generation Aussies. Fiercely proud of his country, Matty had joined the Army at 17 and never looked back. When he was 24, he attempted the Special Air Service Regiment's (SASR) selection course. Matty had been selected on his first attempt and after 18 months of continuation training was finally presented the sandy beret.

Craig had not been as lucky. He had attempted the selection course at 21 and although had completed the course successfully, had been failed on age alone. Attempting again at 25, he was selected. Now at 34 years of age, Craig was a Sergeant, and patrol commander. Both men had shoulder length hair and full beards.

Now at 2,000 feet, a strong head wind had slowed their progress. Craig knew they would not be blown off course. However, he had a strong suspicion they would land a few kilometres short of their target.

Aiming for an open paddock, the soldiers landed and went to ground. The parachute canopy whispered softly as it came to settle around Craig. He pushed the material away from his face and brought his weapon to bear. The men lay silent for several minutes, watching and listening for enemy. Satisfied the area was non-hostile, Craig climbed to his feet while Matty continued to provide cover. Having been disconnected, Craig gathered up the parachutes and moved quietly over to a dark hole in the ground he had spotted earlier.

In the grainy, green glow of the 2-D view provided by night vision, it may have been a dark patch on the ground. But as he knelt beside it, he felt a wombat hole. Stuffing the parachutes into the hole, he pushed them down as far as he could, hiding them from view. With a swift gesture, Craig signalled Matty to his feet and the pair began their patrol. They moved slowly, carefully, but with confidence. Checking the small, hand held GPS, Craig confirmed their location. The screen of the GPS was infrared, so could only be seen with night vision equipment.

Amongst the forest now, the soldiers paused every couple of minutes, took a knee and listened. Noise travelled further at night and a whisper of cloth against a tree trunk, soft snoring, the smell of cigarettes or a quiet conversation would be enough to suggest enemy were in close proximity to them. Progress was slow, but speed was less important than detection and probable capture.

Craig turned his thumb to the ground, the signal for enemy, and quietly lay down on his stomach, staring down the scope of his weapon. Matty did the same. The soldiers waited silently as the foreign voices grew louder, the distinct sound of undergrowth crunching beneath their booted feet echoed throughout the forest. The Indonesians appeared in the near distance, walking quickly along a narrow dirt track, talking and chuckling amongst themselves. They were oblivious to the nearby Australians. Watching them pass, the soldiers made sure the enemy had long departed before they began patrolling forward again.

Their progress was made almost silently and painfully slowly. Checking the GPS again, Craig saw they had covered 500 metres in the last hour. Another 1,500 metres to their target. They would arrive just before dawn, he judged.

Coming across a barbed wire fence, the soldiers stopped. Matty knelt and provided cover, whilst Craig negotiated the obstacle. Once over, he covered Matty. Watching and listening for enemy, Craig heard the fence move as Matty began climbing over. This was followed by a twanging sound as a foot slipped midway over, the tearing of cloth and a soft curse. The twanging sound came again, followed by a dull thud as Matty landed on his back.

Craig held in a laugh. "How's the family jewels?" he whispered into the throat mic.

"I left my fuck'n ball sack back there," came the whispered response.

Craig grinned and shook his head. They moved on again towards their target. The co-ordinates of the target was supposedly the house from which the original call was made. If correct, the people who lived there would be able to take the soldiers to the Indonesian position. However, they needed to be very sure of whom they were dealing with before they showed themselves. The call may very well have been made by either the Indonesian Army themselves, or by pro Indonesian sympathisers. It would be an easy and effective way to lead members of the Australian Army straight into an ambush. It had not happened yet, but was always a possibility.

A distant, but loud laugh broke the silence and both soldiers went to ground instinctively. Craig was worried, there was no cover close by and they were left lying out in the open of a small paddock. He could see several head of cattle standing a hundred metres away. They had been grazing, but now stared towards the laughter with alert interest.

Again the Indonesians swaggered into view. They were no more than 50 metres away and with a sinking heart, Craig realised the lead soldier was wearing night vision goggles. All it would take was for him to look in their direction, spot them and it would be on for young and old. There were five enemy in total. Craig could see an antennae swaying over the shoulder of the middle soldier. A signaller. If a contact began, he would be one of the first to die.

They were still talking and laughing loudly before the lead soldier casually glanced in their direction. He stopped immediately, the soldier behind him almost walking into him. He pointed towards the frozen, silent Australians and whispered quietly. He could see something odd, but could not definitively identify the objects as human. Craig nestled the target reticle over the Indonesian's chest and waited. His comrades laughed and jibed him from behind. Probably taking the piss, mocking him for seeing things, for getting jumpy, nervous or scared. But the lead soldier was adamant. Something about the ground looked wrong. He replied in a rapid, sure fire response. Reluctantly, the Indonesians spread out in extended line and began walking towards the Australians to investigate.

Craig cursed silently, his index finger now resting gently on the trigger. The enemy soldiers were chuckling, talking quietly amongst themselves, mocking the lead soldier. Scared of a couple of logs in the grass. But for the Australians, it was no joking matter. If the Indonesians advanced another ten metres, they would open fire. Still they came forward, right onto the Australian position. Now only twenty metres away, Craig was left with no option. The silenced M-4 sounded like a small cardboard box full of books had been dropped onto concrete. The lead soldier was dead before he hit the ground. The signaller following him almost instantly. Within two seconds all five Indonesians were dead. But for a gentle breeze whispering through the grass, silence reigned once more. The cattle hesitantly began grazing again.

CHAPTER SIX

*"*P*resident Andrew Baker reneges on ANZUS Treaty, stating U.S. public debt cannot sustain another international military intervention."* The Local, Berlin.

Bent Wood Cullen Bone Property

The sky was still dark, although the eastern horizon promised dawn was not far away. Mick stared out at the forest. He had been awoken by a single twig snapping in the distance. If it had been kangaroos, he would have heard further noise as they grazed innocently. He heard no further sound, and his gut instinct told him something or someone was out there, watching. His trusty .303 rifle was cradled in his arms. Although the safety catch was engaged, a bullet was in the chamber. A soft whistle from his left made him jump. Mick whirled in that direction, but saw no one. He walked slowly forward.

"Stop right there," a voice said from behind him.

Adrenalin and fear pumped through his blood stream as he turned towards the voice. A soldier stood before him, rifle pulled into his shoulder ready to shoot. The soldier was slightly shorter than Mick, but well built. He wore chest webbing, dark camoflauge paint adorned his face and a helmet sat on his head. From beneath the helmet sprouted a mess of hair and a full beard suggested he was not a conventional infantryman. Attached to the helmet were night vision goggles, although they had been turned up, away from his face. The soldier wore a heavy looking pack on his back.

A soft boot fall behind him made Mick turn. A second soldier appeared on the other side of him, weapon also ready to fire. The second soldier was dressed much the same as the first, including the messy hair and beard, although he looked of Asian descent. Neither soldier looked concerned, nervous or agitated. Their eyes carried a glint of quiet control.

Mick slowly lowered the .303 rifle and rested it against the wall before holding up his hands in surrender.

"Who are you?" the old veteran asked.

"We're with the Australian Army," answered one. "My name's Craig, this is Matty," Craig gestured towards the soldier of Asian descent.

"Was it you who called the Army?" asked Matty. "You find an Indo comms rig?"

"Yup," Mick replied.

Craig lowered his rifle. Matty did not.

"You alone?" asked Craig.

"No, got my daughter, grand daughter and the boy who saved them in there," Mick gestured to the house behind him.

Craig nodded. "Let's go, take us to the comms rig."

"What, now?"

"No, next week," said Craig sarcastically, his weapon cradled across his chest.

"Ok, let me get a couple o' things and I'll be right with you," said Mick.

Mick went back inside, followed by both soldiers. Matty had lowered his weapon now, although carried it in an aggressive way that suggested he could raise it and fire an accurate shot in less than a second.

Mick swallowed his morning medication, took a swig of water and was ready.

"Right," said the old man, "let's go."

"What the hell?" Ben said as he came stumbling, bleary eyed, out of his room.

"Go back to bed, boy," said Mick.

"Who are they?" asked Ben.

"We're travelling comedians," replied Craig with a straight face.

Mick sighed and introduced Ben to the soldiers.

"We're off, you may as well come with us now that you're up," said Mick.

"What about breakfast?" asked Ben.

"We've had this fuck'n discussion," replied the Vietnam Veteran. "Now get your arse in gear!"

The soldiers allowed the civilian men to carry their rifles, although cautioned them not to fire unless as a last resort. The unsilenced .303 would be heard from kilometres away. Mick drove them as far as possible, before the group advanced on foot into the forest. They patrolled at a steady pace, the soldiers moving with confidence but extreme vigilance. Twice, noises in the near distance made the group stop and go to ground. The first because of a mob of kangaroos, and the second as a result of a wombat. The small tank of an animal moved with slow determination through the leaf litter as it walked back towards its burrow, to sleep throughout the day. Once the creature had departed, the soldiers were the first back on their feet, signalling the others to stand.

As the sun began to rise into the sky, defeating the protection that the darkness offered, the group were lying down in knee high grass, watching the distant Indonesian position, in particular the large twelve wheeled communications vehicle. Craig and Matty whispered to one another, although Mick could not hear what exactly was being said. Within five minutes, the soldiers gestured for the group to depart. Both Ben and Mick were breathing hard as they crawled on their stomachs away from the Indonesian encampment, although they did not turn their back on the enemy. During the lack of light that pre-dawn offered, their approach had been made in a half crouch, which was faster and much easier. Once back amongst the trees, the soldiers allowed a short reprieve for the civilians to regain their breath.

It was close to mid morning when the group arrived back at Mick's home. Mick introduced the newly arrived soldiers to Katie and Jade.

"You need a shave," observed Jade as she looked up at the soldiers.

Craig ran a hand over his beard with a look of shock on his face. "I forgot to shave this morning!" he smiled.

Katie made bacon and eggs for breakfast.

"So what's the plan?" asked Mick, a piece of bacon lanced onto the end of his fork.

"We're gunna blow it up," replied Craig.

"What, just walk in there and blow it to kingdom come?" Mick looked doubtful.

"Pretty much," nodded Matty.

"How? You're dressed like Australian soldiers, you speak English, you carry American made weapons, you'll be spotted from a mile away!"

"Well," said Matty munching on a piece of toast. "It's interesting you should mention that. My oldies are both Indonesian, they came across in the '70s. I can speak fluent Indo. Plus, we had a slight disagreement with an Indo patrol on the way in, so I have an Indonesian uniform to wear," the soldier grinned.

Katie looked at her food distastefully.

Throughout the day, the soldiers slept whilst Mick showed Ben how to service the Navara, changing the oil, coolant fluid, checking the brake pads and checking the fluid levels.

As evening began to fall, Matty and Craig were awake and preparing for their mission.

"So, when do we leave?" asked Mick.

"Soon," replied Craig. "Just need to prep some gear and we'll be on our way."

Matty had donned the Indonesian uniform. Apart from being slightly too narrow across the shoulders, it fit adequately.

"Normally, we wouldn't take civilians with us," said Craig, "but there's only two of us, so a couple of extra rifles will help."

"Makes sense," replied Mick.

The older man did not ask, but he assumed that Australian Special Forces were stretched thin across the country. He knew from his time at Nui Dat as a young soldier in Vietnam, that the Australian SASR usually patrolled in groups of between four and ten. So, for a patrol to only consist of two members, meant that Special Operations Command (SOCOM) were feeling the pinch.

Ben looked nervous. No, Mick corrected himself silently. Shit scared was more appropriate.

"Relax boy," Mick said quietly.

Ben nodded, but remained tense, tapping his fingers against the wooden stock of the rifle cradled in his lap.

"Right, let's have a chat," Craig said, standing and shrugging into his chest webbing. He took Mick and Ben to the dining table where they sat down. Showing them a map of the area, he told them how they would infiltrate the area, where they would be positioned and what they would be doing. For the most part, the two civilian men would be watching quietly. Only if the situation went south were they to consider opening fire with their rifles.

Earlier in the day, Matty and Craig had strung a length of radio cord between two trees near the homestead. Craig had climbed almost six metres up the trees to attach the cord. It would provide much better radio reception explained Matty. However, it was now, just prior to departing on the mission that the soldiers put the elevated radio cord to use.

"Any fast air, any fast air, this is Delta Three, over," Craig spoke into the handset attached to the radio hidden within one of his chest pouches.

For five minutes, Craig attempted to raise any Australian fighter/bombers in the immediate area, without success.

"Right, so the best way to take out the target is for us to lase the Indo comms rig," Craig saw Ben's confused look. "Lase means that we use a special device to place an invisible laser designator on the target. The laser-guided bomb dropped by the fighter will then guide itself onto this signature and turn the comms rig into a fireball. In a perfect world, that's how it should go down. But, no such luck, there's no Aussie fast air in the area. So it looks like Matty gets to use his new uniform and Indonesian language skills." Craig rotated his night vision goggles down over his eyes, "let's go," he said.

Mick and Ben sat on the back seat of the Nissan, whilst Craig drove. The headlights were switched off and Craig was using his night vision to see where he was driving. When they could go no further, the vehicle was parked off the road out of sight and the group continued on foot.

Ben noticed the soldiers were moving confidently, but not as fast as they had this morning. They were walking slowly, being mindful of where they stepped. Ben cursed as he tripped over a log and came crashing to the ground with a grunt. He felt Mick's hand almost immediately on the collar of his shirt, pulling him to his feet.

"Stand the fuck up and watch where you're going," growled the older man quietly.

The group stopped and took a knee, watching and listening for any forewarning that Ben's mishap had been detected by enemy in the area. After five minutes of boring silence, the patrol headed off slowly.

Within a couple of hours they were once again lying in the knee-high grass looking at the distant Indonesian communication vehicle. At least Mick thought he could see the dark outline of the enemy vehicle against the stars in the background.

Craig leaned over to Mick and whispered into his ear, "Matty's on his way in, you two stay put, I'm going to find a better fire position closer to the target. Stay still and stay quiet."

"Yeah, gotcha," whispered Mick, passing the message onto Ben.

Matty crawled forward on his stomach, his helmet, including the night vision, chest webbing and weapon were left behind with Craig. In his trouser pocket was a one kilogram explosive device with a built in timer. Matty carried the detonator in his hand separately from the explosive for safety. It would only take seconds to arm the device. In his other pocket he carried a short fuse grenade that, if necessary, he would use as a decoy.

The soldier froze, listening to nearby Indonesian voices. He was fifty metres from one of the enemy trucks and could now smell the faint aroma of grease and engine oil emanating from the vehicle. They were talking about a girl back home. Movement caught his eye and he saw the dark, almost invisible outline of a soldier leaning against the truck. He cupped his hands, leaned forward into them and ignited the cigarette lighter. Matty quickly shut his eyes to protect what natural night vision his eyes allowed. Even something as small as a cigarette lighter could all but destroy a soldier's natural night vision, taking precious minutes to regain. The acrid stink of cigarette smoke wafted over the prone soldier.

When both soldiers lit up, Matty opened his eyes and moved forward very slowly, inch at a time. Once he was at the truck, on the opposite side of where the enemy stood, Matty quietly stood and brushed himself off. Stretching, he cleared his throat and walked forward loudly. The voices of the enemy on the other side of the truck immediately fell silent.

"Who's that?" asked one.

"Just forgot something out of the truck," Matty said cheerfully in Indonesian. Opening the door of the vehicle, he climbed in, waited a few seconds and then jumped down, slamming the door.

"Got it!" Matty said, walking away.

The conversation on the opposite side of the truck continued as before. Matty walked clear of the vehicle and stopped for a moment, forcing his eyes to focus. The moon was only a quarter full, throwing very little light. Although it made it difficult for him to focus, it also gave him added protection, Matty knew.

In the centre of the ring of vehicles was parked the twelve wheeled behemoth of the Indonesian communication rig. Unzipping his pocket, he took out the explosive device, although he did not attach the detonator. That would be one of the last things to do. Flicking a small switch on the side of the device activated its magnetised underside, which would force it to attach to the metallic surface of the comms rig.

Strolling forward, the Australian moved slowly and confidently, as if he belonged. He cleared his throat, hawked and spat as he walked. As he closed on his target, the outline of the comms rig became darker and more defined. Finally, Matty placed a hand on the cold, thick steel body of the vehicle. He stood still for a moment watching and listening.

He could hear some soft voices in the distance and a few chuckles on the other side of the Indonesian perimeter as a joke was shared. As far as he could tell, though, no one was in his immediate vicinity.

Going down on one knee, he quickly pushed himself under the huge vehicle. Being of such a large size, the clearance was well over one metre in height, meaning Matty could walk in a crouch under the monster. Once he was beneath the centre of the comms rig, the soldier quickly screwed the detonator into place with practised speed and pressed it onto the armoured, metal surface. Activating the weapon, he knew that he now had five minutes before detonation. With a dull clunk, Matty knew the magnetised surface of the explosive was now holding firm. Turning, he quickly made his way back, straightening up once he was clear of the vehicle.

Matty froze as he heard the groan of an armoured door swinging open and the soft thump as someone jumped down from the vehicle. The soldier turned towards the approaching person. Appearing around the other side of the comms rig, the dark smudge of the Indonesian stopped in front of Matty.

"Who are you?" the enemy asked.

"How dare you!" countered Matty confidently in fluent Indonesian. "You know who I am! And why are you not at your station?" the Australian took a step forward, implying a threat.

"Yes sir, of course sir!" the Indonesian hesitated for a second.

"Go!" Matty said in a quiet, but gruff voice.

Without a further word, the enemy soldier turned and disappeared. A soft thud suggested the armoured door had been closed once more.

By Matty's reckoning, only two minutes remained before detonation. Time to go. He moved quickly, but without panic, exiting the Indonesian defensive perimeter the way he approached. The smell of cigarette smoke washed over him. Obviously the two men were still on the other side of the truck. He heard their voices confirming his thoughts.

The Australian knelt down quietly by the front wheel, slowly reached into his pocket and pulled clear the grenade. With a fuse of between three and five seconds, he needed to throw the device very hard. However, the problem was that once he threw it, the handle would detach from the grenade with a relatively loud noise. The enemy soldiers on the opposite side of the truck would know that the grenade had been thrown from nearby, putting Matty at risk of capture or worse.

Pulling the pin clear, carefully and silently, he placed it in his pocket and stood up. Kicking a stone loudly, he opened the vehicle's door with his free hand.

"Forgot one last thing," chuckled Matty as he heard the quiet talking on the other side of the truck fall silent.

"Happens to all of us from time to time," chuckled one.

"Happens to me every day," Matty roared with laughter, making sure he made as much noise as possible. As he continued to laugh, he stepped forward and threw the grenade with all his strength towards where he thought the enemy comms rig would be. The sound of his laughter hid the noise of the handle separating from the grenade. Going to ground, Matty took cover, hearing a dull thud as the grenade landed on the ground in the distance.

One enemy soldier was half way through a reply when the ear shattering explosion of the grenade rent the air. Shouting erupted from all around the Indonesian perimeter, all enemy eyes turning inwards towards the explosion. With the decoy successful, Matty stood and walked away from the enemy position.

Ben jumped as the explosion rolled over him. He looked across at the dark shadow of Mick nearby, but the older man lay still, watching the enemy position. After nearly a minute, Ben was tempted to quietly ask what they were waiting for. There was an explosion, therefore the comms rig must have been destroyed. He opened his mouth and was about to ask when the earth shook, the deafening thunder of a second, much larger explosion ripped the quiet night asunder. The explosion was accompanied by a blinding orange flash that silhouetted the enemy position for a moment. The young man felt the shock wave of the explosion through his body. He lay still, frozen with fear.

Within minutes, the Australian soldiers had returned, instructing Ben and Mick to follow them. Within five minutes, the group had departed the area, leaving the burning ruin of the comms rig behind them, along with the shouting, screaming and dying.

CHAPTER SEVEN

"**US** *Marine Corps base in Australia feared overrun. Don't jump to conclusions advises Major General Davies (USMC)."* New York Times, New York.

Jase conducted G strain as he brought the FA-18 around in a hard break turn. The aircraft juddered violently against the forces placed upon the airframe. Levelling out, he glanced to his starboard side confirming that Mack, his wingman, was still flying alongside.

For almost a week now, the pilots and ground crew of 77 Squadron had been working around the clock. Jase was now beginning to have an appreciation for what the British fighter pilots had lived through during The Battle of Britain. In any given hour of any day, at least two Australian fighter planes of 77 Squadron were flying combat missions somewhere in a 2,500 km radius of the base at Williamtown, NSW.

Jase had shot down five enemy aircraft and obliterated countless Indonesian ground targets. But there was always more. Like a never-ending torrent, the enemy replaced destroyed vehicles or aircraft and continued on without so much as a pause.

Today, another possible Indonesian Communications Vehicle (dubbed ICV by the Australian Defence Force) had been spotted fifty kilometres west of Melbourne by forward air control aircraft. However, the identification had not been confirmed categorically. Rather than send in fighter/bombers, already stretched thin, to neutralise an unconfirmed target, Special Air Service soldiers were dropped into the area. The Special Forces had somehow patrolled through the huge enemy position without detection and now had the target lased, awaiting the arrival of the FA-18s and their deadly payload.

The enemy position inhabited the entire fifty kilometre area west of Melbourne. Dotted throughout the enemy perimeter were surface to air missile (SAM) sites. It was up to Jase and Mack to force their way through in order to deliver their payload. Through his helmet's ear speakers, Jase heard loud rapid beeping which quickened to one long sound. He reacted immediately.

"Break, break, break!" he spoke to Mack.

Several dull thuds in rapid succession confirmed that a string of flares had deployed. Conducting G strain, Jase turned the aircraft violently, the cockpit again juddering violently against the outside forces. He looked quickly over both shoulders in an effort to spot from where the missile had been fired.

"Yeah, seven o'clock," Mack confirmed he had seen the signature of the SAM site.

Looking in that direction, he saw the missile hit one of the flares, which by now were over two kilometres behind them, exploding in a lethal fireball.

The beeping started again. "Break, break, break!"

More flares deployed, another violent evasive manoeuvre and again, the missile was defeated by the Australian pilots.

"Fast, air, air.....over," a very broken, radio message crackled in Jase's ear.

"Say again unknown, say again, over," he said.

"Fast air.......over," again very broken.

"Unknown, you are very broken, say again."

"Fast air, fast air, this is Delta Three Two, we have target lased, over," the voice was much clearer now, giving an indication of how fast the fighter aircraft were travelling.

"Roger Delta Three Two, we are inbound, hot, over."

"Prepare for bomb run," Jase said, activating the five hundred pound bomb with a flick of his thumb.

"Roger that," replied Mack.

Within one second, the bomb was activated, had searched for and acquired the signature being sent by the nearby ground unit. By Jase's estimate the target was three kilometres in front of them. With two loud beeps in quick succession, the bomb confirmed to Jase it had locked onto the target.

"Delta Three Two, danger close, danger close, over," Jase said, releasing the bomb.

"Bomb gone," Jase confirmed, Mack repeating the confirmation, meaning that he too had successfully deployed a second five hundred pound bomb.

"You don't even have a swimming pool," said Ben, picking up a large container of pool chlorine.

"Very observant, boy," said Mick, pouring brake fluid from a large drum into small five hundred millilitre bottles. The two men were outside in Mick's huge machinery shed.

"So why'd you take it from the store? I don't get it."

"I'll show ya," said Mick, gesturing for the younger man to open the chlorine container.

Ben did so, making a face at the acrid smell.

"You bloody sook," growled Mick. "Grab a handful of chlorine."

Ben retreated a step from the powerful odour.

"Man alive, you soft city boy!" Mick said in a loud voice. "Now grab a bloody handful!"

Ben did as requested and as instructed, he poured the white chlorine powder into one of the five hundred millilitre containers. Mick shook the bottle gently and placed it outside the shed at least thirty metres away before returning.

"Now, see that?" asked Mick, pointing to a white smoke that had started to waft out of the open bottle. "That is chlorine gas. The same shit that the Germans used against allied soldiers in World War One."

Ben was intrigued and began walking towards the container to take a closer look.

Mick grabbed the younger man by the shirt and dragged him back. "Hold your horses boy, that stuff will damage your lungs permanently."

"Seriously?"

Mick glared at the younger man.

Ben nodded, taking the hint. "What's that stuff?" he asked, pointing at a number of glass bottles lined up on a distant workbench. A thick, white sludge half filled each bottle.

"Petrol mixed with lux flakes," said Mick, returning to what he had been doing.

"Lux Flakes, as in the laundry flakes?"

Mick stopped and sighed, looking at the ceiling of the shed. "No, the other Lux Flakes. Flam'n heck, are you metrosexual city boys taught anything other than how to dress in pink shirts and smear sludge through your fuck'n hair?"

Ben clenched his jaw. "Alright, I get the point," he muttered.

"Good!" Mick growled. "What you get when you mix petrol with lux flakes is napalm. All you need to do is feed a piece of cloth through the neck of the bottle, light it and throw. The container has to be glass, obviously, otherwise it won't shatter and catch alight."

"How'd you learn all this?" Ben asked, picking up one of the bottles and examining the sludge.

"Combination of a misspent youth and some good platoon commanders not afraid to teach their soldiers some unconventional ways to kill and maim the enemy."

The men remained in the shed for most of the afternoon, Ben helping where he could, although he accidentally knocked over a container of chlorine powder. Mick's rant did not stop for almost five minutes.

As the sun sank, Matty and Craig returned from a patrol. The soldiers departed on patrol every day, usually leaving at sunset and returning at dawn. Sometimes they left at dawn and returned at sunset. They had intended to be exfiltrated so they could prepare for another mission, but had been told by their unit to stay put for the time being. Resources were stretched far too thin for extraction.

"We've found a main supply route," said Craig as the group sat eating dinner that evening.

"How far?" asked Mick, shovelling a piece of broccoli into his mouth.

The soldier shrugged, "about eight k from here, give or take."

"What do you plan to do?" asked Katie, cutting a piece of steak. Mick had killed a beast several weeks before and the freezer was full of meat.

Craig swallowed his food, looking up from his plate. "We want to ambush it, just not sure how, yet. I see you've got some nice concoctions out in your shed, Mick, we might call on you for assistance."

"No worries at all mate. Why ambush them though, what can four blokes do?" asked Mick.

"A hell of a lot," said Craig. "We want to create a decoy, which will be the ambush itself. Once the decoy is underway, Matty will place a tracking device on one of the vehicles in the convoy. The road of the main supply route leads away from where the enemy comms rig was parked. Basically we don't know where they're going, so the tracking device will let our head sheds know where their destination is."

Jade was chewing her food slowly and looking from one adult to the next with large, innocent eyes, listening intently.

Ben nudged the girl's shoulder softly. "Eat up," he said, noticing she was distracted by the conversation.

"It'll be a few days away from the house, though," said Matty, glancing at Ben as he spoke. "You guys are welcome to tag along, but it won't be a Sunday stroll in the park," the soldier warned.

Mick shrugged and nodded. Ben looked down at his plate, continuing to eat in silence.

"When will we leave?" asked Mick.

"I want to spend tomorrow planning, maybe a few rehearsals, then we'll leave the day after. Happy with that?" asked Craig.

"Sounds fair," said Mick. "How 'bout you, boy?" Mick looked at Ben, "you gunna come?"

The younger man shrugged, "guess so," he replied.

"You guess so?" Mick looked away. It was easy to tell he was disgusted. "May as well stay here with the girls then," said the Vietnam Veteran, standing to gather the plates.

"Gee, thanks a lot Dad, way to let your daughter and grand-daughter know they feel useful," Katie said, rolling her eyes.

"Sorry love, I didn't mean it that way, I meant-"

"I know what you bloody meant by it!" Katie stormed. "Cook your own dinner next time!"

"Love!" Mick said as Katie gathered Jade up in her arms and left the room. "Love, come on!" But she ignored him.

"Alright, I'll go along, you old bastard!" snapped Ben.

Diverting his attention back to the young man, Mick held up his hands. "Doesn't bother me, mate. But our country just got invaded and in case you hadn't noticed, we are slowly but surely being overrun by a very persistent enemy. All I ask is you have a bit of conviction, a bit of pride, a little passion. 'I guess so' does not cut it. Now stand your arse up and help me wash up, boy!"

Ben was blushing furiously, he looked angry and embarrassed, but did as he was asked.

"I use it to fertilise resting paddocks after they have gone through improved pasturing," said Mick gesturing towards a large drum full of fertiliser.

Craig nodded, hands on hips, looking at the drum thoughtfully. "Got any diesel?"

"This is a farm, mate, there'd be a problem if I didn't have diesel," Mick grunted.

"Right, well we have ourselves a bomb," replied Craig. "You got any other drums like this one?"

Mick pointed to five other drums hidden beneath a bench top.

"How many you need?" asked Ben, who had walked out with the men.

"Two," said Craig.

"It's gunna be heavy to carry the fertiliser and diesel," observed Mick whistling softly.

"We'll drive most of the way," said Matty, "but like I said last night," he grinned, "it ain't gunna be a Sunday stroll in the park."

The men spent the day preparing the drums of fertiliser, discussing tactics, planning when and where the bombs would be placed and what would happen post detonation. The detonation device would be a small piece of C4 pushed into the middle of the fertiliser and diesel mix. Attached to the C4 would be a small detonator initiated by an electric charge delivered by a small ride on mower battery. Once the C4 detonated, it would cause the forty-four gallon drum to explode.

"So, let me get this straight," said Ben, "you're going to bury the drums almost next to each other?"

Craig nodded.

"Don't you want to hit multiple targets? Wouldn't it be better if the drums were distanced?"

"Yeah, mate, we do want to hit multiple targets, but most of these vehicles are armoured. The first explosion will disable the vehicle, probably won't do much damage to the guys inside, though. We'll hit a vehicle in the centre of the convoy, which will bring the convoy to a halt. Soldiers from the vehicles in front and behind the disabled truck should dismount and approach in a relatively close group to check on the occupants of the target vehicle. Once that group is close enough, we'll detonate the second bomb."

Ben nodded. "Jesus, that's cruel, but effective I guess. They teach you that in the Army?"

"No, mate," replied Craig. "The Taliban taught us that one."

Next day, late in the afternoon, the group set off, Craig driving. They travelled slowly, the engine purring along quietly. The soldiers were armed with their personal weapons, whilst the two civilian men were armed with bolt action rifles. Mick carried his trusty .303 rifle, whilst he had given Ben a smaller .223 bolt action rifle with a scope. Ben had his window wound down, he found the air that wafted in chilly, but refreshing. The journey was long and slow, Craig avoiding driving on the road where possible, favouring instead to dodge and weave through the dense forest. Sometimes where the ground looked boggy, Matty would slowly patrol ahead to check that it was safe to drive on.

"Ah, shit!" Ben swore as a sapling, bent back by the Navara's frame, whipped in through the open window, slapping him hard in the face.

"Yeah, might want to wind your window up," grinned Matty from the front passenger seat.

Mick shook his head. He knew it would be only a matter of time before it happened, but wanted the boy to learn through his mistakes. A tough, but effective way to learn. Grumbling quietly, Ben closed the window, rubbing his cheek where a red welt was starting to form.

The group had discussed what to do if they came across an Indonesian patrol whilst driving. Craig would do his utmost to drive out of the contact whilst the others provided suppressing fire. However, if the vehicle was disabled, or a fast mounted withdrawal was not possible, the group would dismount on the non-contact side and withdraw to safety. Matty still carried three of the explosive devices he had used on the Indonesian comms rig days before. One of these was fitted to the roof of the vehicle, but remained unarmed. If the group were to dismount and withdraw, Matty would arm the device before he left. This would ensure that the Nissan would be destroyed, preventing it from falling into enemy hands. All scenarios had been discussed.

The soldiers had also sat Ben and Mick down where they touched on escape and evasion, and if captured, resistance to interrogation. The SASR soldiers had learned these skills over many, many years spent in the Army. Ben and Mick had only scratched the surface that afternoon, but what little they had been taught was better than nothing.

Growling slowly into a dry riverbed, the Navara came to a halt. Craig had parked the vehicle in a sharp bend where it could not be seen easily. Camouflaging the vehicle took less than ten minutes. When they had finished, it was indiscernible from the surrounding environment. Although Mick grumbled and muttered to himself, Craig instructed him not to carry anything other than the two shovels. The old soldier patrolled at 'tail end charlie', Matty patrolled as scout, whilst Craig and Ben carried a barrel of the homemade explosive between them to the ambush site. Once there, they hid the explosive from sight. Ben's breath came in long rasps, his muscles burned and sweat slid down his face in rivulets. When he had caught his breath, the small group quietly patrolled back to the vehicle. Again Craig and Ben carried the second barrel towards the ambush site. Three times they were forced to stop as Ben regained his breath, stretched his muscles or wiped sweat from his brow.

Allowing the natural sound of the forest to envelope them, the group lay in silence waiting for dusk. Craig had chosen a particularly sandy area of road on which to lay the ambush, for no other reason than it would take little time to bury the explosives. Digging sand was also much quieter than digging soil.

Ben fidgeted with boredom, every few minutes trying to move his body into a more comfortable position, or rolling a little to pull a small rock out from under him. Each time he did so, the leaf litter around him crackled under his body. A tiny pebble struck him in the face and for a moment he thought the object had fallen from a nearby towering tree. As he glanced around to see where it had come from, he noticed Craig glaring at him. The soldier silently mouthed two words that left Ben in no doubt as to what he wanted.

"Keep still!"

Within the hour, dusk had been defeated by night. Hearing quiet movement, Ben knew Craig was on his feet, moving towards the road. Patting the ground next to him, Ben finally felt the handle of the shovel. Climbing to his feet, he tentatively moved out onto the sandy road. Gripping his shoulder, Craig steered the young man before tapping him on the shoulder, the signal to let Ben know that was where he was to dig his hole. The two men worked quickly, stopping regularly to listen for any obscure sounds to indicate things were about to take a turn for the worse.

The holes were dug within half an hour. Ben struggled to keep his heavy breathing as quiet as possible, although he found it difficult. Once again sweat dripped from his face and his muscles burned with fatigue. They carried the barrels out onto the road, gently slid them into position, attached the wire to the small detonators inside the barrels before filling in the holes. Running the wires back to their ambush position Ben lay prone once more, wiping his brow. Craig, however, moved back onto the road and carefully hid both the wire and their footprints from view before taking his place. In front of the soldier was a small ride on lawn mower battery.

The battery would provide a small charge needed to activate the detonator, causing the Improvised Explosive Device (IED) to explode. Because the barrel was buried, the only way for the explosion to travel would be up, delivering all of its kinetic energy straight into the underside of the enemy truck.

Matty had carefully moved from the small group, positioning himself almost one hundred metres away. He had silently placed a claymore mine some ten metres behind him, in case an enemy approached from the rear. The weapon, if needed, would either kill the enemy outright, or provide a distraction giving the soldier precious seconds to turn and fire upon the enemy. The claymore was a precaution, and more than likely, he would not need to use it. Matty hoped that when the convoy was stopped by the group's

IED, the last vehicle would be close to his position, allowing him to move forward and place the tracking device.

Ben was uncomfortable, although he made a conscious effort to remain still. He sighed quietly, boredom washing over him. He reached down and scratched the back of his right thigh, where a mosquito had recently bitten him. It was the engine that made him freeze, however. The noise ebbed and flowed with the gentle breeze. As it grew closer, the sound became more consistent, a single vehicle possibly. The engine seemed deafening to Ben after being exposed to such silence for so long. Then he saw the bright headlights flickering through the forest. It was moving fast. The vehicle was close now, and by the sound of the engine and the distance between the headlights and the ground, it was not a truck. The small four wheel drive tore past the group's position, none the wiser to their presence.

They let the enemy pass unhurt. Blowing up one vehicle was meaningless. After all, the point of the ambush was to create a decoy in order for a tracking device to be placed on an enemy vehicle. Craig was worried that the weight of the vehicle had damaged the detonation wires, in which case the ambush would fail. If both sets of wires were broken, they would have to repair them the following day and try again.

Ben was frozen in place, sweat beading his brow. His itches and discomforts forgotten as adrenalin pumped around his body. For Mick, he was once again lying amongst the humid jungle of Vietnam. Lying in silent wait brought back the memories in a flood. The patrols, fire fights, ambushes and the good times too. His hands were clammy as they clamped the trusty old rifle close to his chest. Without thinking about it, Jonny's face came to mind, clear as crystal. Mick closed his eyes and willed the ghost to leave him be. He could usually control his mind, bring it back to the present, but this time, the face remained, floating in his mind, unwilling to leave. When he opened his eyes again, the dark scrub around him was blurred. A tear slid down one cheek. Jonny Hargraves. Christ, one of the best blokes he had ever met. A brother. A warrior. Killed on a Friday afternoon, an enemy bullet lodged in his guts. Mick shook his head. It had taken him two hours of horrible agony to die. Closing his eyes again he willed Jonny to leave.

Jonny did eventually leave, but not through any effort of Mick's. The noise of the distant engines caused his retreat. There were a lot of vehicles and they were coming towards the group.

"Standby," whispered Craig, "weapons ready."

CHAPTER EIGHT

*"**Police departments across the country struggle against mass public riots demanding action in Australia."* Philadelphia Daily News, Philadelphia.

Concentration Camp Hatta, 5 weeks post invasion

Grant Bridge was starving. Following the assault on Sydney Airport, few knew that it was a decoy for a much larger national invasion attempt. Twenty-four hours later, the Australian Army was fully engaged in combat and on the back foot from the start. Sydney sounded like Baghdad during the peak of the Gulf War, the incessant crackle and pop of machinegun and rifle fire, day after day. In the beginning, Grant tried to keep track of the fighting, listening as it moved from suburb to suburb, sometimes remaining in one place for many hours. On rare occasions, the noise of battle headed back in the direction it had approached, indicating the Australian soldiers were pushing the enemy back.

A black pall hung over the city, growing thicker by the day as ruined residential or business blocks spewed flame and smoke into the sky. On the evening of the fifth day, the noise of the gun battles dwindled away. Without television or radio coverage, Grant had no way of knowing exactly what was happening. Instinct told him the Australian Army had fought hard, that they had fought long, but were no longer. Eight days later, the Indonesian soldiers arrived in his suburb. They swept through the houses like a plague, kicking in doors, smashing windows, burning indiscriminately. Women were raped, men beaten, children led away, departing in trucks, crammed together like sardines. The men and women were separated before they too were driven away.

When his front door was smashed in, Grant kicked the first soldier in the groin, made a grab for his rifle and failed. He was beaten unconscious and dragged away. It was here, in Camp Hatta, with a hammering headache, he awoke. By his reckoning, that was almost four weeks ago. All personal belongings had been stripped from the prisoners, so without a watch, he lost all track of time. One piece of stale bread and a cup of water was breakfast, and at night, they were rationed one boiled potato and another cup of water. Grant was losing what he estimated to be at least five kilograms per week. He felt tired, lethargic and weak.

He had no idea where Camp Hatta was, but it was on the coast, surrounded by open country. Whichever direction Sydney lay, it was far away. He assumed this was planned, so that if any prisoners escaped they could be hunted down quickly. There was nowhere to hide. On the upside, though, the Indonesian guards were not particularly interested in their duty. The prisoners were allowed to wander around the camp's grounds as they wished, during day or night. However, if a prisoner went missing, they had been instructed in no uncertain terms that a prisoner would be shot every five minutes, until the fugitive was found.

No one put this to the test, but Grant had little doubt the Indonesian guards would have any compunction carrying the duty out. His stomach growled loudly again as he sat by the perimeter fence, looking out over the ocean in the near distance. He could not see the water through the dark curtain of the moonless night, but he could hear and smell it. However, that was not what attracted him. It was the sound of battle, very distant, far out to sea, but there nonetheless.

The noise was like waves of thunder, but it was the distant flashes as missiles scudded through the cloud cover, that suggested the event was no act of nature. An Australian ship was out there somewhere engaged in heavy fighting. As each rumble rolled over the camp, Grant silently willed victory upon the Aussie Navy. Occasionally a missile descended with deadly intent, but was met with a long flicker of tracer fire, destroying the warhead before it found its target. Without a watch, he assumed the battle persisted for perhaps two hours. After silence once again descended upon the camp, he could see two miniscule blots of light in the far distance, almost imperceptible to the naked eye. The light was more than likely thrown by burning ships. He hoped the Australians survived, however, had no way of knowing.

Falling asleep against the fence, he remained there throughout the night, eventually stirring with the dawn. Stretching, he yawned, watching bickering seagulls diving and wheeling nearby, envying their freedom. Grant and his ex-wife, Sarah, had parted ways more than five years ago in an angry, bitter and messy divorce. They had not remained in contact. However, as the hint of the coming sun touched the eastern sky, he thought of her, hoping she survived the invasion.

Shouting started in the camp and with a sigh, he climbed to his feet. Head count and breakfast time. Bleary-eyed Australians stumbled out of their poorly built dormitory blocks, being herded into a large conglomerate by shouting Indonesians. Grant joined them, jostling and pushing in an attempt to move closer to the front of the meandering line. One guard handed out breakfast, his face lined with disgust as a second silently counted each man as he moved through.

Once Grant had collected his piece of stale bread and small cup of water, he was ushered over to join the others as they stood and ate in silence. This prevented a prisoner doubling back and either attaining a second helping, or covering for a prisoner who may have escaped during the night.

Trying to ignore the foul taste, he raked his eyes over the area of ocean where he thought the battle occurred during the night. Squinting, he saw two small puffs of smoke where ships were still burning. However, closer to shore he watched as a tiny, grey, sleek ship glided through the water. The battle's victor. Without any way of knowing, Grant hoped it was an Australian ship. A thought occurred to him. Slowly, as to divert suspicion, he looked around the large throng who stood in silence, munching half-heartedly on their meal. Many, more concerned with family, than stale bread.

Keeping his gaze on the dirt, he shuffled forward, until he was standing beside a man whose name he did not know. What he did know, was the man possessed a small torch, which, somehow, had not yet been confiscated.

"What's it gonna cost to borrow your torch," Grant whispered, looking at the ground.

"Your dinner ration," he replied quietly, wiping his mouth with the back of his hand.

"Done."

"Meet me after. But if you break it, it'll be your breakfast and dinner ration for the next week. Clear?" spoke the man, eyeing a bored guard in the near distance.

"Crystal," Grant replied.

With breakfast finished, his stomach still growling with hunger, he found the man in question residing in the dormitory opposite his own.

"How'd you sneak it in?" Grant asked.

The man stopped digging and glanced up. "You don't wanna know."

Seconds later, Grant had his torch. Checking that it worked, he placed it in a pocket and turned to leave.

"By the way, the name's Grant."

"Wayne," replied the man.

Grant nodded and left.

The prisoners were not provided any bedding. They simply slept upon the ground. Within the initial fortnight, many of the elderly men, unable to access their medication, became ill, some of them dying. After the first four weeks, all of the elderly were dead and several of the weaker members of the camp were falling ill. Grant knew it was only a matter of time before they all suffered the same fate.

Twice per week, a supply truck dropped off food and water for the camp before loading the deceased bodies and departing. The truck was not due for two days and as Grant lay upon ground, hands behind his head, he could smell the faint aroma of the dead piled in the distant corner of the camp. How long would it be before he was one of them?

Throughout the day, he strolled outside and without trying to draw too much attention to himself, looked out to sea where the small, very distant grey ship was still visible. It was no longer moving, and may have anchored. That was exactly what he hoped for. Whoever or whatever was looking out for him was clearly listening to his haphazard prayers. As dusk began to fall, Grant willed the ship to remain anchored. Evening fell victim to darkness and he quietly placed himself against the perimeter fence in the same place as the night before.

Whilst he had not studied Morse code in any depth, he did know how to signal 'SOS'. Aiming the torch at the area of ocean upon which he had last seen the ship, Grant signalled the short message with the torch, cupping his hand around the implement so that the light could not be seen by any of the guards in the camp behind him. Not that they would care. The guards would probably be playing cards in their barrack block. Grant signalled the message repeatedly, hour upon hour. Switching hands he continued until the fingers of both hands were numb with exhaustion. At no time was there ever a reply that Grant could see and with a sinking heart, he leaned against the fence, weakness and lethargy driving him into the arms of slumber.

Boomer lay flat upon the sidewall of the rigid-hulled inflatable boat (RHIB), the M4 assault rifle pulled into his shoulder. He stared through the night vision scope fixed to the weapon, but could see nothing other than the ocean speeding towards him before it disappeared beneath the hull of the boat. His driver had the throttle fully open. It had been more than an hour since the SOS signal stopped. Not wishing to take any chances, the hierarchy of the Australian Navy aboard HMAS Newcastle deemed that a single Navy

Clearance Diver would be sufficient to reconnoitre the coast to ascertain from where the signal was coming.

The RHIB throttled back and shut down ten kilometres from the coast. The boat would wait for Boomer's return. The Navy diver slipped silently over the side of the RHIB and began the swim towards the coast. Wearing breathing apparatus meant he would make the swim at sixty feet below the surface. The re-breather forced his exhaled breaths into a storage tank on his back eliminating bubbles appearing on the surface. Boomer's dive mask was fitted with night vision so that he could detect any threats below the surface, including those posed by marine wildlife.

Forty minutes passed before Boomer saw the coast. Surfacing, he advanced slowly, weapon pulled into his shoulder. Once on the beach he crouched, doffed his re-breather, flippers and goggles. Moving quietly up the beach, he scanned his environment. Stopping every few minutes, he took a knee, watching, listening. Within half a kilometre he went to ground, staring through the night vision scope attached to his weapon at a large chain link fence.

The fence was at least twelve feet tall, lined with double barbed wire strands angled inwards, meaning it was designed to keep people inside. What interested him more was the silhouette sitting against the fence. The man's head was leaned against the chain link. He looked asleep. Lying silently, Boomer waited for him to move. He did not stir, although his chest was moving, but slowly. The man was asleep. Moving again, the Navy Diver advanced cautiously, silently.

As the fence became more defined in the grainy, green view of the night vision scope, Boomer saw that the barrier formed one side of a huge perimeter. Against one side of the perimeter were ten or twelve large wooden buildings. Built on the opposite side of the enclosure was a single, large, brick building, far surpassing the poor construct of the wooden dwellings.

Boomer advanced until he was within one metre of the sleeping figure. He crouched behind the sleeping man, sweeping his environment for threats, but finding nothing. Looking carefully, Boomer could see no weapon near the man. In fact, he was dressed in shabby clothes and looked skinny to the point of anorexic. Pushing the barrel of the M4 through the fence, he jabbed the weapon into the man's side. A soft mutter, movement and the man looked in his direction.

"Who's there?" the Australian voice asked.

Boomer released pressure on the trigger.

"Navy, who are you?"

"Grant Bridge, we're prisoners of the Indonesians," the relief evident in his voice.

"Jesus Christ. Prisoners? How many are there of you, mate?"

"Not sure exactly," whispered Grant, "four hundred I'd say."

"Are the Indonesians in that brick building?"

"Yeah."

"Do they patrol the camp? And how many are there?" asked Boomer.

"No, they're lazy, no patrols. From what I can hear, I think they play cards mostly, although they'll shoot one prisoner every five minutes if one of us goes missing. There's between thirty to forty guards."

"Right, I'll be back tomorrow night and I'll be bringing friends. You make sure that you and all the prisoners are inside all night long. If we spot anyone outside in the open, they will be dealt with like an enemy, do you understand what I mean by that?"

Grant was waiting outside as dawn broke, almost an hour before the guards woke the camp. He was excited, nervous and hopeful at the same time. Following breakfast, the prisoners shambled back to their dormitories. Grant returned the torch to Wayne. Once done, he set about visiting each of the accommodation buildings, explaining to his fellow prisoners what had transpired the night before. He also advised it was in their best interest not to wander out during the coming evening.

Hope spread throughout the camp like wildfire, although the Australians were careful not to provide any reason for their guards to become suspicious. However, the news was bitter sweet. Three more prisoners, all elderly men, had passed away during the night. The Indonesian guards ordered several of the prisoners to carry the bodies of the deceased out to the already growing pile of corpses.

Grant knew that sooner than later, hygiene would take a nosedive and the camp would be swept with disease if the deceased were not buried. The guards would not allow this to be done, preferring the bodies to be loaded onto the truck. It was the smell, however, that eventually changed the guards' minds. As the heat of the sun swept over the coast, the sobering aroma of rotting flesh wafted throughout the camp, settling in noses and sinking into clothes.

Providing shovels, they ordered a group of prisoners, of which Grant was one, to the gruelling task. Digging was the easy part. Dragging the dead to their graves was difficult. The fresh corpses proved to be straight forward, but decomposition had settled into those who had died days before and several times arms or legs simply pulled clear of the body. Dry retching and vomiting, the men went about their business. Grant made a conscious effort to hold the contents of his stomach down, not for any show of bravado, simply to allow his body to metabolise any food that may still be in his belly.

As dusk began to paint the western sky in hues of pink and orange, the prisoners, sweating, exhausted and dirty, completed their task. The usual boiled potato for dinner was eaten half-heartedly by some. Grant approached those who were having trouble eating and forced them to finish their meal. Malnourished as they were, one boiled potato was better than nothing. Following the evening meal, the prisoners returned to their dormitories where those who had been digging most of the day collapsed into sleep, exhaustion rendering them helpless.

Grant's eyes snapped open, his heart pounding. He thought he heard something. Rolling over, he looked through the nearby entrance of the dorm, but could see and hear nothing, other than the normal sounds of night. Sighing, he lay down, closed his eyes and began to drift away, sleep engulfing him. A soft click brought him fully awake, his heart thundering once more. It sounded like a fence being cut. Quietly standing, he walked to the entrance and crouched against the frame, eyes wide in an attempt to see through the curtain of darkness.

Boredom embraced him and as Grant was about to retreat to his sleeping area, he saw them. A dark smudge of men, barely visible. They were in a tight group, moving fast. Seconds later they had melted away into the darkness. Try as he may, Grant's naked eye was not effective enough to see where they were.

Boomer knelt beside the door leading into the Indonesians' building. Light was still visible from beneath the door, meaning Rick had not yet located the power box. Small square shapes fixed to the roof suggested solar power was being used. Behind him, four Clearance Divers were knelt close behind one another, ready to follow Boomer into the building to begin the assault. All armed with sub machine guns. None of the men wore night vision. Attached beneath the barrel of their weapons was a bright torch that would be switched on once the assault began. It was this light that would aid their sight, provide easy target acquisition as well as blind the enemy. Boomer crouched ready to advance.

Another small group of Clearance Divers located two more doors, one on the opposite end of the building and another on the far side. Entering the door at the opposite end was fraught with danger as the assaulters would be firing towards each other. The second assaulting group were stacked up outside the side door. The attack would be made from two areas simultaneously causing confusion amongst the Indonesian guards.

Rick's voice crackled through the radio headsets worn by all assaulters present. "Stand by, stand by." A loud snap reverberated from the opposite side of the building and the glow of light emanating beneath the door disappeared. "Go!"

Boomer felt a thump on his back indicating that the man behind held a flash/bang stun grenade ready to throw. Moving swiftly forward, Boomer turned the handle, pushed the door open and heard the stun grenade whirl through the air as it was thrown over his shoulder. The device landed with a soft thud and exploded almost instantly, sending the occupants of the building into a state of disorientation as blinding light and deafening noise filled the building. The device caused little effect upon the Australians as they had trained with flash/bangs incessantly, to the point of desensitisation. The surprise would only last seconds, however, that was all the assaulters needed to enter the building. Switching on the flashlight fixed beneath the barrel of his weapon Boomer brushed through the doorway, fired two shots into a nearby enemy and stepped left, allowing the man behind him to enter.

Gunfire exploded as the attacking Australians forced their way through the building, shooting any and all Indonesian guards on sight. The two-pronged attack lasted less than one minute, leaving Indonesian guards lying lifeless upon the floor or slumped in chairs.

After clearing the building to ensure they had not missed any enemy, the assaulters departed quietly, leaving the building silent and stinking of cordite.

Crowding around the doorway, Grant's entire building was awake, hearts thundering as adrenalin and hope filtered through their veins. Interspersed with several explosions and bright flashes, the gunfire was loud. Lasting only a short time, the Indonesian Guardroom was left standing dark and silent. Gone were the muffled laughs and shouts as cards were played or jokes shared.

Seeing movement in his peripheral vision, Grant squinted through the blackness. There! On the far side of the camp, the same dull, silhouetted smudge of soldiers leaving just as fast as they had entered. Within minutes they had disappeared, without a word, without a trace.

"We're free," whispered Grant.

"Just like that?"

"Just like that!" Grant replied, excitement turning the whisper into a hiss.

"Righto fellas, up ya get!" the loud voice brought them out of slumber.

Bleary eyes and weary brains prepared for head count and breakfast, but as tired prisoners stumbled out of their buildings, much later in the morning than they were used to rising, they were presented with a very different scenario. A large group of grinning, Australian Navy personnel were standing before them and within moments reality sank in once again. They were free!

Tables of food waited before them. Steaming bacon, poached eggs, fresh toast, baked beans and sausages. The smell brought fond memories flooding back. Many of the men could only consume one very small serving of food, their stomachs having shrunk and their bodies beginning to burn fat and muscle in an attempt to survive.

The fresh breakfast was bitter sweet for many as their bodies had not consumed such rich food for so long. A large percentage of former prisoners were left with bellyaches, nausea, vomiting or diarrhoea.

However, concentrating on the calories, Grant ignored both the nausea and bellyache, forcing his body to digest and absorb the energy it so desperately needed.

"Grant Bridge!" a voice called.

Grant did not hear his name as he sat leaning against the perimeter fence, enjoying the feeling of a full belly but staving off nausea.

A gentle kick in the leg brought him around. "Someone wants you, mate," said Wayne. "By the way, you can have your dinner ration back! I got no idea what you did with that bloody torch the other night, but I owe you one," he grinned.

Nodding, he stood and made his way over to a lean, very strong looking man dressed in an Australian Navy uniform.

"That you, Granto?" asked the man grinning.

Grant nodded.

"Boomer," he thrust out his hand and took Grant's in a crushing grip. "Nice to meet you."

Grant tried not to wince, but failed.

"Sorry mate," Boomer released the grip. "Listen, we'll spread the word

82

later, but I thought you should be the first to know. We're on half rations as it is, so we can only provide a limited amount of food. Unfortunately, we can't take any of you guys with us, however, we've brought survival kits, matchless fire sets and fishing kits. We've also brought about twenty osmosis pumps. The osmosis pump will filter seawater and turn it into fresh water, but I'll show you how to use that later. If each man spends five minutes per day on an osmosis pump, you guys should have plenty of fresh water to go around. We've brought some non-perishable food, several semi-automatic rifles and a few pistols."

"I was a security guard at Sydney airport, so I know how to use a pistol," said Grant, weariness enveloping him as his body diverted all its energy to digesting his full stomach.

"Great! You can show the others. We'll spend a short time showing those of you who have already handled weapons before, how to use the rifles. No big drama. However, Granto, you guys need to get away from here, because it'll only be a matter of time before those guys send a truck to resupply and discover what's happened."

Grant nodded. "That truck's only days away."

"Well you need to escape sooner than later in that case. Anyway mate, you look tired, I'll let you get a kip."

Grant smiled weakly. "Boomer!" he called to the man's departing back. Boomer turned. "Thank you!"

The Navy Clearance Diver walked back. "No worries mate." Drawing his 9mm Browning pistol, he slapped it into Grant's hand, closely followed by three spare magazines, each containing thirteen bullets. "Remember, harsh as it might seem, look after number one. Some blokes probably won't want to go too far from this camp. Sounds stupid, but psychologically, this feels safe to them. You're going to have to leave them behind. Get away from here, go as far as you can."

Grant nodded, thanked the man again before turning away.

"Oh and Granto?"

He looked back at Boomer.

"Keep your head down, mate!"

CHAPTER NINE

*"*apital of Australia falls into enemy hands! Contact lost with Australian Prime Minister and his government. They are feared dead."* The Irish Times, Dublin.

The first truck trundled passed their position at a sedate pace. Craig continued to worry about damage to the buried wires. If they were broken, he would have to consider a better way in which to reinforce them before trying again the next night. Acrid diesel fumes wafted over the waiting men as the convoy slowly navigated the sandy stretch of road. The vehicles swept by one after the other, the noise of their engines merging into one loud growl.

With one set of wires clutched in his left hand, Craig pulled the battery closer and brought the first set of wires closer to the power source. Estimating that the middle of the convoy was now passing them, he waited until one of the trucks was almost on top of the buried explosives. With a quiet zap, he touched the first set of wires down onto the battery, one exposed wire touching positive, the other touching negative.

The thunder that followed sounded like a colossal bass drum being struck by God. Throwing sand and flame directly up through the floor of the vehicle, the explosion lifted the front wheels into the air at least one metre. As the roar echoed out over hundreds of hectares, the Indonesian truck, its engine all but destroyed, came to a halt. A new sound replaced the dying noise of the explosion. Screaming.

Coming to a halt behind the disabled vehicle, Indonesian soldiers began dismounting from the rear, running forward to render aid. As comprehension dawned, the entire convoy came to a slow halt. Soldiers came running to their wounded comrades from vehicles both at the front and rear of the convoy. A number of soldiers provided cover either side of the convoy, but being unsure if the explosion had been command or pressure detonated were not certain Australian freedom fighters were within the vicinity or not. Within

84

minutes, a large group had surrounded the stricken truck, dragging out wounded and several dead. First aid commenced, trauma pads and bandages appearing from medical kits.

Watching, the Australians lay silently. Mick and Craig observed events with a detached mind, both considering when the best time would be to employ the second explosive device. However, with wide, disbelieving eyes, Ben felt sorry for the Indonesian soldiers before him. They were confused, scared and on the edge of panic. He felt as if he should run forward and help, but knew how stupid that sounded. A hand clamped on his shoulder and he turned to see Craig watching him. The soldier gave a reassuring nod, as if he were somehow reading Ben's mind.

Craig noticed one Indonesian soldier in particular who was striding around offering words of encouragement, stopping panicking soldiers and reassuring them. It was when the individual began pointing out an area of sand nearby and shouting orders that Craig realised he was preparing a triage area. The enemy were beginning to organise themselves, overcoming their initial panic. Time to hit them again.

Discarding the original wires, Craig grasped the second set of wires and with the same quiet zap as before, he placed them against the battery's terminals. God struck his bass drum once more and the thunder of the explosion shook the ground violently.

Flame, sand and bodies were thrown into the air indiscriminately, broken human forms crumpling to earth with dull thuds. Those closest to the blast simply disintegrated, blood and body parts splattering against vehicles and foliage. The organisation they had so recently developed was destroyed, panic once again flooding through the ranks. A number of troops travelling in the original truck had been wounded by the initial blast. However, the second explosion had decimated their ranks, wounding or killing many soldiers from several trucks.

The decoy was a success. All enemy eyes were upon the devastation before them. No one noticed the solitary figure creep out of the Australian bush into the midst of the Indonesian convoy.

Matty placed a hand on the enemy vehicle, hearing constant ticking as the engine cooled. The shouting and screaming was distant, although he could hear anxious chattering emanating from the cabin above him. Two soldiers from what he could hear. They were talking about the ambush, although the rest of the sentence was muffled and indiscernible. Ducking below the underside, he crept forward until he was beneath the centre of the truck. The tracking device being the size of his palm, was easy to place and invisible to all but the closest inspection.

Pushing the device against bare metal, he activated the magnet, held the small button on the side down until it vibrated gently, acknowledging it had commenced uploading the tracking signal. Matty crept out from under the truck and as he was straightening, he heard the closest door slam and looked at the back of an enemy soldier. Standing statue still, Matty was less than one foot from the soldier, who was staring towards the distant screaming and shouting.

The overwhelming aroma of urine wafted over Matty and he realised the soldier was taking a piss. A quiet zipping noise and the enemy turned around to climb back into the truck, but instead jumped in fright as he looked straight at Matty.

Craig tapped Ben on the shoulder, jerking his thumb in the direction they had approached. Time to leave. As he had been instructed and rehearsed, Ben remained prone, inching his way backwards, away from the scene of carnage before him. Using the tips of his toes and elbows. It was slow, but as close to silent as possible. The enemy soldiers screaming, shouting and dying less than thirty metres away were oblivious to their presence.

Within ten minutes the three men were far enough away that they could move into a crouch and take cover behind trees, waiting for the arrival of Matty, before they departed.

Even though Matty wore the uniform of an Indonesian and looked the part, the enemy soldier seemed suspicious. As Matty was about to engage the soldier in conversation to ease his mind, the enemy shouted a warning to his comrade in the truck's cabin.

Matty reacted instinctively. Punching the man in the solar plexus, he winded the Indonesian, silencing him. A knife appeared in Matty's hand and with a quick step, he was behind his enemy. Plunging the blade into the man's neck below his ear, he ripped the knife forward, severing carotid arteries, voice box and windpipe. The blade sheared through the front of the Indonesian's neck in a spray of warm blood followed by a gush of hot air as the man attempted to scream.

A door slammed on the far side and Matty knew the second soldier had decamped the vehicle and was walking around to investigate. Lying face down, blood spreading out over the ground around him, the enemy had bled out within ten seconds, his weak struggling having stopped.

Matty heard the second Indonesian approaching from the front of the truck, so crept around the rear. Peering from his concealed position, Matty watched as the soldier knelt beside his comrade. Discovering he was dead, the Indonesian looked around suspiciously, before standing. Un-holstering a sidearm, the enemy soldier flicked the safety catch off. Having already walked around the front of the vehicle, he decided that was secure, so began moving towards the rear. Walking faster than Matty anticipated, the Indonesian was standing before him within seconds. Jumping with surprise, the wide-eyed Indonesian pointed his sidearm at Matty's chest.

Matty dropped the knife and raised his hands in the air. He noticed the pistol was shaking. The man seemed nervous, meaning he would probably hold his fire. Probably. The man had not alerted anyone else to Matty's presence. Good, thought the Australian.

"I'm sorry," said Matty in Indonesian, taking a step forward.

The enemy soldier seemed surprised at the fluent speech with which Matty spoke.

"I'm really sorry," Matty's tone suggested deep regret.

The Australian, now less than an arm's length from the weapon, waited for his enemy to speak. When he was about to reply, Matty made his move. With lightning speed, he grasped the barrel of the pistol with his left hand and turned it away. This served to protect him should the soldier choose to fire, however, it also levered the pistol grip out of the soldier's control. With his right hand, Matty grasped the pistol, pulling it clear of the enemy's grasp. Stepping back, he levelled the weapon at the Indonesian's shocked face.

Within seconds, the Australian's brain analysed the risks of killing the soldier. The gunshot would be heard, enemy would investigate, his chances of capture would escalate. But what if he did not kill the enemy? As soon as he withdrew from the area, the Indonesian would alert his comrades and a large hunter force would be gathered. Either way, he was in trouble.

With a snarl, the Indonesian charged, tackling Matty around the waist and driving him to the ground. Even as he was falling, the Australian was looking behind him for the knife. Deciding the noise of a gunshot would place him in even greater danger, he threw the pistol out of reach. Punches rained down upon his torso and face, but Matty ignored them, stretching for the knife. Fingers closed around the hilt and he slammed the blade straight up into his enemy's voice box. Reversing his grip on the blade, he slashed the sharp knife across the man's throat, severing the carotid artery. Rolling away from the Indonesian, hot blood splattering across his face, Matty stood. Kicking the Indonesian onto his face, Matty stepped over him, picked up the pistol and melted into the forest. Collecting the Claymore, he moved slowly and quietly. Within minutes he had joined the rest of the group at the emergency rendezvous (ERV) and they departed silently, leaving the scene of carnage behind.

Jase rolled inverted and pulled back hard, the FA-18 shuddering as g-force assaulted the airframe. Tensing the muscles of his body, relax, exhale, immediate inhale, tense. The G strain was an effective method that kept pilots conscious, but it was exhausting over long periods, placing strain on the body. Looking straight up through the canopy, he saw distant clumps of forest making a last stand against open fields. Within seconds, the ground was immediately in front of him, approaching fast. 6,000 feet and descending rapidly. A brief glance over his shoulder and the persistent tiny black dot rocketing down through the cloud cover told Jase his attempt to shake the enemy aircraft had failed.

Thirty minutes before, he and Mack were flying a routine mission, attacking enemy shipping lines. Within minutes of commencing their first gun run, they had been intercepted by enemy combat air patrol. Seven enemy aircraft in total. Two enemy aircraft were destroyed within the opening moments of the dogfight. However, Mack and Jase had been separated, three aircraft chasing Jase and the remaining two on Mack. Thirty minutes of dogfighting and Jase had defeated two enemy aircraft, leaving one persistent, very skilful enemy on his tail. Low on fuel, ammunition, altitude and with no air-to-air missiles left, Jase was running out of options.

A long, loud tone told Jase his enemy was about to launch a missile. He broke right, leaving a string of flares behind. The cockpit shook under the pressure of the turn, Jase conducted G strain, pulling back as hard as possible. His vision dimmed, Jase's body desperately staving off a blackout. Shooting a look over his left shoulder, he watched the missile explode against a flare. Straightening out and breathing hard, sweat sliding down his face, Jase ascended hard in an attempt to thwart his enemy. But the veteran pilot followed instantly, firing a short burst from the gun.

Tracers flickered passed Jase. He went into a break turn to the left, firing a string of flares, however, only three deployed. Now depleted of flares, Jase was almost defenceless. Throttling back and climbing violently, the airframe acted like a massive airbrake, dumping air speed at an incredible rate. Too slow to react, the enemy fighter streaked below Jase. Pushing down, throttling up, disengaging airbrake, his enemy was now in front and below him. The perfect kill shot. However, out of ammunition and rockets, Jase turned away in a violent break turn in an effort to shake his adversary.

Applying full throttle, the aircraft tore across the sky like some ancient god, landscape slipping below in a blur of green. Trying to place as much distance between himself and his enemy was Jase's last hope, the last resort. A rapid beeping, quickening to one long sound told Jase he had failed. Agility was lost at high speed, and although Jase turned as hard as he could, the enemy missile had little trouble acquiring the heat signature thrown by the twin jet engines of the FA-18 Hornet. The missile took three seconds to travel four kilometres.

Jase felt the explosion, the shock wave hitting his body like a sledgehammer. The aircraft immediately lost power and became unresponsive. Reeling from the explosion, a one second glance at the instruments told him the game was over.

Ensuring he was transmitting on the secure channel, Jase gave his co-ordinates so a rescue force could be launched. Leaning back, pushing his head into the headrest, reaching between his legs, Jase pulled hard on the ejection handle. In less than half a second, a series of small explosive charges detached the canopy from the airframe. Within one second of the handle being pulled, Jase's ejection seat was clear of the doomed fighter. Keeping his head pushed into the headrest, his eyes closed, the rapid ascent slowed and eventually stopped. With heart rocketing into his throat, the descent began and for a moment, Jase thought the parachute had failed. But with a loud snap and gut-wrenching tug, the aircraft seat fell away, leaving Jase dangling below the open canopy of the parachute.

Glancing up, he made sure the lines were not twisted and the canvas had deployed properly. Once done, he surveyed the distant ground below, ascertaining and deciding upon an appropriate landing zone (LZ). With one in mind, he steered clumsily towards his target, being mindful of wind direction and speed. Sweeping his eyes across the terrain below him, Jase watched for houses, vehicles or possible enemy encampments. Nothing of note raised his attention and relaxing a little, he began to enjoy the view. The world was silent at altitude. Jase felt almost detached in some way, as if he was viewing Earth from a great distance, however, was no longer a part of it.

As he descended, the cool air began to flee before heat and humidity. The detached feeling evaporated and Jase began concentrating on the LZ. So far, so good. The coagulated green mash of forest and fields gained definition with each passing minute, Jase being able to identify sugar cane crops, Hoop Pine plantations and wild native forest. Further to the east, in a distant blue haze, lay the ocean, meaning he now knew which direction North pointed.

Rapidly, the ground rose to meet him, he rolled awkwardly, offsetting the jarring impact. Groaning, Jase climbed to his feet, released the parachute and unclipped the harness. Unstrapping his helmet, he dropped it on the parachute. Un-holstering his Browning 9mm pistol, he cocked it, ensuring the safety catch was engaged. The cold metal felt comforting in his clammy hand. Nerves and fear enveloped him as he cast his mind back over the long theoretical lessons of combat survival, escape and evasion, resistance to interrogation. Suddenly it was all real. The combat survival and resistance to interrogation classes were followed by one or two weeks of practical exercise, which, at the time, felt useful. However, now, as reality set in, Jase wondered how well he would cope if captured.

The weeklong practical exercise of resistance to interrogation had been the most daunting. Although the instructors did a very good job of making it as realistic as possible, it was nothing more than an exercise. It was this seed of knowledge that the more astute students kept in the back of their mind. Sleep deprived, exhausted, thirsty, hungry and spending hours at a time in stress positions, they still knew that it would eventually end.

Here, in the Australian scrub, with a very real threat of capture, Jase was not afforded this luxury. If caught and not shot on sight, he might spend the rest of his life a prisoner of the Indonesians. The thought sent a shard of terror down the pilot's spine.

Jase landed where planned, on the outskirts of a native forest. One kilometre to the west lay a large sugar cane crop. Usually there would have been large centre pivot irrigation systems casting water over the crops. The distant growl of a tractor perhaps, as a farmer ploughed in new cane cuttings following a harvest. But Jase heard nothing except the gentle song of the forest canopy as a light breeze drifted through.

To the north, a distant plume of thick, black smoke rose into the sky, no doubt where his downed fighter was burning. The enemy aircraft had long left the area, but probably not before calling in Jase's estimated position. It was time to move. With the 9mm clasped firmly in his hand, he made his way into the native forest. The familiar scent of eucalyptus wafted over him, bringing with it an odd comfort. He needed to move away from his current position in order to conceal himself, however, if he moved too far away, he might miss a rescue attempt.

Jase decided he would hide for twenty four hours within half a kilometre of his LZ . If by the same time tomorrow, no friendly force had attempted an extraction, he must assume he was alone and move on. Shelter, warmth and water would then become his most important commodity, followed by food, which was not as immediately important as the first three.

Approximately four hundred metres from his LZ, Jase discovered a shallow, leaf littered divot in the ground. It was to be here in this silent area of forest that he would spend the longest twenty-four hours of his life.

CHAPTER TEN

"*President Andrew Baker impeached! Baker to be tried by Senate.*" New York Times, New York.

Kane's men rifled through the supplies in short order, discovering spare ammunition, grenades, ration packs, fresh water and several jerry cans of diesel for the Unimog. The ammunition was NATO standard 5.56mm, meaning the bullets could also be used in their own rifles. The Australians discovered a jackpot. With enough supplies to survive at least another month, the Indonesians in the local area could look forward to more ambushes in the near future.

"Bomb up," ordered Kane.

His soldiers refilled empty magazines, placed grenades in vacant pouches, restocked water bottles and prepared for another raid. The recently acquisitioned enemy vehicle worked in their favour, especially at night, allowing them to drive unchallenged throughout the area.

"Orders," spoke Kane, seeing that his soldiers had finished their task.

What was left of the platoon gathered together under the shade of a large eucalypt, minus the two soldiers sitting on sentry duty.

"Right, so after the last couple days of looking around, we now know there's a large Indo camp in this vicinity." He pointed with a small stick to an area of the map laid out upon the ground. "We haven't been able to get a good look at it yet, but it seems to be some kind of staging area. A rest stop for convoys and such to refuel, rest, resupply and carry on towards their final destination. There's good and bad to this. The good thing is that the number of enemy will ebb and flow, meaning we can hit them when they have very few soldiers there. The flip side is that the camp is unpredictable. An enemy convoy can mosey on in at any time of the day or night and catch us unawares. With me so far?"

The soldiers around him were nodding, most taking a deep interest, keen to inflict more damage upon the enemy. One soldier at the back, however, was chewing on a piece of grass and staring up at the forest canopy, his eyes glazed over with either boredom or exhaustion. Neither was acceptable.

"Oi, Bear, when you've finished day dreaming about the fuck'n koalas!" Kane hissed, glaring at the soldier.

Spud smacked the soldier on the back of the head, hard. "Listen up," he growled.

"Sorry sir," Bear replied, snapping out of wherever the hell his mind had taken him.

"Me and Spud have had a chat and Spud's agreed to go and have a looksee at the camp," Kane continued. "Once we have a rough layout of the camp itself, we're going to go in and do some damage, but further details on that when we know more about the enemy camp."

In truth, Spud had jumped at the opportunity, agreeing to the mission before Kane had finished speaking. The soldiers knew that Spud had spent many years in Recon and was adept at the more sneaky side of soldiering. Undetected, he was able to move within pissing distance of an enemy. At thirty-four years of age, Spud was not only the oldest soldier, he was the only Non Commissioned Officer (NCO) left alive in the platoon, and was the next in charge should Kane become a casualty. However, that was a risk that Spud was happy to take.

Later that evening, as the rest of the platoon had departed to their defensive positions, Spud and Kane sat talking.

"You sure you want to do this?" Kane asked.

"Yeah, mate," replied Spud. Out of earshot of the soldiers, he let the formalities drop. Although Kane was an officer, the men had known one another for the better part of a decade.

"Just don't get killed, eh?"

"Kane, there's no drama mate," Spud replied. "I'm looking forward to it."

Spud planned to depart the area at 0100 hours, via the gun position, where a rotating piquet was present throughout the night. Once his reconnoitre was complete, he would return to the platoon, entering, once again, via the gun position. A three quarter moon and clear night sky would provide good visibility.

"I'll draw a rough sketch of the position tomorrow morning. We can make a mud map from that," Spud broke the silence.

"Righto."

"Better go and get ready boss. See ya soon, eh?"

"Ok, Spud, keep your head down mate," said Kane.

"Roger that," Spud replied, the grin in his voice evident.

At 0050 hours the platoon stood to, meaning all soldiers were awake, lying prone and facing out in all round defence, weapons pulled into shoulders ready to fire should the need arise. Spud departed the position quietly. Within minutes, he disappeared into the blackness of the surrounding forest.

Spud moved along the sandy, dry creek bed slowly, ensuring he was as close to the left bank as possible. The trees growing above the bank cast shadows upon him, making him more difficult to see should enemy be on sentry on the opposite side. However, with another few kilometres to cover before reaching the Indonesian camp, there was no reason for enemy to be guarding an empty creek bed.

Although he was leaving a trail of footprints, the sand meant almost silent movement. Normally, a creek bed was considered not only an obstacle by a passing platoon, but the perfect fire lane for enemy soldiers and was to be avoided, or crossed with caution. A fire lane was a direct line along which a machine gun could fire persistently with devastating results. Roads, creek beds, even fence lines were all considered potential fire lanes. Alternatively, a fire lane could be man made by simply stamping down long grass in a straight line leading towards a likely enemy route.

However, as a lone soldier, Spud was not concerned. At times, he left the creek bed to patrol through the forest for long stretches. Returning to the dry creek hours later, he knew this would assist in throwing off a possible hunter force.

A dry branch snapped with a loud crack nearby and Spud slowly and silently went to ground hidden within the shadow of a nearby boulder. Closing his eyes and opening his mouth slightly, he allowed his ears to take control. Silence. Spud was in no hurry. Lying still, but for the slow movement of his chest as he breathed, he waited for foreign noise. Nothing. Feeling the frustrating sting of a mosquito on the back of his neck, he ignored it, maintaining noise discipline. Another branch snapped, further away this time, followed by the rustle of leaf litter as man or animal moved through the forest. Spud closed his eyes once more and listened to the soft crackle of leaves. There was a rhythm to the movement and he listened to it for almost five minutes. Soft crackle, louder crackle, slide, over and over. A kangaroo, he knew. The soft crackle was made as the front paws took the weight of the animal and the louder crackle and sliding noise were made as the powerful hind legs and tail moved forward. The animal was relaxed, head down to the ground, grazing through the leaf litter, chewing on grass and shrubs alike.

Spud pushed himself into a kneeling position, happy that the animal was unaware of his presence. Patrolling quietly around the boulder, he continued on his mission, ensuring he was concealed by shadow. For close to half an hour, he continued patrolling, once leaving the creek bed to lay a false trail should an enemy follow up occur.

The proceeding kilometres were covered slowly, methodically and most important of all, silently. So it was that as the moon reached its peak and began to descend towards the horizon, Spud was lying hidden within twenty metres of the enemy perimeter. The naturally flat ground inside the fenced area was massive. He estimated the compound to be at least two kilometres long and at least the same distance in width. Four or five square kilometres of empty ground. The camp was quiet. There were very few vehicles parked, suggesting the enemy vehicles were flat out. Spud crept closer in order to obtain a better view. As he advanced, he spotted three enemy trucks parked together beside a large single story building in the far distance. Adjacent to the building was a mammoth warehouse, which looked to be at least three storeys high and perhaps half a football field long. More than likely, this was stored with supplies and fuel to resupply the endless convoys passing through.

He guessed the single storey building belonged to the soldiers who were stationed here on a permanent basis. Each truck could potentially carry twenty-five soldiers. The calculations were stacked heavily against the Australians he knew. Smiling, Spud knew this would have no effect upon Kane, who would attack the compound regardless, and his soldiers would willingly follow. Kane was a good leader, even a brilliant leader.

After ninety minutes Spud patrolled carefully along the length of the compound until, finally, he located the main gate. Facing East along a compact, neatly graded, wide dirt road, the tall, steel chain link gates were padlocked. Armed with this new knowledge, Spud made his way back to his original position. Dawn was less than an hour away and although it was time to depart, the overwhelming urge to take a look inside the enemy compound overcame him.

Now very close to the fence, he studied its structure. Steel chain link at least twelve feet high, two strands of razor wire ran along the top. Spud cast his eye along the length of the fence looking for any signage that may indicate it was charged with high voltage electricity. Nothing that he could see. Nor could he hear the telltale buzz of electricity at work. Advancing at a crawl, the soldier touched the fence with the back of his hand. Cold steel.

Pushing himself into a kneeling position, Spud reached into a pouch and withdrew a pair of wire cutters. Quietly placing the tool into place, a piece of chain link wedged between the blades, he watched the distant building, waiting for enemy movement or sound. When neither was evident, he cut the fence with a snap. Working quickly, he cut only enough of the fence required to push his body through.

Forcing his body through the hole in the fence, he grunted as a jagged edge of wire ripped his uniform and dragged along the skin of a calf. Cursing silently, he lay on the enemy side of the fence, weapon pulled into his shoulder, watching, waiting and listening. Scanning his surroundings, Spud looked for any other buildings or vehicles he may have missed on the original sweep. However, it seemed the two buildings in the near distance were the only in the immediate area. No guard towers were evident and he could see no enemy patrols, static or roving. Deciding to gain a closer view, Spud advanced. He patrolled slowly, cautiously, sweeping his environment for threats.

The strong, acrid aroma of cigarette smoke drifted over him and Spud slowly and silently went to ground. Lying prone and pulling the rifle into his shoulder, he scanned the building. There was no movement or sound, however, the unmistakeable tang of cigarette was evident. Someone, not so far away, was enjoying a cigarette and Spud had no idea where the enemy stood. He felt exposed and for the first time, fear settled upon his skin, soaking into his flesh with cold finality.

The scuff of a boot against dirt! Adrenalin began pumping through his body, driving the fear away. Spud remained silent and motionless. The enemy soldier was closer than he thought. Movement caught his eye and Spud watched the dark form move towards the building. Hidden within the shadow cast by the building, it had been impossible to detect the enemy soldier. Bright light exploded from the building as the soldier opened the door and disappeared inside, the painful brightness vanishing as the enemy slammed the door behind him. Spud blinked, his night vision ruined by the bright light. Remaining where he was, he waited for his vision to readjust.

After what seemed a lifetime, his night vision corrected, Spud moved into a crouch and crept closer to the enemy position. Knowing dawn was close, instinct told Spud it was time to exfiltrate the area, however, something drew him closer, urged him to place caution to the wind.

Creeping closer, the building now less than twenty metres away, seemed larger than life. Hearing muffled laughter and the dull thump of booted feet walking around inside, Spud ran in a crouch along the side. Ducking below the windows he swiftly moved to the far end of the building. There, before him was the wide road that led in from the front gate, where he had stood some hours before. Enjoying the adrenalin coursing through him, Spud grinned. He took a deep breath, knowing if he stayed any longer, he would be seen. Letting the breath out slowly, he heard the quiet crunch of nearby booted feet. Swiftly turning, his heart stopped as he looked into the face of an enemy soldier. The butt of a rifle slammed into Spud's face and the last thing he saw was a bright explosion of light, and then darkness. Silence.

"He should have returned hours ago," Kane pulled his sleeve back over the watch. Movement caught his attention and Lance Corporal Mathers sat down beside him.

"Sir, the men are worried. Spud should be back," Mathers' alert, dark eyes bored into Kane.

"Yeah, I know mate," Kane replied softly. He shook his head, "I know."

Mathers nodded. "He's in trouble, sir."

Kane took a deep breath. "Prepare the men, be ready to move in five."

Mathers, who involuntarily had now become the next in command after Kane, stood and moved away to instruct the remaining members of the beleaguered platoon. They might have been hungry, thirsty and tired, but they were motivated, and that counted for everything. They were ready to move in two.

"So, Mr. Spud, what were you doing creeping around last night?" the accent was heavy and difficult to understand. Spud could not see the speaker, the dark, cloth sack on his head blinded him with simple efficiency. His hands were bound behind him and they in turn to the steel chair. His feet were tied together.

Under the Geneva Convention, Spud was unable to answer the question, nor did he want to. His head throbbed with pain and he could feel severe swelling around his right eye.

"No? Nothing to say? Well, Mr. Spud, we can change that, believe me!"

Spud held back a smile as the Indonesian used his nickname. Even through the dark situation in which he found himself, it provided him with some morale.

"When were you born?"

The Australian rattled off his date of birth in quick time, hearing pen scribbling on paper behind him. At least two enemy were in the room.

"Religion?"

"Can I get a drink of water?" he asked, "mouth's so dry."

A moment later, the hood was ripped from his face and he squinted against the blinding light. The steel cup was forced to his lips and tilted back. Spud quickly swept the room, surprisingly it was full of enemy soldiers, all armed, all watching with amusement. Water spilled down his front, but Spud drank as much as he was able before the hood was replaced.

"There, better? See we are not savages, are we Mr. Spud?"

That's fuck'n debatable, Spud thought to himself.

"Now, religion?"

Spud ignored the question.

A moment's pause before the interrogator continued. "You don't have one, do you?" He spoke a loud, short sentence in Indonesian and the room filled with mocking laughter.

"Why don't you have a religion?"

Spud ignored the question, knowing the interrogator was trying to draw him into conversation. He was able to give four responses, date of birth, name, rank and regimental number. If he responded to any other query, he was stepping into dangerous water.

"Untie him," commanded the voice. Shortly afterwards, Spud was rubbing his wrists.

"We have given you water, we are treating you well, and what have you given us?" the interrogator's voice had taken on a harder tone. "Nothing!" the Indonesian shouted.

I'll give you a mouthful of fist in a minute, Spud thought to himself, enjoying the freeing feeling it brought. The hood was ripped from Spud's face and the interrogator's face was inches from him.

"Why were you here?" growled the Indonesian.

Your nose is too fuck'n small, Spud thought silently. Even as a prisoner of war, with an uncertain future, the self-dialogue ensured the Australian remained mentally empowered, making it more difficult for the enemy to break him.

The Indonesian shook his head in disgust, "put the hood back on," he shoved the material into Spud's hands. The Australian relaxed his hands and allowed the hood to fall to the floor. Such a small gesture carried two messages. They might have Spud prisoner, however, one, they could not control him and two, he was not afraid of them.

"Pick it up!" the Indonesian roared, thumping a hand onto the table.

Sniffing, Spud looked over the interrogator's shoulder and stared at the wall. Behind him the metallic sound of a rifle being cocked echoed around the room.

"Pick it up," the interrogator said through clenched teeth.

Spud sat, unmoving and counted to five. Then, very slowly, he reached down to the hood. Even as he obeyed his enemy, Spud made sure he carried out the command in his own time. He dropped the hood onto the table.

"Now, put it on!" snapped the interrogator.

Picking up the piece of dark cloth, Spud fumbled it, dropping it to the floor. He sat staring at the hood for several long seconds before slowly reaching down again.

Gesturing to a guard, an enemy soldier stepped forward picked up the hood and shoved it onto Spud's head without ceremony. Whether the interrogator was aware of it or not, what had transpired was a battle of the wills, one which Spud won, regardless of his current situation. That was important, more important than most of the Indonesians in the room that day knew.

"Take him away!"

His hands were rebound tightly before he was grabbed from either side and pushed, stumbling, from the room.

"We shall talk again soon!" the interrogator's voice drifted to him as he was pushed down a small flight of stairs. Stumbling, he lost his footing on the top step, hitting the ground hard. It took all his effort to keep his pain hidden from the guards, who, chuckling, descended the stairs behind him. Spud felt the warm trickle of blood oozing from his nostrils, but remained still. The Indonesians, still chuckling and talking in their native tongue, hefted Spud to his feet. A sharp blow to the small of his back and Spud was stumbling on his way again. Within minutes, the Australian was thrown into a room, the door slamming behind him. A loud click indicated it was locked. He sat against a wall, groaning softly. In silent darkness, Spud contemplated his future. It did not look bright.

CHAPTER ELEVEN

"*New Zealand SAS reported to be involved in heavy fighting against Indonesian forces in Australia.*" New Zealand Herald, Auckland.

"Prime grass fed," said Mick, placing the steaming steak on Craig's plate.

The Special Forces soldier nodded appreciatively. "Thanks mate."

"Aren't we going to say grace?" grinned Matty before the group started eating.

"Grace," growled Mick and began shovelling food into his mouth like a front-end loader.

The SASR soldiers had placed two claymores at opposite sides of the house. If they were to come under attack, the closest person to 'the clacker' was to fire the device. This was not necessarily to cause casualties amongst the enemy, but to create a distraction for the attacking force. Theoretically, the decoy would provide sufficient time for the occupants to exit, in order to affect either a counterattack, or a withdrawal.

"This is yummy Grandad!" Jade said, her mouth full of mashed potato.

"Don't talk with your mouth full," Katie chided the child gently.

"It is yummy," agreed Mick.

Yummy, that word which belonged firmly in the land of frivolity and childhood innocence, spoken by a tough old man, sent Jade into hysterics. Mick grinned at the girl and winked. He loved that even in such hellish circumstances, his granddaughter could still feel safe and loved.

"Good job love," Mick said, gently squeezing Katie's hand.

She smiled, but remained quiet.

"So where to from here?" asked Ben, polishing off the last scrap of food on his plate.

"We're keep'n an eye on the tracking device," replied Craig. "Looks like the convoy is heading east of here closer to the coast. They were moving pretty slow earlier today. They stopped about an hour ago and haven't moved since. Where they stopped is about seven kilometres east of here. We'll check their location again tomorrow. If they're still in the same place, it might indicate an Indo camp. We'd be stupid not to go have a look being this close to them." Craig pushed the plate away from him and ran a hand through his beard. "Thanks for that," he nodded. "Bloody beautiful."

"You mind if we tag along again?" asked Mick.

"The more the merrier," smiled Matty.

It was obvious earlier on, that the SASR soldiers were hesitant taking Mick and Ben with them. However, now, after having met the enemy and living to tell the tale, they were more trusting of the civilian men.

"Just be careful," said Katie.

"We will," replied Mick.

Mick did not notice that Katie had been looking at Ben as she spoke.

Sodium Pentothal was a powerful drug that had been ordered stocked in all first aid kits prior to the invasion. It had taken Major Taufik Simanjuntak almost half an hour to dig through the large first aid kit to find the tiny vial he now held before his eyes. The drug was used by some countries as a truth serum. Allegedly the CIA still used it. However, if a large dose was given, it would kill the subject, hence Sodium Pentothal's use as a lethal injection in thirty-four states across the United States.

Theoretically, lying was a more complex endeavour than the truth, requiring higher cortical brain function. Sodium Pentothal neutralised this higher brain function forcing the subject's hand.

Major Simanjuntak, a short, but powerfully built man, glanced down at the captured Australian soldier slumped in the chair before him. The man had been beaten and abused over the last forty-eight hours, bruises adorned his face, dried blood was crusted around his nostrils, not to mention the stench of shit and piss. But still he would not break.

Opening the vial, Simanjuntak drew the drug up into a small syringe.

"We will make you talk," he said softly to the Australian.

The soldier remained silent, ignoring him.

The major nodded at a nearby soldier, who stepped forward, pulled up the prisoner's sleeve and wiped the skin clean with a wet cloth. Simanjuntak expected the soldier to struggle, however, he instead sat still, allowing the drug to be injected without complaint.

"How do you feel?"

The Australian continued to ignore him. How long would the drug take to work?

"Keep an eye on him," ordered the major, "I'll be back soon."

The guard nodded and looked disdainfully at the Australian.

Ten minutes passed before the prisoner leaned back in his chair and glanced around. The Australian tried to stand, but the bindings stopped him. Placing a hand on his shoulder and pushing down, the Indonesian guard, in his native tongue, growled at him to sit still.

Major Simanjuntak returned to see the Australian fighting against his restraints. He smiled. Good, the drug was working.

"Back in the land of the living, I see," smiled the major, standing before the soldier.

The Australian looked up slowly. His eyes burned with anger, hatred and violence, a look that sent a chill down the major's spine.

"Now, we shall talk as friends," Simanjuntak said.

"Friends?" spat the prisoner, "you ain't no friend of mine."

Ignoring him, the major signalled for the guard to depart the room.

"Now, Spud, why were you here? And were you alone?"

"Why was I here," said Spud, grinning, showing blood-stained teeth. "I was here havin' a look around so the rest of my platoon knew what they were dealin' with, and yeah, I was alone."

"Good, we are getting somewhere," said the major. "What were your platoon going to do with this knowledge?"

The restrained soldier shrugged. "Attack the camp, do some damage, I dunno what Kane's plan was, but if I know that bloke, it wouldn't have been pretty for you fellas."

Major Simanjuntak reached into a pocket, pulled clear his notebook and flicked to a blank page, writing the name down.

"Kane, platoon commander," he said softly as he wrote. "How many soldiers in the platoon?"

"We're probably at half strength," replied Spud. The soldier hawked and spat on the floor.

Simanjuntak looked distastefully at the blot of bloody phlegm. "I wish you wouldn't do that," he said.

"I'm goin' ta kill you, you know?" Spud spoke quietly and very directly, derailing Simanjuntak from his original line of questioning.

"Why is that?" was all he could think to ask.

Spud was glaring at the little major, his eyes burning with bloody murder.

"You're asking me why?" asked the Australian through clenched teeth. "You invaded my country and killed my brothers," he spoke softly. "You have burned my cities, pillaged the homes of my people," his voice was louder now. "My people," he shouted. "You murdered innocent men, women and children, and you want to know why I'm going to kill you?" Spud roared.

"Guard!" shouted Simanjuntak, taking a step back and checking the prisoner's bindings.

The guard burst into the room.

"Take him away," Major Simanjuntak waved at the Australian, struggling to remain calm.

"You're gunna meet my platoon sooner than later," said Spud.

The guard, unable to speak English, had no idea what was being said, he simply obeyed orders given him, untying the enemy prisoner.

"They won't stand a chance," replied the major, but he sounded nervous.

Spud threw his head back and roared with laughter. "You haven't met them mate," he sneered. "But you will," he said, "you will."

The guard released the bindings and Spud exploded out of his chair, tackling the major to the floor. Simanjuntak covered his face, or tried to, but the powerful Australian rained punches down on him, dislodging teeth and fracturing his nose. For a moment the Indonesian guard stood rooted to the spot, but sprang into action a moment later, delivering a powerful butt stroke to the back of Spud's skull.

The Australian lay limp, blood oozing from his scalp. Major Simanjuntak pushed the prisoner aside and climbed slowly to his feet, groaning in pain. He held his nose gently.

"Take him away," muttered the major.

The guard dragged Spud away, his head mopping a trail of blood onto the floor.

Jase opened his eyes and checked his watch. 06:23 am. He slept fitfully throughout the night, always keeping an ear out for radio traffic or aircraft noise, but heard nothing. No rescue was going to be attempted he knew. What little the Australian Defence Force had left at their disposal was stretched to breaking point. Common sense told him no resources would be utilised to rescue one man.

He stretched, the leaf litter beneath him crunching. Jase froze, his eyes opening wide. Slowly, he reached for and grasped the 9mm Browning pistol. In the divot nearby, his back to Jase, sat a man looking out at the forest. The initial panic, however, passed as Jase realised the man wore the camouflage of an Australian soldier. The soldier looked around at him as he heard Jase stir.

"Hello young fella. Wake now mate?" asked the soldier. "I'm Jimmy."

He was a middle aged, fit, very strong looking full blood Aboriginal.

"G'day, I'm Jase. How'd you find me?"

"Watched you get shot down."

"I didn't think I was that far north," said Jase, realising Jimmy was more than likely a Norforce soldier.

"You're not. Me and some fellas were flown south to fight the invasion. Darwin and the top end weren't hit too bad. A few Caribous took a heap of us to different areas of the country, you know? To lend a hand. Me and my boys came 'ere."

Jase waited for the soldier to say more, but only silence followed.

"What happened?" he asked.

"We was landed and got ambushed straight away. Plane got shot down as it took off. A few of us that survived got away and took a car, you know? We drove south and got ambushed again. Two of us got away. Me and," Jimmy paused, "another fella. He was hurt bad, real bad. Got him as far as the scrub before he died."

Jase seemed to remember that in the Aboriginal culture, they preferred not to speak the names of those who passed away.

"So what now?" asked Jase.

Jimmy glanced out towards the forest for a moment before looking back. "I've heard about this camp, it's not far from here. Like a big Aussie army camp, you know? Full of soldiers and weapons. Word is, they fightin' back against the invasion."

"How'd you hear about this?"

"Somethin' the aircrew was sayin' before we landed," said Jimmy, "nothin' left to lose," he shrugged. "May as well go find out, you know?"

"Yeah, why not?" said Jase.

"You hungry?"

"Starvin'!"

"Know much about bush tucker?" asked Jimmy.

"We did some basic stuff in combat survival, but not much more than that."

"Ok, see that over there?" Jimmy was pointing to a large shrub from which plum coloured berries were hanging in bunches.

"We call that Burdekin Plum, good tucker. Those ones are ripe. If they're not, we usually bury 'em to ripen 'em quicker. I'll stay 'ere you go have a feed ay?"

The berries were packed with a bitter sweetness that Jase found irresistible. After eating his fill, he returned.

"Time to move," Jimmy said quietly, standing. "From now on, no talking."

Jase nodded his understanding and the Aboriginal soldier led the way, his rifle held at the ready and his dark eyes scanning the surrounding environment, missing nothing.

Once again, the four men climbed into Mick's old Nissan Navara and the vehicle grumbled away from the homestead, leaving Katie and Jade watching the vehicle growing smaller as it swayed and rocked across the rough ground, eventually disappearing around a bend in the road.

Matty held the tracking device in one hand, occasionally glancing down at it, checking the location of the convoy, his rifle lying across his lap, ready to use at a moment's notice. Again Craig drove the vehicle, his weapon gently wedged on his right side, between the door and his seat, the barrel leaned up against the dashboard so that he could quickly and accurately take hold of the rifle and shoot through the windscreen at a target.

"Ok, like we rehearsed, if we get ambushed, Craig'll try and drive us out, if not, get out on the non-ambush side and we'll engage and break contact. Maybe set up a counter ambush if the terrain and time is right," Matty was looking around at the two men in the back.

They nodded. "Gottcha," said Mick.

"Yeah, no worries, we'll be right," said Ben, sounding more like he was trying to convince himself that everything would be ok.

Mick rolled his eyes and muttered under his breath.

"What was that?" Ben looked across at the older man.

"I said," Mick returned the younger man's stare, "you better not fuck this up city boy."

Ben shook his head and looked away.

"I mean there's no reason that you should," Mick continued to stare at Ben, "you've had breakfast and you've rubbed gel through your hair," the Vietnam vet sneered. "Did you bring your comb and mirror?"

"Alright, fuck you old man!" Ben snarled, whirling on the older man, his fists clenched.

"Oi, you two," chuckled Craig, looking at them in the rear view mirror. "For fuck's sake, you're carrying on like a couple of-"

The soldier did not have a chance to finish the sentence as bullets thudded into the vehicle. Matty brought his weapon to bear and fired three shots in quick succession, the sound deafening in the close environment.

"Ambush left!" roared Matty.

"Hold on!" Craig shouted, steering the vehicle violently away from the enemy, dodging trees. A loud thud reverberated throughout the vehicle as it hammered over a fallen log. Low hanging branches and native shrubs clawed along the side of the vehicle with screeches and scratches. Ploughing through a long stand of shrubs, everything went silent as the vehicle became airborne for a second. Launched into thin air, they had driven over a dry riverbank. Seconds later, they slammed into the sandy riverbed. The engine stalled, steam pouring from beneath the closed bonnet. Try as he may, Craig could not start the engine.

"Out! Now!" yelled Craig, flinging open his door and exiting the vehicle.

Moments later, Matty was gone and the two civilian men sat like stunned mullets for a second, before Mick launched into action, opening his door and running clear of the Navara. Ben slid across the seat and exited on the non-ambush side, as he had been taught. As he ran clear, he noticed the two soldiers had already sprinted up the far riverbank and were nowhere to be seen. He suspected they were lying hidden, providing cover for the lagging civilian men.

As Ben was about to shout a question, the Australian soldiers opened fire from their concealed positions, bullets hissing and cracking at close range over the young man's head. Mick had taken cover behind a large boulder in the creek bed and was looking back towards Ben, rifle pulled into his shoulder.

"Get behind cover!" roared the older man, the loud, deep report of his .303 rifle making the quiet popping of the silenced weapons sound like toys.

Ben glanced over his shoulder and noticed Indonesian soldiers lining the opposite side of the dry river. Several of them lay dead, however, the majority began opening fire.

Bullets whizzed around Ben. Fear enveloped him like a water sodden blanket. His legs felt heavy, lungs burning, hands barely holding onto his rifle. Ducking behind a boulder, the deafening whine of a ricocheting round caused Ben's ears to ring. More rounds slapped against the rock and the young man lay still, wishing he could dig a hole in the ground.

Again the .303 spoke. Ben shifted slightly, craning his neck around the boulder and watched Mick fire another shot. More than five enemy soldiers were down, the hot, dry sand drinking their blood. The Australian soldiers were yelling something to the civilian men, but over the noise, it was impossible to hear.

Kneeling up, Ben brought his rifle into his shoulder and stared down the scope. With shaking hands, he settled the target reticule over the chest of an enemy soldier and took a breath. The air around the young man suddenly came to life as bullets hissed, whizzed and cracked. Ben threw himself to the ground, winding himself. Closing his eyes, he willed himself to kneel back up. He convinced himself to ignore the area of his brain responsible for self-preservation. It was near impossible to do, but Ben succeeded, he must have done, because without knowing how, he found himself kneeling, staring down the scope once again.

Squeezing the trigger, he ducked behind cover as return fire chipped the boulder. Pulling the bolt back and making sure the next bullet engaged the breech, Ben pushed the bolt forward, sweat beading his brow. The heavy blanket of fear had fallen away to be replaced by the aggressive heat of adrenalin. His legs now felt light and powerful, lungs inhaled fresh air and his rifle held tight.

The sound of Mick's .303 rifle became background noise, the young man finding himself in his own world. Kneeling up and pulling the weapon into his shoulder, Ben fired another shot, watching his victim drop like a rag doll and sliding down the steep riverbank. Working the bolt, he fired again, again and again. Sliding against the boulder, he ripped the empty magazine out of the weapon, reloaded and slapped it back into place.

Adrenalin was now mixing with anger, a dangerous, yet effective mixture. Kneeling up, Ben saw the riverbed was now littered with enemy dead. He fired another bullet, taking an Indonesian through the throat. A round hissed close to Ben's face, making him go to ground. Anger faded and was replaced by fury. That close relation of blood lust. Sometimes the two were indistinguishable.

With a long bellow of anger, weeks of rage burst their banks and swept over Ben. All logical thought fled before the onslaught. The young man charged forward like a madman.

Katie hummed softly as she washed up dishes, cutlery and cups. With the task done, she pulled out the plug, let the sink drain and dried her hands on a tea towel. She could still hear Jade playing outside. Her daughter was close to the house, as she had been told, playing with a barbie doll. Katie popped her head out the door, to see her daughter deep in conversation with her plastic doll. They were both sitting on the veranda steps. Smiling, Katie went back inside and began folding clothes she had recently brought in from the washing line.

It was when the muffled voice of Jade fell quiet, that Katie stopped to listen, waiting for her daughter to begin serving imaginary cups of tea, or muffins.

"Who are you?" she heard Jade ask.

Katie frowned and straightened.

"My name's Jade, what's yours?" Jade asked.

Katie walked back out onto the veranda and supressed a gasp as she watched an Indonesian soldier slowly climb the stairs towards her. The unshaven soldier was filthy, his camouflage uniform almost black with dirt and dried mud. One hand was placed on Jade's head, the girl looking up at the newcomer. His other hand held a knife.

"What do you want?" Katie asked.

The man remained silent, simply grinning, showing yellowed teeth.

Jade screamed as the man grabbed her by the hair, dragged her close and held the knife to the girl's throat.

"Please!" Katie said, holding out her hands. "Please don't hurt my daughter, I'll give you anything. Anything!"

"Makanan!" he snarled.

"I'm sorry, I don't understand," said Katie.

The soldier pressed the knife harder against Jade's throat, bringing another scream from the little girl. "Makanan!" he said again, he made a chewing motion with his mouth.

He wants food, thought Katie. That must be it.

"Come inside," Katie said, gesturing for him to walk in. "But let me have my daughter back." She held out her hand to Jade, indicating he should let her go.

Chuckling, the soldier released Jade and pushed her towards Katie, who swept the girl up into her arms and kissed her cheek.

"We'll be ok darling," Katie whispered into the sobbing child's ear. "It's over now."

Anger boiled inside Katie, but she did not let it show, instead inviting the soldier into the house.

"Go to your room and lock your door," Katie spoke quietly and calmly to her daughter, placing Jade down on the ground.

Wiping tears from her face, Jade sprinted for her bedroom, slammed the door, a loud click following shortly after.

Katie emptied a can of baked beans into a bowl and turned to open the cutlery drawer, but before she could find a spoon, the Indonesian had lunged for the bowl, using his fingers to shovel food into his mouth. Barely chewing, he finished the meal within minutes. Katie gave him another can of baked beans, which he took from her with equal fervour. Finishing that, he threw the bowl aside, gesturing for water.

After three cups of water, he slammed the cup down onto the counter and grinned again, staring at Katie. Before she could react, the man had slapped her across the face, spinning her from her feet. She hit the ground hard. Strong, rough hands grabbed her by the shoulders and lifted her violently to her feet. Clutching a fistful of material, he ripped the shirt from her, staring lustfully at her breasts hidden scantily beneath the bra. Katie back handed him, and ran passed him. Within seconds, the Indonesian regained his composure and gave chase.

Tackling her in the corridor outside Jade's room, both fell to the ground. Wriggling free of his grip, Katie kicked him in the face, climbed to her feet and ran towards her father's room. He always kept a handgun under his pillow. As a child, if she needed to go to the toilet during the night, she would often have to call out to him, letting him know it was her walking around the house. Although he had improved ten-fold over the years, the Vietnam War had left a lasting effect upon her father.

Anger fuelled her now, she had two lives to protect. Barging through the half open door, she leapt onto the bed, jumped onto the furthest side. Pushing her hand under her father's pillow she felt the cold steel of a .357 revolver. Bringing the weapon to bear, supporting it with both hands as her father had taught her, she pointed it at the soldier's chest. The Indonesian halted, still grinning, knowing she would not fire.

"…and most importantly of all, don't bloody hesitate, love," her father's voice drifted from her memory banks.

Pulling the trigger, the weapon bucked in her hand, the gunshot deafening in such a small area. Ripping through the soldier's chest, the bullet hammered into the wall behind him. Dropping to his knees with a groan, he fell forward, lying prone as the carpet around him slowly turned claret. Coughing loudly, frothy blood slid from the corner of his mouth.

Standing over him, Katie, grim faced, pointed the weapon at her assailant's head. She fired again, his skull opening like a melon. Leaving the soldier where he lay, Katie strode over the corpse to make sure her daughter was safe.

"Ben!" yelled Mick, "get back here!"

However, the young man was oblivious to his surroundings. As bullets ripped past his face with whip like cracks or loud thuds as they slammed into the soft sand about his feet, he sprinted up the riverbank and fired point blank into the chest of the closest soldier. Loading the next round he shot another enemy, scooped up his automatic rifle and sprinted forward, barging through a thick shrub. Sliding to a halt he stared down the iron sights of the Indonesian weapon and fired burst after burst, until the weapon fell silent. The enemy soldiers were concentrating on Mick and the opposite bank, where they knew the Australian soldiers were somewhere lying hidden. Ben's flanking attack took them by complete surprise and most of them were killed within the first ten seconds.

Throwing the empty enemy weapon to the ground, he picked up another. Several quick thinking soldiers had retreated and taken cover from the new attack. One was killed as a round fired from Mick's weapon slammed through his chest with a loud, meaty thud. Teeth bared like some rabid animal, Ben sprinted into the forest, low hanging branches scraping the skin of his face. He ignored the pain, thought nothing of the loud hiss as a bullet cut a sapling down in front of him.

Within the minute, he had approached the remaining Indonesian survivors from behind. Still the fury was upon him, making it seem that those he opposed moved in slow motion. With a roar reminiscent more of some great war hound of old than a human being, Ben gunned them down, his weapon singing in a long, loud, chatter until the magazine was empty. Slowly lowering the Indonesian automatic rifle, he stared through the steam wafting from the hot barrel. At his feet lay the remaining five enemy. They never knew what killed them.

"Ben!" Mick's distant voice shouted, "Ben! Are you ok?"

The younger man did not reply. As the fury began to wain, nausea swept over him and weakness filled his limbs. He knelt and vomited onto the dry leaf litter, stomach acid burning his throat. Taking a great gulp of air, he leaned forward and vomited again. Staggering to his feet he wiped his mouth with the back of his hand.

"Ben!" Mick was closer this time. "Ben!" the Vietnam Veteran brushed passed a towering Iron Bark and seeing the enemy were dead, lowered his rifle. He clamped a hand onto the young man's shoulder, "you alright?"

Ben nodded, but did not speak.

"Come on, let's get outta here," Mick suggested, steering Ben towards the river bed. "Not bad for a pansy city boy."

Ben stopped and glared at the older man. The Vietnam Veteran noticed the twinkle of false bravado he had seen in Ben's eyes, not to mention many young men his age, was gone. In its place smouldered a glint of controlled violence. Something had changed in the young city boy and given Australia's current position, it was for the better.

"You know much about the ANZACs Ben?"

Shaking his head, he shrugged. "A bunch of Aussie and Kiwi soldiers who landed at Turkey during World War One." He was surprised. Today was the first day Mick had ever used his first name.

Mick nodded. "Yeah, you're not wrong there." Mick stopped walking and looked across at the young man. "More than half of 'em were city boys." He slapped Ben on the shoulder and continued walking, "you did well out here today," he called over his shoulder.

CHAPTER TWELVE

*"*A*ndrew Baker, first President in US history to be convicted by the Senate!"* Al-Sharq, Doha.

Lying amongst tall ferns, long dead musky smelling leaf litter surrounding him, Grant Bridge listened to the foreign language. He remained frozen, barely breathing as he heard the Indonesians walking along the dirt road. It was the third time in a week since escaping Concentration Camp Hatta he had come in close proximity to enemy soldiers. Grant was sure it was only a matter of time before he was captured. They were talking in loud voices and obviously held no concern of alerting any Australians. In their minds, it seemed, the brief war had resulted in victory and Australia was theirs for the taking.

Eyes wide, he stared hard at the fern reaching up out of the leaf litter in front of him and noticed a grasshopper sitting on one of the fronds, returning his intent glare. The insect was frozen in place, hoping that the giant newcomer had not seen it and would soon leave. Grant in turn lay still, silent, adrenaline quietly leaking into his bloodstream as he willed the enemy to depart.

As the minutes passed and the voices grew faint, eventually fading into the distance, Grant began to relax. He was bone tired and knew his body was still recovering from malnourishment. His food intake had slowly increased day by day, until he was comfortable eating a normal diet once again. Although, eating well came at a price, especially when one had escaped as a prisoner of war and on the run. Grant shifted under the weight of the pack and grunted as it moved into a more comfortable position. The pack was full of non-perishable food. Boomer had also provided him with a reverse osmosis pump that he could use to help purify water from rivers, creeks, even puddles of muddy water. However, Grant had been advised to boil the water before drinking whenever possible. When lighting a fire was not possible, Boomer had given him several boxes of purification tablets. One tablet dropped into a bottle of drinking water was enough to remove all impurities and render the water drinkable.

"They make the water taste like shit, but they work," Boomer had chuckled. Grant would be ever grateful to the Navy Diver, and if he ever came through this, had intentions of buying him a beer.

With chafed shoulders, a sore back, utter exhaustion dogging him, and the fear of capture or death at any moment, Grant pushed himself into a kneeling position with difficulty. Clasping the pistol in his hand, he scanned the environment quietly, watching and listening. A flock of Kookaburras began asserting their domination over an area of the forest in the near distance. The noise sounded so much like laughter that Grant felt they were almost laughing at him. Grunting, he pushed himself into a standing position and quietly walked through the ferns. He could see the road appearing through the forest as he advanced. It was a narrow dirt track. It had been more than an hour since he consulted his map, however, he knew that he must cross another track after this one before he arrived at a small creek, where he would refill his water bottles.

Before Grant departed Camp Hatta, Boomer advised him he had heard rumours of a large Australian encampment within the Royal National Park, twenty kilometres south of Sydney. Boomer had informed him he had been held prisoner on the coast side of the Kamay Botany Bay National Park some twenty kilometres from the Australian camp as the crow flies. However, with a bay full of ocean in the way, he was forced to traverse east into suburban areas and follow the coast south towards the Royal National Park, adding an extra fifteen to twenty kilometres to the journey. Grant knew it would be a difficult and perilous hike.

Apparently there was scattered guerrilla-type resistance occurring all over the country, but this large encampment was one of the very few left in Australia offering any real large scale challenge to the foreign invaders. A second, similar camp was located somewhere in Queensland, or so Boomer gathered.

Grant recalled the conversation as he glanced down the track in both directions. Boot prints left by the enemy soldiers were still evident in the soft earth. The Australian scuttled across the road, fearing a shouted challenge, but none came. He pushed through the bush on the other side.

As dusk arrived, Grant dropped his pack and knelt by the gently flowing creek. Deciding not to use the reverse osmosis pump, he filled his water bottles, dropped a purification tablet into each and lay back, rubbing his shoulders. Staring up through the forest canopy, he watched a flock of cockatoos fly above him, screeching and calling amongst themselves. They seemed so carefree, he thought, blissfully unaware of the wholesale destruction happening throughout the country.

Exhaustion swept over him as silent and unnoticed as an assassin. Laying his head back against the soft bank of the creek, he closed his eyes and relaxed.

"And when you stop to rest, for Christ sake get into cover, out of sight," Boomer's distant voice echoed through the vaults of his memory.

Burbling quietly, the gentle voice of the creek willed him to sleep, caressed him like a new born, driving reality further away.

"If you get caught, mate, it's over. They'll probably kill ya," Boomer's tiny voice whispered from somewhere deep within his mind.

The creek's song defeated the warning, however, and Grant slipped deeper into slumber.

"…for Christ sake get into cover," the familiar voice whispered.

Crickets added to the creek's persuasion and the deep, resting blanket of sleep would not be lifted.

"…out of sight," the voice said. Was it Boomer's voice? The lethargic, distant question moved sludge-like across his mind.

Sleep took him then and his surroundings retreated in a gentle blur until he was held prisoner within the dream world of which he would have no recollection. Grant did not hear the Indonesian vehicles rumble passed in the distance, was oblivious as the diesel fumes wafted over him and had no idea of the mosquito sucking blood from his cheek. His body was in recovery mode, and he needed sleep to recuperate. It was a dead branch crashing onto the forest floor in the near distance that woke him.

"For Christ sake get into cover," the familiar voice echoed as his eyes snapped open, lethargy draining from him as adrenaline took over.

Sitting up, slumber slipped away from him like a thief, his eyes and ears focusing upon his surroundings. It was night and with a silent curse he realised he had been sleeping for hours. The crickets were in full chorus and select stars twinkled between the thick canopy, reminding him that the sky was somewhere up there. Pushing himself into a sitting position, he quietly dragged the pack to him, stood and moved further into the vegetation, boots crunching upon dead leaves and half rotten branches. When he was surrounded by thick shrubs, giant trees and chest tall fern fronds, he dropped the pack gently and lay back down. Unless an enemy stumbled directly upon him, he would be invisible.

"Ssshhh," soothed Sarah, "you're safe now," she whispered.

"Nowhere is safe," Grant said. He was lying on the couch and tried to sit up but found it impossible.

"You're safe now," she repeated. He had forgotten her beauty. With long flowing auburn hair, dark green eyes, an inviting smile and shapely figure, he wondered where they had gone wrong. On the verge of asking that very question, she spoke.

"Stay quiet my love, go to sleep now," her hair was draped gently upon his face. "Go to sleep," she said, stroking a hand across his cheek.

Grant's eyes snapped open, a gentle breeze stroking his cheek. Dawn spoke in the eastern sky and it was time to move. Breaking open a can of baked beans, he ate the cold contents quietly, enjoying the feeling of food in his stomach. As he donned the pack, hues of pink and orange streaked across random areas of the sky visible through the forest canopy. Kookaburras laughed nearby and in the far distance a flock of cockatoos shrieked, bickered and called among one another.

Before he moved, Grant checked the map followed by his compass. When confident of his location and direction of travel, he set off, moving through the national forest as quietly as possible. Butterflies, native bees, birds and the single goanna he spotted, treated him with indifference. The flies and mosquitos, however, treated Grant with a special attention he found frustrating.

A sudden movement in front of him gave Grant reason to freeze, and for good reason as he watched the snake slither away amongst the leaf litter. He had little knowledge of snakes and as such, chose to treat all of them as venomous, to be given a wide berth whenever possible. When the reptile had departed, Grant advanced once more.

As the sun reached its zenith and Grant's stomach growled with hunger, he leaned against the trunk of a large Bangalay tree and looked out upon the ocean. Now as the forest gave way to the beach, he knew he had walked as far south as possible. Out in the open, surrounded by enemy, he would be at his most vulnerable, but he knew he must make the journey in order to link up with the Australian camp. Ducking against the tree, he listened to the powerful scream of jet engines roar above him, the fighters tearing past at tree top level. They were Indonesian.

The Australian soldiers patrolled ahead of Mick and Ben, melting into the forest, disappearing for long lengths of time, before reappearing with a thumbs-up or wink. They had been unhappy with how the fight with the

Indonesians had progressed and had told the two civilian men as much. In future, they would withdraw quickly, not stand and fight. Contact drills had not changed much since the Vietnam War and Mick knew that outnumbered and outgunned, they should have withdrawn from the vehicle fast. He had turned to provide cover fire for Ben, who was lagging behind and as such, their withdrawal became bogged down. Mick did not have the stomach to tell Ben, however, he felt confident Ben would not make the same mistake again. The young man had changed, a steely determination emanated from him.

Walking backwards for several moments, Ben, who was tail-end-charlie, watched for enemy behind. Turning around, he continued to patrol forward, seeing Mick twenty metres in front of him and to the right, disappear behind a shrub. A soft click brought the young man's attention to Craig, who was in the near distance, knelt by a tall grass tree. He signalled for the civilians to stop and go to ground. When the soldier was happy that they knew what he wanted, he turned and patrolled forward, disappearing from sight within seconds.

Craig and Matty were gone for close to twenty minutes before they quietly came back into sight. Tapping his head, Craig signalled for the Mick and Ben to approach him. Matty knelt close by providing cover while the three men talked in hushed whispers.

"We got the enemy encampment within a hundred metres of here, lots of vehicles parked up in convoy fashion, just as we expected. Not an alarming find in itself, but we've scoped a large group of Australian soldiers lying in extended line watching the camp. We think they intend to attack," Craig whispered.

"So, what now?" asked Ben quietly.

"We wanna link up with them," replied Craig, "you boys are more than welcome to stay here and wait for us, there's no pressure to join in, we certainly don't expect it."

Mick looked across at Ben and found the young man watching him, his eyes glinting with a resolve that had up until recently been absent.

Mick nodded, "we'll come with you," he whispered.

Craig grinned. "Thought you'd say that."

The four men moved off slowly, each step taken carefully so as not to create too much noise. Ben's index finger rested comfortably upon the trigger guard. The rifle that had so recently been heavy, cumbersome and foreign, now fit snug against his body. It felt like an old friend. Slung across his shoulder was one of the Indonesian assault rifles.

Being so close to the enemy, the soldiers forced the civilians to move slowly, the group taking almost fifteen minutes to cover one hundred

116

metres. Ben remembered what he had been taught by Matty. Placing the ball of his foot down first, he rolled his foot, much like someone would when they accidentally rolled their ankle whilst playing sport, however this was controlled. Then he slowly flattened his foot. If pressure was felt beneath his boot, like a dry branch, which might snap and cause undue noise if he placed his full body weight upon it, the foot was raised and placed elsewhere and the process repeated. It was very slow going, but as close to silent as humanly possible.

Staring through the binoculars, Kane watched enemy soldiers coming and going, checking engines, tyres, refuelling vehicles, standing in groups joking. But when the Australian prisoner, hands tied, hessian sack hiding his face, was pushed and prodded towards the main building, his interest was piqued. Squinting through the binoculars, he sharpened the focus and saw dried blood spattering the uniform, noticed the obvious limp, and knew that Spud was injured. Anger washed over him.

"Sir, visitors." Mathers thumped him on the arm, breaking his concentration.

Dropping the binoculars from his eyes, Kane watched a small group of men join them. Three of the four went to ground and joined the right flank, whilst the fourth man crawled towards the officer. Minutes later, he was lying prone beside Kane. He was a relatively short, very well built man. Dressed in Australian Army uniform, his hair was long, reaching half way to his shoulders and he sported a thick beard. Probably a Commando or Special Air Service Trooper in a previous life, before the Indonesians made landfall, thought Kane. His intent, dark eyes bored into Kane.

"G'day," grinned the man. "Name's Craig," he said holding out a hand.

"Kane," he responded with a nod, shaking the offered hand. "Where'd you come from?"

"Long story," replied Craig. "You want a hand?"

Kane nodded and gestured towards the Indonesian stronghold in the near distance. "They've got one of my men prisoner. He's inside that main building right now, probably being interrogated."

"Righto," said Craig softly, "what are you planning to do?"

"Wait 'til dark and then move in through the wire, I was thinking of causing a diversion and making a grab for Spud and withdraw back to the vehicle."

"Vehicle?" asked Craig with interest.

"Yeah, we managed to acquire an Indonesian Mog a little while ago."

"An Indonesian vehicle," said Craig thoughtfully, followed by a grin. "Wait here, Kane and hold off for the time being, I'm going to go chat to my mate for a sec, I think I might have an idea."

Once again Spud found himself in the fun chair as he silently called it. His enemy had questioned him at length, shouted at him, slapped, punched, kicked and even bitten him. However, they could not break him, a fact that constantly frustrated Major Taufik Simanjuntak. Sodium Pentothal had simply unlocked the prisoner's inhibitions, which the drug was supposed to do. However, instead of making the prisoner speak about information of an operational nature, it simply made him speak his current thought pattern, most of which was related to his immediate thoughts of Major Simanjuntak.

"So, Spud, here we find ourselves once more," Simanjuntak said.

Spud nodded.

"Are you ready to talk yet?"

Spud was silent for a long while. "I don't understand," he began. "I've been nothing but co-operative. I've given you lots of information."

"Have you?" the major sounded unconvinced as he paced around the prisoner, hands firmly clasped behind his back. The bruise around his right eye was fading with each day, but the pain in his cheek remained, a sour testament to the hail of punches Spud had landed upon him.

"Yes."

Simanjuntak stopped pacing. "I don't think you have," he said softly. "No, you haven't," he said louder.

Spud nodded but remained silent.

"Why were you here?"

"I already told you," replied Spud in a weary voice, "I was having a gander."

The major frowned at the last word in confusion, although he assumed it was Australian slang for reconnaissance.

"What were you going to do?"

"Find out what sort of threat you are," replied Spud.

The Australian knew not to give any information away within the first several days, however, there was a fine line. On one side of the line, the enemy may consider the prisoner useless, just another mouth to feed and kill him if he were not talking. It was important to start giving information after the first few days, in order to make the captors think they were breaking their prisoner. The trick was to divulge enough information to make the enemy think the captive was important, but not give information that may be considered mission critical.

"Yes, and then report back to your superior officer, but what then, Spud? What then?" Simanjuntak stopped pacing and stared at the back of Spud's head.

"Make trouble," replied Spud. The major did not see the snarl on Spud's face.

"I fear you and your men would have been sadly mistaken," said the major in mock sadness, shaking his head. "They wouldn't have lasted five minutes."

Don't bet on it, thought Spud silently, clenching his jaw.

An engine rumbled outside the building, followed closely by the hiss of air brakes as a vehicle came to a stop immediately in front of the building.

Spud had been expecting to be transported sooner rather than later and his time had come. He knew that once he was transported deeper into the Indonesian network, the chance of him being rescued would be slim to impossible. With a quiet sigh, he closed his eyes for a moment so as to reinforce his dwindling mental fortitude. The next man to interrogate him would be a true professional. A man or woman trained specifically for the purpose of extracting information from prisoners of war. His time here would seem like a holiday, he thought.

The door exploded inwards and smashed against the wall, its hinges complaining with a loud groan. Major Simanjuntak watched a well-built Indonesian soldier stride into the room. With long messy hair and unkempt beard, the man did not appear to be particularly disciplined. A large stain of dried blood was splattered across his chest. But his eyes exuded authority and unconsciously, the major's hands unclasped from behind his back.

"Is this him?" the man asked in rapid Indonesian, gesturing aggressively towards Spud.

"This is an Australian prisoner of war, captured by my soldiers some days ago."

"Yes!" snarled the newcomer. "I have heard all about him."

"May I ask why you are here?"

"I am Colonel Hartono."

"Forgive me," said the major gesturing towards the man's shoulders. "Where is your rank?"

Hortono glared at Major Simanjuntak for several moments. "Excuse me?" he asked.

"I only ask why you do not wear your rank, it's just that-"

"How dare you!" roared Hortono. "You dare challenge my authority?"

Major Simanjuntak had made a snap judgement based on the man's messy uniform and scruffy appearance. He knew he was incorrect. The weeks following the invasion had been difficult for the Indonesian Army. Lesser tasks like shaving and haircuts had taken a backseat to fighting the Australian rebels.

"Sir, I apologise," he began.

"Forget it!" the colonel replied abruptly. "I am here for this filth," he said, Hortono's face contorting in hatred. "I'm going to personally interrogate him."

"Yes, of course sir," said Simanjuntak.

With fear ebbing and flowing through his body, Spud kept his chin against his chest and stared at the floor in a pose he hoped passed for submission as the two Indonesians shouted at one another in their native tongue.

He watched the progress of the argument in his peripheral vision and with sinking heart saw Major Simanjuntak walk away, disappearing through the door. In the world of the POW, Simanjuntak had been his best friend. He was now in no-man's-land, with a man who could very well kill him outright. He certainly seemed to be a man of short temper.

Continuing to stare at the floor, he tried to breathe deeply, willing himself to relax as he watched the newcomer turn towards him and with a shriek of anger, charge. The Indonesian collided with Spud heavily and for a moment, he was airborne before he smashed into the floor. Pain shot through his left shoulder and he felt the chair to which he was tied, shatter.

"You Australian dog!" he roared in a thick Indonesian accent. "I will make you talk, do you understand?" The man's snarling face was close to Spud's ear. "Understand?" he yelled.

With ears ringing, Spud simply nodded.

"Right, I'm with the Australian Army," a thick Australian accent whispered in his ear. "We're getting you outta here. You do what I say when I say, got it?"

Spud was speechless as he tried to fathom what had just taken place.

"Got it?" the voice growled.

Spud nodded, still speechless.

"Up!" said the Australian.

Powerful hands grabbed Spud and pulled him to his feet. With several deft knife strokes, he was free of what was left of the chair. He stood staring at his grinning saviour.

"Name's Matty," said the man holding out his hand.

"Spud," he muttered in disbelief.

THE RECKONING

at his grinning saviour.

"Name's Matty," said the man holding out his hand.

"Spud," he muttered in disbelief.

CHAPTER THIRTEEN

"*United Nations talks stalled as Indonesia rejects all diplomatic attempts.*" Toronto Star, Toronto.

Trying to keep track of the days had been close to impossible, but Jase was sure they had been patrolling now for eight days. Eight days did not sound long, but it felt like more than a month. Jimmy had driven him hard, pushing on through the Australian bush, avoiding roads, open ground and any remote buildings, of which there had been several. For every five kilometres gained, there were perhaps another five kilometres in addition as the duo avoided Indonesian camps and permanent bases. Jase found it sobering just how much of a foothold the enemy held upon Australia.

"You look stuffed," grinned Jimmy one afternoon after they finished patrolling, the sun setting in a dull orange.

"I feel it," he replied, lying heavily upon the leaf littered ground of the native forest.

Resting hands behind head, he stared up at the swaying canopy of eucalyptus trees high above him, their whispered song gentle in the soft breeze. The distant, high-pitched shriek of what sounded like an eagle echoed. With a huge mountain range towering over them to the west, it was no surprise that eagles were present. He closed his eyes and listened to the powerful birdcall again. It was further away.

"Bandits, bandits, bandits, three o'clock low!" Mack's voice burst into his ear.

Jase heard the call but continued to fly straight and level, he felt numb, unable to make his body respond.

"Can't shake him!" Mack's voice held genuine fear. "Jase, got two on my six, engage, engage!"

Clenching his jaw, Jase struggled against his lethargy but failed, his aircraft continuing to fly straight and level. A deep, thundering explosion reverberated over him and he instinctively knew Mack had been shot down.

Jase's eyes snapped open, heart thundering, adrenalin pumping through his body, he noticed it was pitch black and the night's silence was only broken by the rhythmic chorus of crickets. He wiped cold sweat from his brow and slowly sat up. Jimmy was asleep nearby, although his weapon was within arm's reach. Yawning softly, Jase felt exhaustion sweep over him. Reaching into his pocket where he stowed some berries earlier during their patrol, he munched on the fruit, enjoying the punch of flavour. When he finished, his stomach continued to growl and he looked forward to one day enjoying a breakfast of fresh bacon, soft eggs, tomatoes, sausages, toast and fried tomatoes. His mouth watered at the thought. It seemed such a small ask before the invasion. But now, he knew it would be a long time before he ever ate like that again, if ever. Lying back, he knew he might not even survive.

A heavy blanket of exhaustion crept upon him, moving over his body like a shadow. The tiny amount of star riddled sky he saw between the forest's canopy disappeared behind closing eyelashes and sleep came for him faster than a wraith. Neither of them awoke as the distant crackle of gunfire broke out in the north. It was almost discernible to human hearing, but there nonetheless. A testament to the fact that no matter how strong a foothold the enemy had upon the land, subjugation would be more difficult than the Indonesians first assumed.

Grant slept under the shade of the Bangalay tree throughout the day. He needed the rest, but he was also aware that he would be able to move faster and silently by walking on the beach, rather than stumbling through the forest. As such, he would only be able to move over the open expanse of the sand by night. Yawning softly, he sat up, stretched his aching back and slowly climbed to his feet. His body argued, willed him to lie back down and return to the comforting arms of slumber. Ignoring the compelling thought, Grant slipped the pack onto his back, checked that the beach was clear and stepped out onto the soft sand.

Although he needed the rest, especially as his body was still recuperating, he knew the longer he lingered in one place, the more chance he had of recapture. He walked close to the water's edge, as the sand was more compact there and easier to move along. The incoming tide would also wash away his footprints.

Grant walked at a steady speed, he guessed about six kilometres per hour.

On a normal night, he could cover the curve of beach around Bate Bay in two hours, but on many occasions, he was forced to slow or even stop at some sudden noise nearby. Once, he thought he heard the mewl of a feral cat, although he could not be sure. A feeling of utter disbelief crept slowly over him as the night progressed. More often than not, he heard the faint crackle and pop of automatic gunfire. Twice low flying jet aircraft screamed overhead and as the moon began to rise, its light gently glimmering upon the Tasman Sea, Grant watched tracer fire flicker up into the sky over Sydney, reminding him of television footage from Baghdad city during the Gulf War.

A dull, reverberating explosion swept over the peaceful beach. He strangely found the sound, which months before would have resulted in the screaming sirens of police and bomb squad vehicles, comforting, because he knew a person or group, somewhere in Sydney, was resisting the Indonesian invasion.

It was a strange mix of the peaceful ebb and flow of the sea on his left, and the constant chatter, crackle or boom of distant fighting on his right. There was one thing of which he was sure. Sydney would be a ruined city. Even time, that great healer of all wounds might not be successful. Amongst the sound of warfare spattered about the city, Grant could see the warm, orange glow of fire dotted along the horizon. Sydney was burning. She was hurt and hurt badly. Nearby gunfire exploded and Grant hit the wet sand instinctively. Distant gunfire sounded surreal, almost like a child cheekily walking along a length of bubble wrap. Close gunfire had a decidedly different sound and feel. It was much more threatening. Drawing his pistol, he felt comforted by the cold metal of the weapon.

Distant voices shouted, followed by the staccato of gunfire, a scream, two quick gunshots and then silence. The cold wet of the sodden sand soaked through his clothes, but he remained still, quiet, safe. His index finger slowly slid onto the trigger and Grant pointed the pistol towards the approximate direction where the recent gunfight had taken place. Apart from the ever present crackle, pop and rattle of distant gunfire, his immediate vicinity remained silent. Grant waited for voices, more shots, but none came.

He remained prone for an indeterminate length of time, probably twenty minutes he assumed, before he slowly climbed to his feet. Holding back a groan as his body protested strongly against the move, he began walking again, index finger never leaving the trigger and the barrel always pointing inland. An unassuming enemy would receive an unfortunate surprise should they stumble upon Grant. He would of course be outnumbered should enemy soldiers discover him, but what counted was the first, and perhaps even the second soldier would be worm food.

It was a far cry from working as a security guard at Sydney Airport. There were days he complained about the hours, the lack of breaks, and the length of the breaks they were allowed, however, the invasion had brought everything into perspective. He wished he were a security guard again. Even if they were given no meal breaks at all, it would be far better than the situation in which he currently found himself.

Grant recalled the fateful day that the Indonesian Army made landfall at Sydney airport. Many security guards lost their lives that day, and if it were not for the fast acting anti-terrorist element of the Army, he would have died as well. Swallowing hard, he shrugged the backpack into a more comfortable position and glanced at another length of bright red tracer shudder into the sky over Sydney, followed by the almost inaudible shriek of jet engines. Grant stopped in his tracks and cocked his head, trying to acquire better hearing, but the sound did not return. Hope filled him that the Australian Air Force, or at least part of it, was still active.

Feeling lethargic, noticing the moon was passed its zenith and on the way down, he decided it was time to rest. From what he could see, Grant had made it most of the way around the crescent shaped Bate Bay, however, tomorrow night would command much more concentration. Tomorrow, he would travel into the built up suburban beachfront areas of Cronulla, which he was certain would be filled with Indonesian soldiers. He knew recapture meant death. The pistol clasped in his hand ensured he would be a marked man and he vowed that the invaders would recapture him over his dead body. Literally. Grant's attitude had changed vastly whilst on the run. If discovered by the Indonesians, his one enduring thought was the number of enemy he could kill before he was shot, and if that wound was not fatal, he liked to think he could continue the fight.

Most red-blooded males thought they were tough and made of stronger stuff than the next man. However, it was not until they were mentally and physically tested that the truth was revealed. The truth was usually disappointing. Grant was going through the process and was beginning to find all sorts out about himself and disappointment was not amongst them. Given a life or death situation, he was not found wanting, but had instead risen to the challenge. Moving carefully up into the tree line, he walked into the forest and found an area he thought to be hidden from view. When the sun rose, he would re-evaluate. Darkness changed the environment, making an area look very different than what it would have during bright sunlight.

Sleep took him quickly, its blanket settling upon him with a heavy weight. Before he knew it, the gentle warmth of dawn warmed his skin, waking him. Bleary eyed, survival always at the back of his mind, Grant peered around him and noticed that his current position was not as hidden as he had first thought. Rather than move, he lay on his side and dug out a hollow in the sand the length of his body. With shoulders and arms burning, he rested every few minutes before continuing. When he was happy, he rolled onto his opposite side and dug out a hole for his pack. This done, he dropped the pack into the shallow hole, covered it over and rolled into the man sized trench.

Sweeping sand upon himself, he lay back, attempting to make himself as camouflaged as possible. From a distance, he was invisible. However, if an enemy soldier decided to investigate more closely, Grant would be discovered. With pistol resting on his chest, at least the first Indonesian to stumble upon him would receive a hole in the face. After what he had lived through, recapture was not an option. Grant was sure of that. If found by an enemy hunter force, he would die fighting.

With that in mind, sleep gently crept upon him, bright red erupting in front of his eyes as eyelashes closed before the blinding sun. He slept fitfully, waking several times during the day to gunfire, a close birdcall, distant shouting, the deep reverberation of an explosion, jet engines, or as dusk began to settle, Grant's own snoring woke him from sleep. With a soft yawn, a quiet cough, stretch and silent groan, he slowly sat up and climbed out of the sandy trench. Pulling his pack clear of the ground, brushing it off, he sat, enjoying a quick meal and drink, before hefting it onto his back. Shrugging the pack into position, he walked to the edge of the tree line.

Leaning against a tree, he knelt in the soft sand and spent several minutes watching the length of the beach in both directions, watching for movement and listening for sound. When he was sure the coast was literally clear, he walked out upon the beach and moved down to the water's edge, so that once more the incoming tide would hide his footprints.

A long burst of tracer sputtered through the night sky over Sydney, followed seconds later by the distant chatter of the heavy machinegun responsible. Sporadic gunfire continued relentlessly throughout his journey, the wet sand squelching softly beneath his boots. Whoever was responsible for the distant fighting had given the Indonesian Army pause. They were resisting doggedly. Not an hour would pass without some area of Sydney subject to gunfights, explosions or aerial attack. Grant was not sure whether the fighter jets he heard periodically were Australian or Indonesian.

He was forced to duck to the sand as one jet shrieked low overhead. Almost a minute later a bright orb of light silhouetted Sydney's high rises against the horizon, followed by the deep, rolling thunder of the explosion. Not long afterward, the jet shrieked past in the opposite direction. With a wince, Grant pushed himself back to his feet and began walking, his wet boots feeling heavy in the sodden sand. Close to midnight, he stopped and ate another meal, aware that feeding his recovering body was of the utmost importance.

Taking a deep breath, he glanced inland and realised he was entering the beachfront suburb of Cronulla. The houses were blacked out, their power having failed long ago. Nonetheless, he still heard muffled sounds of people in a closer vicinity than he would have liked. It was almost impossible to determine whether they were friend or foe and Grant did not want to find out. He continued walking, ignoring the burning in his legs and trying to forget the ache in his knees.

Working through the pain and the reluctance of his mind, Grant was able to actually increase his pace, in an effort to pass through the built up area as fast as possible. A nearby drunken shout followed by more yelling sent Grant diving to the ground, the air leaving his lungs in a rush. Brushing sweat from his brow, he watched the dark objects run onto the beach in the near distance. There were perhaps five people he could see, all shouting abruptly in Indonesian. Drunk Indonesian soldiers. Just what he needed, thought Grant, dampness seeping through his shirt, cooling the skin beneath.

One of them was being dragged forward by the others, almost as if he was a prisoner. Grant squinted through the darkness, not able to make out any distinct definition. Had the group just forced the man to his knees? The prisoner shrieked something in Indonesian before a loud pistol retort echoed out over the beach. Grant flinched, adrenalin sweeping through his veins.

"Holy shit," he whispered, watching the kneeling man flop forward onto his face, where he remained silent and still.

The four remaining soldiers stumbled from the beach, talking and laughing. In minutes they vanished amongst the houses. Well that certainly answered the question as to who inhabited the suburb. If there were still Australians around, there would not be many of them, not in Cronulla anyway.

Picking up the pace, the man's execution style murder still fresh in his memory, Grant pushed on. He glanced at the dark smudge lying on the sand, but there was no movement. Within the hour, the houses closed in, moving closer and closer to the water. Rocks replaced the easy sand of the beach and Grant found the going hard. Twice he came close to rolling an ankle, or slipping off balance on the smooth surface of the sludge covered boulders. The tide was out and would not return for many hours. He looked out to the sea where light from the moon twinkled upon its surface. Grant knew he must cross Bundeena Bay tonight, or risk recapture and death. If the Indonesian soldiers could kill one of their own so callously, what would they do to a foreigner? A foreigner? He stopped mid-stride, *I'll be bloody damned if I call myself a foreigner in my own country!* He clenched his jaw, the warmth of anger flooding his body, lending him strength.

Hearing a soft cacophony of waves clashing against one another off shore, he assumed he was passing Shark Island. It was not an island as such, more a large sand bar, where waves clashed and competed against one another. Again he met soft sand, and remembered just how hard it actually was to walk across in comparison to rock. As sweat began beading upon his brow, he found a large rocky outcrop and strode on. Muscles ached, joints rebelled and his mind complained, though Grant knew just how important crossing Bundeena Bay was to him. If he failed to swim across tonight, there was nowhere to hide come dawn.

Twice he was forced to stop or even lie down as the sound of nearby people radiated down to the beach. He struggled to hear what they were saying, but could not distinguish whether they were Australian. Ignoring his body, Grant forced himself to walk on, leaping over small rock pools, slipping on algae covered rocks and clambering over boulders. Suddenly the ocean seemed to envelope his position. The sea no longer flanked his left side, but now lay before him as well. He knew that finally, he had reached Bundeena Bay.

He sat heavily upon a flat rock and let the pack slide from his shoulders. Boomer had given him a waterproof piece of material he called a hootchie, explaining it could be used as a shelter by tying the corners to nearby trees, saplings, boulders, fence lines and so on. However, in the event of a river crossing, wrapping his pack in the hootchie, turned the pack into a buoyancy device in order to help him make the crossing.

Once he caught his breath, he took a long drink of water before delving into the pack for a meal. Although he did not feel hungry, Grant knew that he needed the energy, especially with the swim ahead of him. The packet was a cold ration meal Boomer had given him. The night Australian Navy Divers liberated him from Concentration Camp Hatta felt like a lifetime ago. Lamb and rosemary by the taste, he thought, munching on the processed meat. Using his fingers to scoop up the food, he forced the cold meal down his throat, crushed the packet and buried it.

Taking another long swig of water, he finished the bottle before closing the lid and pushing it down the front of his shirt. The swim was at least seven hundred metres. Before the invasion, Grant had received the Bronze Medallion in recognition of his strength as a swimmer. Now, however, tired, weak, hungry and half the size of his former self, the long swim would be an incredible physical and mental challenge. A challenge that might end him. As he glanced over his shoulder and watched another long string of tracer soar into the sky over the city he once knew as Sydney, Grant knew the swim was worth it. There was nothing left for him here.

Placing his pack in the middle of the hootchie, he pulled the watertight material up around the pack, tying the parcel closed at the apex. As long as the apex of the waterproofed pack remained upright, no water would leak in.

"Christ help me," he whispered.

Wading out into the water, he pushed off from shore towards his invisible destination.

CHAPTER FOURTEEN

*"*M*artial law declared in Florida! Riots out of control, 51 dead, 279 injured. Senate is urged to act now on crisis in Australia!"* Florida Today, Tallahassee.

Matty withdrew a sidearm. "Put this over your head and walk in front of me," the Australian newcomer said, throwing the hood at Spud.

Spud caught the material deftly and pulled it on over his face.

"Clasp your hands behind your back like they're tied."

A cold sense of dread descended down Spud's spine as he felt his hands bound tightly behind him.

"Yup good," Matty shoved Spud in the back, "let's go."

Spud shuffled uncertainly towards the exit. He heard Matty stride past him, opening the door and latching it.

"Come on mate, hurry up," hissed Matty, "the longer we take, the greater the chance of those bastards getting suspicious."

Spud quickened his pace, feeling Matty's hand in his back, relentlessly urging him forward. When he arrived at the top of the stairs, he slowed to a halt and was about to feel his way down when Matty shoved him in the back, hard.

"I don't have time for this, dog!" Matty shouted in a thick Indonesian accent.

Spud was airborne for less than a second before he slammed into the ground, pain exploding through his jaw. Seeing stars before his vision, he blinked them away, spat out a bloody tooth and climbed to his feet with a groan, shaking his head. It was a small price to pay for the sake of authenticity. He knew Matty was making a show for those Indonesians in the immediate vicinity and being a life or death situation, he was not about to complain. Clasping his hands tightly behind his back, he allowed Matty to shove him forward towards the truck.

Spud could smell the acrid, greasy smell of a heavy vehicle nearby and knew that freedom was close. With heart hammering in his chest, adrenaline and excitement swept over him. He felt alive. Strength enveloped him and with his face hidden behind the hood, he grinned, blood dribbling down his chin and dripping onto his neck.

Matty opened the passenger side door and pushed Spud up into the cabin, "get up there," he growled. "Hurry the fuck up!"

"My hands, though," said Spud.

The bindings were cut free within seconds.

"Take your hood off, and get the fuck up there!" said Matty.

Ripping the hood from his face, Spud clambered up into the seat, slammed the door behind him and hoped they would make it out safely. He heard Indonesian shouting nearby and looked around, his hand closing around the cold metal of a sidearm resting on the dashboard.

"Where are you taking the prisoner?" shouted Major Simanjuntak, who stood nearby, the smoke from his half-finished cigarette clasped between index and middle finger drifting in the slight breeze.

"I told you I would interrogate the prisoner," responded Matty. "I have been instructed to bring him to HQ for more rigorous questioning."

"HQ?" asked the major, dropping his cigarette. Clearly the term was foreign to the man.

He watched the glint of suspicion enter the major's eyes and Matty's hand dropped to clasp the pistol grip of his sidearm. One second. That was the length of time it would take the Australian soldier to draw, aim and fire a lethal shot, and Major Simanjuntak instinctively knew it.

Matty strode around the back of the vehicle, never turning his back on the Indonesian officer. Finally turning, he ran to the driver's side, pulled open the door and climbed into the seat. The engine roared to life and Matty dropped the clutch, the vehicle lurching forward, accelerating violently.

"Stop them!" roared Major Simanjuntak, gesturing towards the fast departing truck.

Soldiers in the near vicinity looked at the officer in confusion.

"Shoot them!" he shouted.

Weapons were unslung as soldiers made ready to fire.

"Forget that," Matty said, snatching the pistol out of Spud's hand. "Use this!" he reached down and pushed an Indonesian automatic weapon at him. "Safety's off, mag's full, just aim and pull the bloody trigger!" he said, bringing the truck around, the back end almost sliding out as they careened towards the front gate of the compound.

Loud thuds exploded along the metal skin of the truck as bullets hammered home. Matty glanced in the side mirror and saw they were being fired upon from behind. He almost lost control as a bullet lodged in the rear left tyre. Maintaining control of the steering wheel, he planted the accelerator to the floor. With a stink of burning rubber, the tyre tore from the rim and Matty found himself driving on three wheels.

"Is that all you got?" shouted Matty, grinning.

Spud glanced across at his saviour in disbelief, Matty was enjoying this! Forcing himself to concentrate on the task at hand, he watched as the front gate came rocketing towards them. The guards had taken kneeling positions and were firing upon them. Many of their bullets zipped passed the vehicle, but three smashed through the windscreen, lodging into the dashboard, seat or rear wall, narrowly avoiding both men.

Spud pulled the rifle into his shoulder and fired through the windscreen. The noise of the gun shots were deafening in the enclosed space. Aiming along a metal gun sight posed more challenging than using a scope. Taking a breath, concentrating, Spud aimed carefully and fired again. The gate guard on the left dropped like a ragdoll, and with silent satisfaction, Spud turned his attention to the guard on the right and saw that he was already down, clutching his leg.

It was then Spud realised Matty was half hanging out the vehicle, firing his sidearm at the enemy soldier on the right. Ducking down into his seat, Spud flinched as the vehicle rammed through the tall gate, bursting through the compound and into freedom. The bullbar was bent and twisted up at an unnatural angle. Fighting the steering wheel, which juddered violently in his grip, Matty kept the vehicle on the road.

Several kilometres further, Matty slowed and turned onto a narrow, rough track. Bouncing in his seat, Spud remained silent, his mind continuing to analyse what had just taken place. He was still coming to grips with the fact that he was free again.

Matty slapped him on the arm. "You alright?"

"Yeah, mate," Spud said, a grin slowly spreading across his face. "Bloody oath, I'm alright!"

Within minutes the vehicle came to a slow halt. The tailgate swung down with a slam and soldiers began boarding the rear of the Unimog. Snatching the passenger door open, a large, older man stood looking up at Spud, a trusty, well used .303 bolt action rifle cradled across his chest.

"Move over, mate. Make room for an old bastard," said the old man.

He climbed up into the cabin and slid into the space vacated by Spud. "Name's Mick," he said offering his hand. Turning his attention to the Special Forces soldier, Mick nodded and said, "g'day Matty. I see you made it out in one piece."

"It was touch and go for a moment there!" grinned Matty.

Shifting it into gear with a crunch and accelerating away, Matty was eager to place as much distance between themselves and the enemy. A loud knock on the rear glass of the cabin made Spud turn. On the other side of the glass Kane grinned, giving him the thumbs up.

"Welcome back!" mouthed Kane.

Spud returned the thumbs up.

Mick leaned forward to address Matty. "We had a chat to Kane," he said. "We're gonna head back to the farm. There's plenty of food there. We'll just have to slaughter a couple of cattle."

Matty nodded thoughtfully. "Yeah righto. Not sure how long we'll be able to stay there though, mate. Those Indos will really have a bug up their arse now and will be searching high and low for us. Only a matter of time before they find us."

Mick shrugged. "It's safe for now. We can talk more about what to do when we're back there."

Matty nodded dubiously, but remained silent. He knew well enough the official motto of the SAS was "Who Dares Wins." The unofficial one was The Six P's, "prior preparation prevents piss poor performance". A prepared strategy now meant that should contact with an enemy force be established, they could withdraw rapidly and in good order.

A kangaroo bounded in front of them, disappearing into the bush with a crash as a rotten log snapped. Matty swerved violently to miss the animal.

"Stupid bloody animals," he muttered. Kangaroos resting on one side of the road usually had a habit of fleeing onto the road in front of traffic.

"Not the most forward thinking animals God shovelled guts into," agreed Mick.

The journey took less time than Spud expected, the Unimog's headlights sweeping across a large, lowset homestead. Standing on the veranda watching them arrive stood a woman and beside her, clutching her leg, a young girl.

With a loud hiss, the Unimog came to a halt and as the engine shut down, silence enveloped them. The tailgate was lowered quietly and soldiers disembarked from the rear. Mick climbed down from the cabin, stubbornly waving away a helping hand. Jumping to the ground with a grunt, he slung the rifle and walked towards Katie who had run to greet him. She flung her arms around him, sobbing.

"What's wrong?" he asked, rubbing her back.

"It's terrible Dad," she cried into his shoulder. "I shot someone."

Mick held her at arm's length. "Whaddaya mean?"

"He attacked me. Tried to kill me. Tried to kill us!"

Mick knelt and dragged the tearful Jade to him, kissing her cheek and lifting her into his arms, standing. Pulling Katie to him, he hugged her tightly.

"What happened?"

Katie took a deep breath as she struggled to control her emotions, before explaining what had taken place.

"Did Jade see it happen?" he whispered into his daughter's ear.

She shook her head. He seemed relieved.

"Where's the body?" Mick asked, Craig and Matty now standing close by, listening.

"In your bedroom. I shot him with your revolver."

"It's okay Katie. It's okay my girl. You stay here, I'll go take care of it."

Kissing Jade, he placed his granddaughter onto the ground and walked towards the house.

Craig approached Kane, explaining what had taken place and requesting he place his men in all round defence around the house. The two Special Forces soldiers followed Mick into the house.

"Are you okay?" a soft hand touched Katie on the back. She turned and found herself being pulled into Ben's embrace, his acrid aroma somehow soothing. Relaxing in his arms, she pulled him tight, enjoying the feel of skin beneath her hands.

"I'm fine," she replied, smiling.

"Shit she doesn't muck around!" Craig said, looking down at the corpse. Blood had soaked into the carpet around the body.

"Nope, that's my girl," replied Mick, pride evident in his voice.

"This bloke didn't stand a chance," said Craig, nudging the cold body with a boot. Squatting down, Craig rolled the corpse over. "I'd say he's a deserter by the look of him. Obviously hasn't seen a decent meal in a while. Nevertheless, just goes to show, we're no longer safe here."

"My bloody sheets are ruined!" Mick said, flicking pieces of brain matter from the bed.

"You sound like my Mum," smiled Matty.

"Yeah, you'll have to remind her to return my watch. It's still sitting on her dressing table." Mick turned to Matty, grinning. The men chuckled.

"You got a tarpaulin or something?" asked Craig.

"Yeah mate, out in the shed, near the main work bench."

Craig left the room, returning minutes later with a large blue tarpaulin tucked under one arm. Rolling the corpse onto the tarp, they wrapped it up and carried it from the house, using the rear door so as Jade would not see. Within the hour, the trio had dug a suitable grave in the forest, burying the deceased Indonesian.

Later in the evening, the dining room was transformed into a briefing room. Around the table sat Mick, Ben, the two SAS soldiers, Kane and Spud.

"First logistics," said Mick. "We need food to feed all the new mouths. Me and Ben'll slip out in the morning and round up a couple of cows. We'll butcher 'em back here and store the meat. That should keep us fed for close to a month."

"I'll send a couple of diggers to help you out," said Kane, "if only to help manhandle the carcasses."

"Righto," said Mick, feeling awkward accepting the help. "Thanks."

"Logistics is the stuff that makes or breaks wars," said Craig. "I won't deny that. But we've given the Indos in the local area a right bloody flogg'n in recent weeks. They know we're here somewhere, and after breaking out young Spud here, it might be the straw that breaks the camel's back. We need to consider moving on. Especially after Katie's encounter."

"But where?" asked Ben.

Craig shrugged. "That's why we're here. We need to at least consider the option, and steps to make it happen very quickly should a full Indo patrol stumble on this position. Because sure as shit, if we've got no plan in place, at best we'll be overrun in a matter of hours."

Mick nodded thoughtfully, but remained silent.

"I heard about a place," Spud spoke quietly, his body still aching. "I heard the Indos talk about it on several occasions. Apparently it's an Australian stronghold in the middle of the Cordalba State Forest north west of Childers. Thousands of people fighting against the invasion. That's only thirty kilometres north of here."

"As the crow flies," replied Matty. "Definitely worth a look though. We'll need to travel by road, though, and that in itself is not only a longer way around, but it means we'll be exposed to greater dangers."

"Although, like you said, definitely worth a look," smiled Kane.

"Hang on," said Craig, pointing at Spud. "You understand Indonesian do ya?"

"No, they spoke in piss poor English, but I made sure I listened."

"Yeah, righto. No offense mate," Craig glanced at Spud. "But we'll give that camp a miss, especially since they were speaking in poor English. All we need is a bit of misinformation and the next thing we know we're walking into an ambush or a bloody concentration camp."

Silence emanated around the room.

"You reckon we can retrieve the four wheel drive from the creek bed?" asked Craig.

"Yeah, maybe, depends what's wrong with her," replied Mick. "Don't see why not though."

"Day after tomorrow, we'll go see if we can retrieve it," said Craig.

"What's wrong with tomorrow arvo?" asked Ben.

Mick chuckled. "Obviously you've never butchered a beast before Ben, never mind two. That'll take most of the day. Day after tomorrow sounds good."

The men talked long into the night, discussing ideas, agreeing on plans, ironing out problems and deliberating on what Australia might be like after it was all over.

Mick, Ben and a quarter of Kane's platoon boarded the Unimog early the next morning. The twenty minute journey took them into the middle of Mick's closest paddock. Before the invasion, two thousand head called it home, but as they looked out over the herd, Mick knew less than half that number stood before him. The Indonesians had slaughtered his livestock in their hundreds. He had no idea how the cattle roaming the twelve remaining paddocks fared. At that rate, the paddock would be empty inside a month. As Craig pointed out, logistics made or broke an army, and soldiers needed to eat.

Two large heifers were chosen. The Unimog reversed up to the closest stock ramp. Half the soldiers set up a defensive perimeter, watching for enemy. Try as they may, they were unable to load the beasts onto the unimog. Eventually they were forced to use their last resort. The cows were shot with Mick's .303 ensuring an instant death, before the carcasses were dragged up the ramp onto the Unimog. Departing quickly in order to avoid tangling with curious enemy patrols that may have heard the shots, they returned to the house an hour after dawn.

With the help of Ben and several soldiers, the beasts were butchered by lunch. No easy feat. Most of the meat was stored in Mick's freezers, giving the solar power a real challenge. Some of the meat did not fit, which served as the evening's meal.

Craig and Matty appeared after dinner had been eaten. They had departed on patrol before the sun rose that morning.

"They're search'n high and bloody low," said Craig, sitting at the dining table and placing his weapon on the floor beside him.

Matty nodded his thanks as a plate of warm food was placed in front of him.

"Yeah?" Mick sat with the men as they ate.

Craig nodded. "Like a dog with a bone, mate. We're used to seeing convoys come and go along the rat lines, but it's the first time we've seen aggressive foot patrols." Craig used the term rat lines to describe nearby supply routes used by the Indonesians.

Mick knew the term aggressive patrolling from his days as an infantryman in Vietnam. A technique used whereby a section, platoon or company patrolled an area of ground known to be held by opposing forces in order to force contact with the enemy.

"It's only a matter of time," Craig said, chewing on a piece of steak. "Damn that's good!" he added, cutting another piece.

Mick nodded, his mind reeling. He had hoped to wait the invasion out in the safety of his home, however, that seemed to become less likely by the day.

"I don't know what's going to happen," said Katie, leaning her forearms on the veranda rail. They had spent the afternoon ripping the blood stained carpet out of Mick's bedroom.

"Neither do I," replied Ben shrugging. "All we can do is our best, day after day." He looked up at the silent night sky, watching the stars twinkling at him. To the east, a single, low cloud slowly crept towards the horizon. "I wish I could say everything will be alright," said Ben, "but I'd be lying."

They both heard the shriek from Mick's room, a deep inhalation, followed by the sound of soft sobbing. Katie sighed and closed her eyes.

"He has nightmares about Vietnam," she whispered. Opening her eyes she looked at Ben. "One of his best mates died there. Jonny Hargraves," she chuckled humourlessly. "Even though he died long before I was born, I still know his name. I used to hear dad calling for him in his sleep sometimes. Pleading with him not to die. When I was a girl, before mum and dad's divorce, I would wait in the car while dad visited Jonny's grave. I sat there for almost two hours once. Dad eventually stumbled back to the car, drunk."

Ben frowned a silent question.

"He used to carry a hip flask everywhere he went, drank day and night." The sobbing had subsided to be replaced by gentle snoring. "But he cleaned himself up when mum left."

"Wasn't enough for her to come back though?"

Katie shook her head sadly. "Nope. I went with her, mainly because she had sole custody of me. Visited dad every second weekend. I used to love it out here. The day after my 18th birthday, I moved back with dad," she smiled, looking out into the darkness. Before Ben could ask, Katie continued. "Mum had a major stroke three years ago. The hospital had her on life support for 48 hours before we decided to have the machines switched off."

Ben suddenly saw Mick in a new light. The old man was tough, no doubt about that. But he now took on a more human aspect to the younger man.

Silence descended upon them as each became lost in their own thoughts. A soft breeze drifted across them, sending a chill down Katie. Ben was watching a satellite drift silently across the night sky. With all the horror surrounding them, the satellite continued oblivious to it all, unaware of the tens of thousands of Australians who had been killed, or the hundreds who would be dead within the following hour. Ben wished he could drift away with the satellite. Closing his eyes, he relaxed and found himself reviewing recent events. The hiss, crack or whizz of bullets at close range, the acrid smell of cordite, the sickly sweet aroma of death wafting gently on the breeze, but most of all, he remembered the eyes of the dead, they stared lifeless beneath half closed eyelids. A hand rubbed his back and he jumped in shock, adrenaline pumping through his body.

"Are you okay?" Katie asked softly.

"I'm fine," he replied, a little more sharply than he intended. Enjoying the warmth of her hand on his back, he smiled at her. "I'm fine," he repeated, more gently this time.

They stared at one another for a long time before Ben leaned forward slowly. Their lips touched gently, and the moment seemed over before it began. Cupping her face in his hands, Ben kissed her again, more passionately this time. As they kissed softly, Ben became acutely aware of Katie's body pressed against him, her soft skin, the bulge of her breasts and the heady aroma of her perfume.

A loud giggle burst out behind them and Jade, with hand clasped over her mouth, ran inside the house. "They're kissing! They're kissing!" she shrieked.

They pulled away from one another and laughed quietly. Jade's distant, muffled voice continued to echo as she ran through the house, from room to room, telling anyone who would listen.

"I'm half expecting your old man to come out here and knock my block off," said Ben softly.

"He wouldn't dare!" Katie grinned. "He'd have me to contend with!"

"He can be kinda scary though," replied Ben.

"Only to those he doesn't like. You're fine," she winked at him.

"Oh well, I s'pose we should make the most of it then," he said softly. "Everyone knows anyway," and pulled Katie to him, kissing her.

Jade scrambled back out onto the veranda, dodged a half-hearted kick from Katie before sprinting back inside shrieking with laughter. Neither of them cared. The world as they knew it was going to hell, and with little to no privacy as it was, they each enjoyed the intimate moment.

As Kane pissed against the trunk of an Iron Bark, the crickets in his immediate vicinity fell silent. The house some hundred metres behind them sat quietly, only a gentle flicker of light suggesting there was a building there at all. Kane's platoon was spread out around the homestead in all round defence, providing security for the position. Looking up at the half moon through the light canopy of forest, he sniffed, zipped up his trousers and unslung his weapon, master hand instinctively snaking around the pistol grip of the weapon.

A loud laugh erupted in the distance, followed by Indonesian voices. Kane froze and slowly descended onto a knee, finger disengaging the safety catch. Although silence surrounded him, he knew his soldiers heard the voices and were ready. It seemed they were about to be evicted from the homestead. If the enemy thought they would leave quietly, they had another thing coming. A grin slowly spread across Kane's face as the voices grew ever closer.

*"*espite best efforts, UN insider states Indonesian sanctions have failed."* Daily Record, Glasgow.

Two weeks of hard slog saw Jase and Jimmy safe in the largest camp they had ever seen. Nestled in the most southern part of central Queensland, the resistance encampment was hidden amongst the remote Cordalba State Forest. Jase, however, was less than impressed by their leader.

"I'm Barry," said an obese man in a New Zealand accent.

Barry was relaxed in a camp chair, looking at the newcomers standing before him. His moustache looked like a large, brown slug had oozed out one nostril and perched itself above his top lip. An ugly, bulbous nose, tiny red veins flanking his nostrils, suggested he was an alcoholic. The man boasted an enormous beer gut, an arrogant attitude and an air of distrust. Something about him spoke of a two-faced buffoon whom was not to be trusted, not even on a good day.

The men uneasily introduced themselves, Jase's pistol still gripped tightly in his hand. Jimmy allowed his weapon to point at the ground, although his finger rested upon the trigger. With a great groan, Barry pushed himself to his feet and limped forward awkwardly, holding out a hand. His grip was soft and weak, and Jase disliked him instantly. Maybe it had been instinct, or maybe his father's voice silently whispered to him in his subconscious, but in his opinion, a man with a weak, soft handshake indicated either abject weakness, or had no interest in making the appropriate greeting and thus offered disrespect from the outset. Either way, Jase took a step back and looked away.

"You'll like it here," said Barry, sniffing, hands on hips.

Obviously the newcomers were boring him, and after their introductions, it seemed he did not want them taking up any more of his valuable time.

"How often you fight?" asked Jimmy.

"Me?" said Barry, "I don't need to fight boy, I'm in charge here," Barry parked himself back in the camp chair with a great groan.

You wouldn't even know how to fight, thought Jase quietly, looking around the forest.

"No, the camp, you know?" said Jimmy, an edge entering his voice. "How often they give them Indos a kick'n?"

Barry shrugged. "Most days I think. Listen, I only plan the major campaigns," he said airily. "You'll have to talk to Mark to get the ins and outs."

Jimmy nodded and fell silent, although Jase knew the Aboriginal soldier was angry. Barry had started something he likely would never be able to finish.

"Nice meeting you, anyway," muttered Jase, not particularly bothered if he sounded genuine or not.

"Yeah, you too!" offered Barry, who was now reading a book.

"Wanker," said Jase as the pair walked away.

"Oi! You two!" called a voice.

Jase and Jimmy saw a tall man striding towards them through the thick forest to their left, an Indonesian automatic rifle cradled across his chest.

"Mark," offered the man, holding out his hand. Jase almost winced at the grip.

"So, you've met our illustrious leader?" asked Mark with a knowing smile.

"Yup," replied Jase evenly, not knowing where Mark's loyalties lay.

Life was so much easier on the run. Stay quiet, low, slow and alert.

"Yeah, I can see he impressed you no end. Righto, the camp is hidden amongst the forest. We're in all-round defence and the circle is about one kilometre wide. Where possible, we've kept friend and family groups together. There's always eyes out, but every second day sentry duty is changed and those on piquet move back into depth to rest and relax. We plan missions when and where we see fit. Mostly we move on targets of opportunity."

"Sounds pretty well organised," said Jase, nodding.

"We try our best," replied Mark. "Barry's just a self-proclaimed figure head, he's bloody useless. The man couldn't walk more than ten metres without losing his breath, let alone running. The safest place for him is at the centre of the camp, out of the way, thinking he runs the show. There's a lot of former and current military members spread throughout our number, all the way from Vietnam Vets to Iraq and Afghanistan veterans. They come in handy from time to time."

"Sorry boss, you have any water?" asked Jimmy. "I wanna refill me water bottles."

"Right this way fellas," Mark led the way through the forest.

The camp itself was hidden away exceptionally well. Jase noticed disguised trails in the leaf litter leading in many different directions. The longer they spent in location, the more they realised just how intricate and complex the camp had grown over time.

In the beginning, it was probably no more than a conglomerate of several people clinging together for safety. However, as needs must, out of such humble beginnings, an entire guerrilla camp had formed.

"This is the water point," said Mark, pointing at rows upon rows of full jerry cans. "Each morning, empty jerries are carried down to the river nearby and refilled. We all take it in turns, but you can expect to restock the water point at least once a week."

Jimmy nodded his thanks and refilled his bottles, but not before taking a long, fulfilling swig.

"Gees, that's better eh?" Jimmy grinned.

"I'll take you out to the south side of our position. It's where we're most thin in number. I'll introduce you to some of the people there."

Walking to the position took the best part of fifteen minutes, and as they closed upon their destination, Mark slowed the pace, becoming more cautious, making less and less noise. Jase noticed families sitting together beneath tents, hootchies or tarpaulins, whispering amongst each other, sleeping, eating or playing cards. He steered the two newcomers to the most furthest tent. It was a ten by ten foot khaki coloured military tent sheltering one man.

"This is Steffan Wyatt," said Mark, gesturing at the single occupant by way of introduction.

The men shook hands.

Steffan was a well-built man standing six feet tall, with short cropped dark hair and cruel dark eyes. The corners of his mouth turned down in a permanent sneer.

"What brings ya here?" Steffan asked curtly.

"The Indonesians, I guess," replied Jase, taking an instant dislike to the man.

Wyatt chuckled humourlessly. "The Indonesians," he repeated, "fuck'n smart arse," he said turning away.

"I take it this is our new home?" Jase asked.

Mark nodded apologetically. "For the short term, this is the most secure area of the southern boundary. Once you've got a feel for our tactics and routine, I'll move you out further."

The former fighter pilot swore silently to himself.

"And don't think you're sleeping, there, there or there," said Wyatt matter of factly pointing to an empty stretcher and two other empty bed spaces. "You can sleep over there," Wyatt continued, indicating the two furthest stretchers from him.

Jase nodded, biting off a rebuttal.

"Ay boss, can I speak to ya for a sec?" Jimmy asked Mark.

The two men moved away from the tent to talk privately.

"That Wyatt fella's a prick, you know? I don't wanna sleep near 'im."

Mark held out his hands in appeasement. "Listen, I know and I'm sorry, it's the best we can do at the moment."

Jimmy's eyes glinted fiercely. "Well you bloody do better then, coz I'll kill 'im before mornin'." Jimmy tapped his rifle. "I've killed eight fellas so far. One more won't make a difference. I don't care whose side he's on, you know?"

Mark's eyes widened slightly as he realised Jimmy was deadly serious.

"Jase, there," Jimmy continued. "He's a fighter pilot. He's killed fellas too. We're not pampered puppies. Get us up front and we'll hold our own." Jimmy leaned in close and dropped his voice to a whisper, turned slightly and gestured towards Wyatt who was facing away. "Most of all boss, get us the hell away from this joker!"

Mark could see that Jase and Wyatt were already exchanging words. "I'll see what I can do."

"Righto, you see what's what. In the meantime, me and Jase are moving out of 'ere."

"Wait! You can't do that!" said Mark sharply.

"Bullshit boss! You watch us!"

Mark caved. "Alright, alright! I'll take you up the front, but you gotta be quiet, no talking, I expect…"

Jimmy cut him off. "I'm a rifleman, lead scout and assaulter. I know how to be quiet!" he hissed. "Do you?"

Mark appraised the Aboriginal soldier and finally nodded. "Alright, let's go."

Jimmy pushed past Steffan Wyatt, picked up his pack and swung it onto his back.

"Oi! Watch where you're going!" said Wyatt.

"Wise words," replied Jimmy glaring at Wyatt. "Keep 'em in mind."

The trio moved south away from the tent, well spread out, patrolling slowly and near silent. A distant shriek of military jets forced them to a knee. Evidently, fast air was still active. Jase hoped the aircraft were Australian, although he knew the chances were slim at best.

Another two hundred metres saw them on the southern-most perimeter of the Australian camp. Mark indicated their new home by pointing at a nearby gun pit dug into the ground. The gun pit, or trench, was roughly half a metre wide, two metres long, one and a half metres deep and camouflaged to a professional standard. The pit was difficult to see until they were almost on top of it. All that was missing was the gun.

Climbing into the pit, Jimmy mouthed a curt "thanks" to Mark. Mark nodded and moved away quietly.

Before long, all the men could hear was the soft breeze moving through the forest canopy like silk across a tiled floor. Occasionally, birds called to one another as they flew in formation high above the forest, oblivious to the inhabitants below them. A loud, bickering flock of galahs landed in a nearby Eucalyptus tree, their noise a breath of fresh air. Jimmy knew he would rather listen to the birds than endure Steffan Wyatt's arrogance. It was strange how things had changed. On the run, in a land controlled by an occupying force who outgunned, outnumbered and surrounded them, Jase and Jimmy now felt imprisoned by this new 'safe haven'.

Clinging to the hootchie enshrouded pack, Grant caught his breath. The water of the river enclosed around him, threatening to drag him below the surface. His brain shouted for survival, to push on and live, but the cold water tugged at his clothes, weighing him down and whispering for him to release his grip on the floatation device. Let go of the hootchie and it would all be over. A silent death, an end to the pain. Groaning through chattering teeth, muscles shivering in an attempt to keep warm, he opened his eyes a slit and saw the dark smudge of the opposite bank. Grant realised he was more than half way across. Slowly glancing over his shoulder, he saw how far he had swum. And you want to give up now? You want to bloody give up now? Kicking his legs out behind him, he pushed himself onward, the groan turning into a snarl.

"You ain't giving up," he hissed to himself, anger warming his body, driving him through the cold water.

Muscles aching, lungs burning, his breathing coming in short rasps, Grant was forced to stop and rest again. The river's water began whispering to him once more, gently pleading with him to release his grip and let himself slide below the surface. All his worry, pain and struggle could be gone in an instant. No more fighting. No more hiding. Just quiet, soothing eternity amongst the river weeds drifting along the bottom.

"Fuck you," growled Grant through clenched teeth, kicking his legs out behind him and forcing himself onward.

Pain consumed him as his body defied his will. Nevertheless, Grant's mind was victorious as the red hot burn of muscle fatigue faded away to a dull heat. Ragged breathing became deep, rhythmic breaths and before he knew it, Grant was staggering along the riverbed, wading through chest deep water. Waist deep water. Knee deep water. Ankle deep water. Then the pebbles of the riverbank met his face with a dull thud.

"Come on," he muttered to himself, commanding his body to stand, feeling cold stones against his cheek. Aching muscles rebelled and won a small victory, Grant collapsing back onto the ground.

"Get up," he said quietly, teeth once more beginning to chatter. "Come on, get up!" his lips pulled back in a snarl reminiscent of an attack dog, rather than a human.

Now on his knees, he forced his legs to move and the muscles' act of rebellion failed as he staggered to his feet with a quiet groan. Dragging the hootchie wrapped pack up the riverbank into long grass, he flopped into a sitting position. Unwrapping the pack, he pulled out a spare pair of dry socks. Undressing and cursing the cold night air, he used the socks to dry himself as best he could. Then he dressed in dry clothes. Throwing caution to the wind, he lit a fire and heated a can of food before forcing the warm meal down his throat. Filling the can with water, he placed it back on the fire and heated it. When the water was warm, he lifted the can from the flames and taking care of the sharp edges, drank the warm water down. Already he could feel energy recharging his body.

Once finished, he scattered the fire, packed the hootchie away, slung the pack and walked deeper into the forest. When he was satisfied, Grant set up camp, climbed into his sleeping bag and welcomed the relaxing approach of slumber. As he slipped away, one last fleeting question flittered across his mind. Would he wake up in the morning?

Now lying prone with eyes closed, and his assault rifle pulled firmly into his shoulder, Kane allowed his ears to engage the night's quiet atmosphere. The Indonesians were within four hundred metres of their position, but did not seem to be coming closer. Aware that the noise the enemy made might be a decoy for a much larger attack, the officer swept his eyes across the dark environment surrounding his immediate vicinity. At night, the senses provided by the ears and nose was invaluable. For instance, an enemy smoking a cigarette could be detected almost half a kilometre away. The ears detected movement and were usually able to differentiate quickly between noise caused by an innocently grazing animal or that of a deliberately moving enemy soldier. These senses provided direction and a rough distance, giving forewarning and allowing soldiers to set up deliberate ambushes, or simply to remain hidden and silent.

Index finger gently resting on the trigger, Kane listened as the enemy skirted within two hundred metres of their perimeter, unaware of their presence. Twenty minutes passed before the enemy's noise drifted into silence. However, the Australian soldiers remained alert, silent and ready to fight for almost an hour afterward. When they were sure the threat had departed, they relaxed slightly.

Kane rose smoothly to his feet and walked quietly through the forest towards the house. As the distance to his destination closed, Kane slung his weapon and let his empty hands fall beside his body, allowing the occupants know he was not a threat.

Climbing the short flight of stairs onto the veranda that hugged the house's perimeter, he nodded a greeting to the couple who stood close together, leaning on the rail. They offered a quiet greeting, though it was obvious they were more interested in time together and alone.

Removing his boots, Kane walked into the house and made his way to the living room. Hearing voices from the kitchen, he walked in to find the pair of SAS soldiers finishing off a meal. Kane pulled up a chair, sitting at the table.

"Just had enemy pass within a couple hundred metres of here," he said.

Matty, the man responsible for freeing his soldier from enemy captivity, looked at him thoughtfully. "How many you reckon?"

"Maybe platoon strength. Hard to tell."

"You see 'em?" asked Craig.

"No. Certainly heard 'em though. Loud as a bloody toddler throwing a tantrum," Kane replied, immediately feeling a pang of longing to hold his three-year-old daughter. He wiped the thought from his mind.

Craig pushed the empty plate away from him, made a noise to suggest he had immensely enjoyed the meal, reached into a pocket, and pulled out a folded map. Flattening the paper across the table, he picked free a piece of meat wedged between his teeth, then pointed at the map.

"Where'd they pass?" Craig asked.

Kane moved around the opposite side of the table in order to better view the map.

"Right along here," Kane said, leaning over Craig's shoulder, pointing to a portion of light green with a steak knife.

"Right." Craig leaned back in his chair, and placed his hands behind his head. "We'll set up an ambush somewhere near that location, knock at least half the Indos over and then withdraw in the opposite direction from the homestead. It might help throw them off the trail and buy us some time at least to work out where we go from here." Craig looked at Kane and Matty. "Thoughts?"

"Worth a try," said Kane, shrugging.

Matty nodded, shovelling the last portion of food into his mouth.

"I'll get your guys to remain in position," Craig said, looking at Kane. "We'll take a small group, hit 'em hard and withdraw fast. It'll work a lot better with a small group."

Kane thought about it for a moment. "True, but if you end up getting in a sticky situation, withdraw to our position."

"Don't worry mate, I had every intention of doing just that," Craig grinned. "But if that happens, once the Indos have been taken out, we'll have to move on. It's not worth risking one enemy soldier we may have overlooked escaping and bringing an entire regiment down on us."

Kane nodded. He did not share the same seemingly carefree attitude the Special Forces soldiers carried. After all the long weeks of running and fighting, Kane finally found a more permanent location for his men, where they enjoyed fresh food, routine and restful sleep. It had been a small taste of normality. However, with the Indonesians encroaching closer with each passing day, he knew it would not be long before they were on the move again.

"**US** *Senate convenes to receive resolution from the Senate Foreign Relations Committee authorizing use of American military forces in Australia."* New York Times, New York.

The distant call of Kookaburras brought Grant gently from slumber. A light, cool breeze drifted across his face. Streaks of bright orange spanned the eastern sky, heralding the arrival of the sun. Yawning silently and stretching, Grant winced against dozens of aching muscles. Lying awake, silent and still for almost ten minutes, he enjoyed the soft sand beneath him and the warm comfort inside the sleeping bag.

Forcing himself to move, Grant subdued a groan and awkwardly sat up before rising to his feet. With back burning, legs aching and sharp pain shooting along his arms, Grant stooped down and gathered up his sleeping bag. He moved slowly, overworked and injured muscles rioting.

"Pain tells ya you're still alive," echoed the voice of Grant's father from the vaults of his memory.

He smiled weakly, missing his old man, claimed by pancreatic cancer less than two years before.

"I owe it to you mate," he whispered to his father, slinging his pack without complaint and limping deeper into the forest.

The kookaburras had long departed, leaving only a gentle whisper of breeze stroking the forest canopy. It seemed like a new world, far removed from the ravages of Sydney. Grant felt at peace within the forest. Apart from only the faintest crackle or pop of distant gunfire, one could be forgiven for even thinking Australia had been invaded.

Pushing past weeds, ground creepers and saplings, he attempted to remain as quiet as possible. Somewhere in this forest hid a large Australian resistance group. Although moving as near to silent as possible held benefits, if he surprised them, they could be forgiven for shooting him on sight.

Leaning against a tree, Grant watched a pair of sea eagles soaring high above him until they were lost amongst the thick forest canopy. Pushing on, he ignored a long burst of distant gunfire behind him. Sydney, or at least the Sydney he had known growing up, would never be the same again. She had been tainted, washed down with violence and blood. Her grand allure was fleeing before her newfound darkness, like an innocent young girl transforming into a teenage Goth.

Grant pushed through a thick hedge of saplings woven together by ground creepers. Just when he thought he had successfully negotiated his way through, his foot became entwined by a vine and he found himself on all fours. Cursing softly, he attempted to stand, but instead fell forward under the weight of the pack. He became aware once more of the pain pulsing through his body. Closing his eyes and clenching his teeth, he pushed through the pain as his legs raised his body up. Grant stood with a growl, exhaling sharply.

"Halt!" a voice shouted.

Grant needed no second warning. He dropped the pistol instinctively and raised his hands, offering empty palms in an attempt to show he was no threat.

"Advance slowly!" the voice commanded. "You try anything and I'll drop ya like a sack o' shit, you got that?"

Grant nodded his understanding and walked forward slowly.

"Stop there! You alone?"

"Yes," Grant called, knowing several loaded weapons were pointed at his head or chest. One wrong move and it was over.

"Take your pack off!" ordered the voice.

Grant obliged.

"Walk forward. Faster! Keep your hands raised."

Grant crunched across leaf litter, long dead bark and rotten logs before two men suddenly tackled him to the ground. Air exploded from his lungs as he hit the dirt, his face buried in a mound of decomposing leaves. That was just what his aching muscles didn't need. Trying to relax and keeping his hands out to show he offered no threat, Grant waited as they conducted a thorough body search. Having served as a security guard at Sydney Airport, he knew they were not only looking for concealed weapons, but detonators, initiating devices, wires or even small, basic booby traps. After finding nothing, his hands were tightly zip tied behind his back. When he was lifted to his feet, he watched as another searched his pack for similar threats.

A hand shoved him from behind. "Move!"

Staggering forward, Grant ignored the pain racking his body and limped through the forest. In his mind, he imagined this meeting would be different. However, given recent circumstances, an amount of controlled aggression at this early stage showed a healthy level of distrust.

They had barely started walking when Grant found himself flanked by another four men who seemed to melt out of the forest around him, military assault weapons held professionally. Grant noticed the weapons were immaculately clean, safety catches off, index fingers resting gently on the trigger. Even here, now, if he made a move that was perceived to be a threat, he was dead. The men would shoot him, and by the look of them, sooner eat lunch than bury his corpse. A good thing, thought Grant, for it was people like the men escorting him who could win Australia back. Tough, uncompromising, yet professional. It may take months, years, even decades, but it was possible. Of course, Australia as he knew it before the Indonesians, was gone, never to return. However, a new land might be carved from the old, and he found himself amongst pioneers.

Twenty minutes of brisk pace brought him before the commander. A middle-aged man standing just over six feet, light orange hair and beard, both dappled with grey, lent his face an unforeseen menace. He glared at Grant for some time before he offered him a chair with a nod. Grant remained standing for no other reason than his body still hurt.

"I'll make you sit if I have to," the man said quietly, nodding once again at the empty chair.

Stifling a groan, Grant sat heavily in the chair, his boots feeling like they had been filled with lead, the muscles of his legs as if red-hot pokers had been slid into them. Closing his eyes, he clamped his mouth shut and remained silent, defeating the pain.

The commander nodded to a man standing behind Grant, who sliced roughly through his bindings. Relieved of the tight zip ties, Grant rubbed his aching wrists.

"Just who the fuck are you?" asked the commander by way of introduction.

Grant introduced himself, leaning forward, trying to alleviate the discomfort spreading across his back.

The leader nodded, but remained silent for a moment. "You came outta nowhere, son! Lucky you weren't shot outright. Where'd you come from before this?"

Grant looked up at that question, holding the man's gaze. "Where'd I come from?" it was a rhetorical question. He chuckled, shook his head and stared at the ground.

"Camp Hatta," said Grant slowly, looking back up. "Sheer fucking hell."

Several soldiers in the near distance who had been talking amongst themselves fell silent and turned to watch proceedings.

"A concentration camp?"

Grant was not sure, but he thought the man's voice softened slightly. He nodded wearily in reply.

Noise exploded in the area at once as men surged forward towards Grant, shouting over one another. Had he seen a wife, girlfriend, mother, child? Instinct took him over and he slid from the chair, protecting his face with his hands and rolling into a foetal position, sure he was about to be attacked. Just for a moment, a terrible dark moment, Grant's mind cast back to Camp Hatta. He screwed his eyes shut and clenched his jaw against the onslaught.

"Shut the fuck up, all of you!" roared the camp's leader, his voice echoing around the forest like a gunshot. In the distance, a flock of cockatoos frightened by the shouting, took to flight, shrieking as they departed.

"Get back," the man muttered to those surrounding them. Squatting beside Grant, he spoke softly. "It's okay mate. We ain't going to hurt you," he said placing a hand on his shoulder.

Coaxed back onto his chair, Grant took a deep breath to fend off the impending feeling of claustrophobia. Hands shaking, the warm ebb and flow of adrenaline flowing through his system, Grant no longer felt the pain which had so recently disparaged his body.

The commander introduced himself. "Just call me Bluey," he said. He turned towards the men standing nearby. "This is my original crew. We once belonged to the Second Commando Regiment. Those days are dead and buried now. We were the few able to fight clear of Holsworthy Barracks when the invasion happened. Slowly we've increased in numbers as men, women and children fled out of Sydney looking for a place to lie low, to call safe."

Grant nodded, the adrenaline wearing off, his pain returning.

"Got room for one more?" he tried to smile.

"Bloody oath, mate," said Bluey. "We're over a thousand strong and growing by the month, although there's good and bad to that."

"Logistics," Grant replied, having seen how poorly Camp Hatta had been run as far as food and hygiene were concerned.

"Exactly, my man!" said Bluey, gesturing him to stand. The bigger man helped Grant to his feet. "We got a raid going into Sydney the week after next looking for food and fuel for the vehicles. You're welcome to come along if you're up to it."

"I'd like that," said Grant. "Might not be able to walk and run, but I can definitely shoot!"

Bluey saw the fire in the man's eyes and grinned. "Come on mate, we'll sort out your sleeping area, introduce you to some of our people and get some fuck'n weight on those bones. Jesus mate, you look anorexic!"

"I've stacked on kilos of weight since Hatta."

Bluey clenched his jaw and looked away, remaining silent. Grant knew Bluey felt angry by what he had gone through at Camp Hatta. He was even angrier at what a large portion of Australia was experiencing right now. As an Australian soldier, Bluey had sworn to serve the Queen and protect Australia from all enemies, both foreign and domestic. In this, in his mind at least, he had failed. Grant suspected that Bluey felt like a father who had been unable to protect his child from violence, abduction or worse.

"You can sleep here for now," said Bluey, pushing through the entrance of a large tent hidden within the forest. He noticed at least twenty other such tents scattered randomly throughout the forest in a two hundred metre diameter.

Although he was introduced to the occupants, at least thirty of them in number, for now Grant found remembering their names impossible.

"We house the newest arrivals in these tents," explained Bluey. "Once you've got some experience under your belt, we'll move you out to the perimeter where you'll be a kept a bit more on your toes," he grinned, passing him a large can of baked beans and a plastic spoon. "I know it's not a fresh, hot meal, but it's better than noth'n."

Grant grinned like a child, taking the food eagerly, "you're not wrong, mate, I'm bloody starving!"

"Anyway, kip down for the night, try and get a good night's sleep and I'll see ya in the morning." Bluey slapped him on the shoulder and left.

Sitting down on the stretcher that was now his bed, Grant dropped his pack on the ground and tentatively unlaced his boots. He winced as he pulled them from his feet. Slipping off his socks, he rubbed the sore, blistered skin. Over the next several hours as the sun descended towards the horizon, Grant sadly looked at a seemingly endless string of photos of people's family, shaking his head or explaining that he had not seen them.

"I'm sorry," he muttered, looking at the distraught couple standing before him. "I haven't seen your daughter."

Another man made to approach Grant but was stopped by an elderly lady. "Let him rest," she spoke softly. "Ask him in the morning."

The man looked as if he would argue, but finally closed his eyes and nodded, moving away. Grant slowly lay back on the stretcher, gritting his teeth against the pain slithering throughout his body. Finishing the last scraps of baked beans from the can, lay his head upon the folded hootchie, released a long, drawn out breath and closed his eyes, the soft talking around him soon melting into the background as sleep crept over him.

He dreamed of concentration camps, the smell of death and the taste of boiled potato mixed with terror.

"What happened Ben?" Mick asked the younger man in mock surprise, staring at his head. "Where's your hair product? Your hair's a mess!" Mick turned to his daughter. "Love, you got any hair gel you can lend him?"

Katie stood nearby, hands on hips smiling as she shook her head in disapproval.

"I'm all out old man," replied Ben, "I used the last of your stash."

Mick laughed. "Let's go mate, Craig and Matty'll be waiting for us."

Ben pulled Katie to him and kissed her softly. "I'll be back soon," he said quietly.

"Careful son, that's my daughter," grinned Mick.

"Give us some bloody privacy Dad," frowned Katie.

"Righto, righto," he waved at them as he departed.

"Take care out there," she said, cupping his cheek with her hand.

"Always," Ben replied, grinning. "You take care too."

Mick had made her a special belt to which he had attached a holster to carry the .357 revolver. On the opposite side, Mick had made a small pouch in which were three speed loader clips. Kissing her again, Ben followed Mick.

Kane offered the service of several of his soldiers, however, Craig politely declined. Over time, the four men had learned to work as a silent, cohesive team. Not quite as silent or well-oiled as a complete SAS patrol, but given the circumstances, the two civilian men certainly stepped up as far as Craig was concerned. The patrol left in the opposite direction of likely enemy advance and continued for several kilometres, before deviating around in a large loop. They patrolled slowly, deliberately and methodically, taking almost three minutes to travel one hundred metres. Hours later, they set up an ambush on the far side of Bentwood Cullen Bone property.

Ben lay still, ignoring the annoying tingle as an ant crawled across the skin of his neck. Gone were the days of squirming, cursing or trying to move into a more comfortable position. Ignoring discomfort, his hands gently clamped the Indonesian assault rifle ready to fire. Safety catch disengaged, finger resting on the trigger. The only part of his body that moved constantly were his eyes, scanning, watching, gauging shadows, flitting back to a moving branch in the near distance to ascertain whether it moved as a result of a breeze or enemy movement. It was the former, and Ben relaxed again.

Jonny hadn't aged a day. The young soldier's grinning face was back, haunting Mick's thoughts. He missed his mate, and wondered what Jonny would look like today, had he survived 'Nam. Sure as shit, he'd be lying beside them right now, weapon in hand. But that NVA bullet had changed all that. They had tried to stop the bleeding, and for a time, Mick thought they had succeeded. With the dust off still hours away, they tried their best.

'We tried our best,' Mick thought silently to Jonny's grinning face.

He remembered the moment when the light left Jonny's eyes forever. With dust off still an hour away, Jonny's pale face, tensed in pain, relaxed for the last time. Dead, half open eyes staring at the jungle canopy above. Mick had punched the ground. He remembered that much. Mick rubbed his eyes quietly, sniffed and cleared his throat softly.

Voices! Faint and difficult to hear, but voices nonetheless. Almost five minutes passed before Ben could discern that the language they spoke was Indonesian. The enemy patrol moved from right to left in front of the Australian ambush, but were too far away to engage. Within ten minutes their voices and clumsy movement through the bush had faded to silence. The Australians remained in position for a further hour, withdrawing only when the dark blanket of night's protection grew thin. Dawn was breaking as they returned to the homestead.

"Have a gonk. We'll go out again later tonight," said Craig.

"Have a what?" asked Ben.

The soldier chuckled. "A sleep," he explained. "You look like you need it!"

Ben nodded and slung his weapon. "Too right," he muttered.

When the civilian men had disappeared into the house, Craig turned to Matty. "Get a couple of hours, mate, then I want to have a look in daylight. Might be they've created their own little track through the forest. If they have, we'll find out where it is and then hit them tonight."

Matty nodded. "Thought crossed my mind too, especially now that they've been in the same area of forest two nights in a row."

As the sun conquered noon and began to charge for the horizon, Craig and Matty melted into the forest. They were careful to inform Kane of their intentions so as they would not draw fire from the Australian soldiers who might confuse them with enemy. They moved slowly and quietly, stopping often to look and listen.

At last, Craig, thirty metres in front, signalled halt and took a knee. Eventually he signalled for Matty to join him. When the soldier reached him, Craig pointed to a narrow track in front of them. The grass and weeds had been trodden down by numerous pairs of feet, making the track obvious.

The crushed foliage had yet to yellow and die, suggesting the track had only been created in recent days.

They silently withdrew. On approaching the house, they held their weapons above their heads, an agreed signal for friendly forces. Kane's soldiers allowed the pair through the perimeter.

"I think we should let them be for now," suggested Craig later that evening.

"You don't reckon they know we're somewhere close," nodded Mick.

Craig shrugged. "If they did, they'd be sending out constant patrols in organised patterns across the terrain. They're not. It just happens that one of their newly made supply lines runs relatively close to the house. They're none the wiser we're here," he said looking around the table. Even Katie and Jade had joined the discussion, the girl sitting on her mother's lap.

"If we ambush them now, all we're doing is making them aware that our base camp is somewhere in the vicinity," said Matty. "If we let sleeping dogs lie, they continue using their man made track as some minor grade rat line between encampments and they'll leave us alone."

"For now," added Ben, arms resting on the table.

Craig nodded. "For now."

"They'll find us," said Mick, hands on head, looking at the ceiling.

"Have no fear of that," replied Craig softly. "But in the meantime, we can prepare rapid withdrawal plans, booby traps, counter ambush drills and so on. The most important thing at the moment is the Indos don't know we're here. That gives us precious days, maybe even weeks."

"What's an ambush?" asked Jade, wide eyes focused upon Craig.

"Shoosh, adults are talking," admonished Katie quietly.

Craig smiled at the little girl. "An ambush is like a big bad surprise."

"Oh," Jade said, playing with her hands and nodding knowingly. "My mum's like a cowboy now, except she's a girl," said Jade, pointing to the sidearm Katie now wore on her hip.

"She's a cowgirl," said Ben.

"A cowgirl?" Jade looked up at Ben.

"Yup, that's what she is."

"Oh," Jade nodded knowingly again.

"A hot cowgirl," Ben whispered into Katie's ear.

"So, I think you guys should all go and get some rest in warm comfortable beds while you still can," advised Craig. "I hate to say it, but there're dark days ahead."

"You're not wrong," yawned Mick. "I'm not as young as I used to be."

"True," said Ben softly.

"What's that you say?" Mick asked mid-stretch.

"I said you're old," grinned Ben.

"Yes I am," the older man said, slapping Ben on the shoulder, chuckling. "Night all."

The others remained talking quietly around the table before retiring. Ben climbed into bed, groggy with exhaustion, while Katie gently rocked Jade to sleep in the second guest bedroom. As for Matty and Craig, they slipped out into the night on patrol. With plenty of sleep under their belt, they moved into the dark depths of the forest to observe the enemy.

Ben lay on his back, arms splayed out beside him. A soft, cool breeze drifted through the open bedroom window and across his face. Sleep eventually claimed him, her heavy, silky arms drifting through the vaults of his mind. Gunshots rang out, deafening in the enclosed bedroom. Bullets ricocheted from the roof, and suddenly an Indonesian soldier stood over him, a sharp knife in hand and a wicked grin illuminating his face. The enemy stepped forward and let the flat, cold metal of the knife slide across Ben's face. The blunt weapon slid across the skin of his cheek and slowly headed towards his throat.

Ben thrashed in bed and awoke with a start, taking in a sharp breath.

"It's okay," soothed Katie, her hand stroking his face. "It's okay."

"Thank God, it's you," breathed Ben. He pulled the young woman to him and kissed her fiercely. She pushed him back to onto the bed and they kissed passionately. Undressing each other clumsily, Ben eventually ripped Katie's knickers off, throwing the torn material aside. They giggled like teenagers and then made love as quietly as possible. Ben felt like he was in a dream. A wonderful, pleasure filled oasis. As they lay in each other's arms, sleep drifting across them blissfully, neither of them heard the distant gunshots that shattered the night.

CHAPTER SEVENTEEN

*"*__UN__ *refuses to intervene in Australian crisis, stating it is against UN mandate."* Ekstra Bladet newspaper, Copenhagen.

Grant sat in the tray of the ute as the vehicle sped along the pothole riddled highway. Almost two weeks had passed since his arrival and he felt much better. His body almost completely recovered. Sometimes he grappled for a handhold as they skidded around the perimeter of a bomb crater that nearly destroyed the road. He shared the tray with six other men, all armed with weapons. The others were calm, leaning against the metal body of the vehicle, watching outwards, weapons ready to fire. Obviously, they had made this trip many times before.

Nervousness swept through Grant, clammy hands clinging weapon against chest like a newborn. Brakes brought the vehicle's speed down rapidly and a screech of tyres rent the air as the vehicle dodged a large pothole that had not been present during their last run into Sydney. Grant clamped a hand onto the wall of the ute's tray, fingernails turning white as he disobeyed gravity and remained seated and intact.

Food was their mission. Non-perishable food of any description. The camp employed daily hunting, gathering and fishing parties, but the food that was procured was almost never enough to feed the entire camp for half a day, let alone half a week. Now they resorted to commando type raids into enemy occupied Sydney. A much more profitable venture as far as food was concerned, but at great cost. Invariably, at least one or two men were killed each time a raid was launched.

To begin with, Grant had asked and even expected to be included on the next food raid into Sydney. At this moment, as he watched the tracer lace across the city, it became that much more real. The bright orange strings of tracer seemed much larger now than they had when walking along the quiet, private beach.

Wind roared in his ears and hair as they disobeyed the speed limit, bitumen blurring beneath the vehicle as they pushed 180 km/h. Speed and surprise were key. Before Grant could ask, two of the men knelt up and fired, the retort of gunfire strangely distant thanks to the wind screaming in Grant's ears. He looked towards their direction of travel and noticed they were quickly approaching an enemy vehicle checkpoint. The vehicle accelerated and Grant watched as Wayne leaned out the passenger window and fired a long burst from his M-4 assault rifle.

The boom gate shattered as they ploughed through, Grant snapping his head around to see enemy guards shrink rapidly into the distance. He observed as guards pulled weapons into shoulders and ducked as the distinctive crack, hiss, buzz and snap of bullets shrieked close by his head. Even at 180 km/h, the noise brought back memories of Sydney airport that fateful day. The day Australia fell.

Some of the men in the ute returned fire, but without a clear sight, Grant's weapon remained cold and silent. Seconds later, the enemy vehicle checkpoint was a dot in the distance, and something they would encounter on the way back.

Slamming into the tray's wall, Grant scrambled for a handhold as the ute swerved violently, narrowly missing an Indonesian military truck. Before anyone could engage the enemy vehicle, it was the size of a matchbox car, disappearing into the distance, brake lights blazing as it came to a slow stop. Within several short minutes, the Ute skidded to a halt outside a large Woolworths supermarket somewhere on the outskirts of western Sydney. As Grant was scrambling to stand and jump over the side, three of the men, weapons pulled into their shoulders, had already entered the building. As Grant's boots thudded onto bitumen, a short exchange of gunfire erupted inside, and although all his instincts told him to withdraw or take cover, he and the remaining men advanced into the building. Several Indonesian soldiers lay scattered near the vacant checkouts, fresh blood pooling beneath their inanimate bodies. Finger resting on the trigger, Grant heard more gunfire, this time from the rear of the supermarket. The gunfight lasted almost a minute before silence reigned.

"Clear!" shouted a distant voice.

The remaining men surged forward, scooping any and all non-perishable goods into shopping trolleys. All the supermarkets of inner Sydney had been cleaned out Wayne had explained earlier in the day. Now only those on the outskirts stocked anything of worth, and those stocks were running low.

Only another couple of raids would be fruitful for provisions. After that, all the supermarkets would have been stripped bare by both Indonesians and Australians alike. For now, however, it was like a grand final episode of My Kitchen Rules as people rushed trolleys to and fro.

"Here," hissed Wayne, pushing an empty trolley towards Grant. "Fill 'er up!"

Grant ran forward, almost colliding with another man.

"Sorry!" he called over his shoulder, disappearing down the cooking aisle.

Anything and everything was thrown into the trolley, it was the way he always thought a food shop should be done. Heading up the refrigerated aisle, Grant held his breath as the stench of rotten meat emanated from the last few packs remaining in the butcher section. The loud buzz of blowflies accosted him and maggots writhed on the ruined cuts of meat beneath the clear plastic of each pack.

Withholding a dry retch, he ran down the aisle, eventually confronted by what remained of the fruit and vegetable section, which was almost as bad. His lesson learned, Grant rapidly withdrew from the perishable areas of the supermarket, their stink thankfully departing as he jogged down the canned food section. Most of the area had been cleaned out, but what little remained soon found a home in Grant's trolley.

"Here mate, get a bit o' that into ya," said someone running past, dropping a stinking packet of minced beef into his trolley.

"For fuck sake!" he muttered, the stench assaulting his nostrils. He reached for the packet as vomit ascended towards his mouth. Holding it at bay, he grabbed the putrid packet and flung it away over into the neighbouring aisle.

He heard a wet splat followed by an unimpressed voice. "You bloody mongrel! Who did that?"

Grinning, but saying nothing, Grant fled to the safety of the next aisle. Within five minutes, his trolley was full and he ran back to the ute waiting out the front, Wayne standing guard. Two trolley loads of food had already been emptied into the back. As Grant ran closer, several men grabbed the trolley, picked it up, upended it until it was empty, and then threw it out onto the street where it landed on its side with a loud scrape.

In less than ten minutes, the supermarket had been stripped clean of the few non-perishable items that were left. Grant found himself sitting uncomfortably high in the tray of the ute as he attempted to wedge himself amongst packets and tins.

"Wasn't expecting that VCP on the way in," spoke the man closest to Grant.

"Vehicle check point," explained another, noticing Grant's look of confusion.

"Sure as shit they'll be expecting us on the way out."

Grant asked a question, but the vehicle was travelling much too fast now and the words were ripped from his mouth. Minutes later, the hulking darkness of Sydney was behind them. Not a streetlight twinkled. Skyscrapers stood silent and abandoned, their electricity supply having been severed weeks prior. Apart from the intermittent glint of enemy headlights as distant convoys negotiated decimated buildings and concrete rubble, Sydney appeared dead. Australia's premier city brought to her knees in preparation for the killing blow. Grant swallowed and looked away.

Screaming along the highway, the distant roadblock appeared in the far distance, an enemy truck parked beside it. Feeling a hard slap on his arm, Grant tore his eyes from the fast approaching enemy vehicle checkpoint and noticed one of the men gesturing for him to prepare his weapon. Disengaging the safety catch, he slapped the underside of the magazine, ensuring it had fully engaged the breech and was not about to drop clear of the weapon.

Several men were standing, leaning on the roof of the cab to steady their aim. Grant pushed himself into a kneeling position, slipped on a can of baked beans and ended falling heavily on his bum. A shrieking sound close by his face indicated the enemy had opened fire. Scrambling for purchase, and finally succeeding, he knelt up only to duck as loud hisses and cracks ripped over his head. He realised he was the only one not returning fire.

Grant steadied his aim, stared down the scope and fired a short burst knowing his rounds had gone well wide of the enemy roadblock. However, any rounds going down range at this point was better than nothing he thought. A loud thud, clearly heard even above the noise of the speeding ute and one of the men fell back, dropping like a rag doll. Eyes rolled back in his head, Grant saw he had taken a bullet in the middle of his chest, claret slowly soaking through his shirt around the bullet hole.

Things just got real. Adrenalin and fear sweeping his senses, he pulled the weapon into his shoulder, knelt up and fired a long burst directly at the vehicle checkpoint. Firing another burst, his weapon fell silent and he ripped the empty magazine free, reached for another and pushed it into the weapon's recess. Pulling the cocking handle back, he let the working parts slam forward under their own power. The ute streaked through the vehicle checkpoint, enemy bullets thudding through the thin metallic skin. Grant fired several short bursts at the dwindling enemy, watching one man fall to the ground clutching his leg.

Within a minute, they were out of range and slowing down. Looking around, he noticed black smoke streaking from beneath the bonnet and heard the unmistakeable flapping of a flat tyre. The stench of burning rubber and the tyre crumbled on the road behind them, the bare metal rim throwing sparks as it screamed along the bitumen. They pulled off the road, the driver attempting to accelerate off the road and into the concealment of the forest, but the engine stalled and remained silent. Steam drifted from under the bonnet. They disembarked.

"We're in serious shit," spoke one man, jumping down from the rear of the vehicle.

"Really?" one asked sarcastically.

"Fuck up, both of ya," shouted Wayne. "Jonno, Blocker, you two get back to camp quick as ya can, pick up another vehicle and get back 'ere. We'll try and hold 'em off."

The two fittest men disappeared off the highway and ran through the darkness. With more than twenty kilometres of ground to cover, Grant had serious doubts of surviving the night.

"Don't worry," grunted Wayne, noticing Grant's anxiety. "They'll be back in just over an hour."

"That's bloody quick running," said Grant doubtfully.

Wayne shrugged. "They're fit blokes."

It was the distant engine roaring into life that brought silence among the men. The men scattered off the road, finding cover or concealment where possible. With sinking hearts, they watched the enemy vehicle which had so recently been parked beside the VCP turn around towards them. With headlights blaring, the vehicle began accelerating violently in their direction.

Grant lay hidden behind a small shrub, safety catch disengaged, finger resting on the trigger, heart thundering in his ears. With nowhere to go, it was only a matter of time before the Indonesians hunted them down, slaughtering them all. He closed his eyes and took a deep breath, trying to hold off the body numbing fear that assaulted him, threatening to engulf him completely. The truck's engine grew louder with each passing second, a loud rumble of heavy tyres mingling with the engine's growl.

He wished Boomer and his silent, invisible team of killers were present. Grant cast his mind back to the night the Navy Diver and his team had assaulted the guards' building, killing them all and setting the prisoners free. A terrible nightmare brought to an end. The hiss of air brakes brought his mind back to the present. Flicking open his eyes, he watched the enemy truck on the highway. The Indonesians had stopped short of the abandoned ute. Obviously, they were being cautious, knowing the Australians could not withdraw very far and had nothing to lose.

Silence claimed the night once more as the truck's engine died, although the headlights remained alight. Grant heard laughter and shouting in a foreign language. The quiet night seemed to somehow transform into something deeply sinister.

A deafening shriek ripped across the sky above Grant's head and the enemy truck exploded in a mighty, earth-shattering explosion, which left ears ringing. The laughter and shouts were instantly replaced with the burning, hissing metal mess that had once been an Indonesian truck. The stench of rubber mixed with burned flesh was almost enough to make Grant gag.

"There!" whispered Wayne nearby, pointing in the direction the two Australian soldiers had so recently departed.

They can't have been that quick! Thought Grant to himself. No way!

Following Wayne's finger, Grant saw a tiny flicker of red light, indicating there were friendlies close by.

"Up! Let's go!" hissed Wayne to the remaining Australians.

They moved as a staggered group, advancing with caution, weapons ready. The torch flashed discreetly at them, before fading into darkness.

The group advanced carefully, a distant, deep judder of heavy machinegun fire blasting somewhere from within the depths of Sydney, making them pause. Grant slipped on a rock and landed heavily, pain exploding from his left elbow. Silently cursing himself, and ignoring a nearby chuckle, he clambered to his feet.

"Friendlies coming in!" hissed the voice from their front.

Wayne instinctively raised his rifle, pulling the weapon into his shoulder, finger resting upon the trigger.

"Who are ya?" Wayne asked.

"Friendlies! You fuck'n deaf?" asked the voice.

Two men appeared out of the darkness and advanced, stopping in front of the group. They wore Army issued uniforms, assault helmets, from under which sprouted long, thick, unkempt hair. Both wore beards, their faces stained with dirt and mud. The first held an assault rifle across his chest. The night vision goggles attached to his helmet were turned up away from his eyes. The second soldier cradled a long rocket launcher in his arms. Slung on his back was what appeared to be a sniper rifle. The weapon, with silencer attached, must have been close to five feet in length.

"Bob," the man said by way of introduction, "and Snapper," he said, jerking a thumb at the man behind him.

Wayne made the introductions on their side, noticing the newcomer's distinctive New Zealand accent.

"You a Kiwi?"

"Yeah, we both are," replied Bob. "Don't hold it against us," he grinned.

"Army?" asked Wayne.

"Yup," replied Bob and fell silent.

Wayne was astute enough to know the pair were not alone. More than likely, they were New Zealand Special Air Service and were part of a larger patrol who were lying low somewhere nearby, watching.

"Thanks for saving our arses back there," said Wayne. "Not sure we would've survived that one."

"No worries," replied Bob.

Wayne spent the next few minutes explaining to the pair about the nearby Australian encampment. Although the newcomers listened quietly, when Wayne asked them to join the camp, the New Zealand soldiers politely declined.

"We work on our own," said Bob quietly. "Sounds like you've got a good setup, but we're better off out here living off the land."

"Fair enough," replied Wayne.

The men talked softly for a while before a deep, rhythmic juddering swept across the landscape.

"You're fuck'n jok'n," said Wayne turning towards the sound. They all could see a single, very bright search light in the sky sweeping the ground.

"Chopper," said Bob, and with that, he and Snapper were gone. Like apparitions they had disappeared into the dense underbrush.

"This just gets better and better," muttered Grant, watching the helicopter streak towards them.

The men scattered, spread themselves out and went to ground behind cover or concealment, fingers never far from triggers. They heard soft footfalls in the distance behind them where Bob's patrol was more than likely withdrawing from the area. The loud whine of the chopper's engines was loud now, drowning all other sound out. The blades slapped the air with violent ferocity and within minutes, the monstrosity was hovering over the stricken white, Holden ute in the near distance.

Grant physically jumped in surprise as he felt a slap on his arm. He turned, heart thundering in his chest, and saw Wayne kneeling beside him.

"Aim just above the search light," he yelled over the scream of the chopper. "Shoot single, well aimed shots and empty yer bloody magazine!"

Grant tapped the man's shoulder to let him know that he had understood the instruction.

Breathing out sharply, Grant brought his weapon up, pulled the butt into his shoulder, stared down the sights and squinted against the bright searchlight. He thought he heard rifle cracks nearby as the others opened fire, though he could not be sure. Ignoring the deafening helicopter, he aimed above its search light, weapon bucking against his shoulder. The aircraft swerved away from the area, the aircrew aware they were taking fire. Grant continued to shoot, although he found it more difficult with the chopper now flying away from the area. A high-pitched scream mingled with the growl of the helicopter and Grant noticed an orange glow trailing from the diminishing beast. The flame from the engine threw enough light to outline the body of the aircraft. Obviously, a bullet had lodged somewhere important. Grant watched the helicopter slowly descend towards earth, the orange glow now a bright red spout of flame. Lazily, the aircraft turned into a nosedive and slammed viciously into the ground, disappearing behind a massive fireball. Almost two seconds passed before the thunder of the explosion rolled across them.

"No way they're walk'n away from that!" said Wayne triumphantly.

The small group remained prone, silent and frozen, waiting for the next surprise and hoping it never arrived. Once the ringing in their ears dissipated, it was replaced by silence, not even the crickets were game to make a noise.

Twenty minutes later the replacement vehicle arrived, an old Toyota Hilux dual-cab utility. Food from the nearby stricken Holden was transferred across. Grant dropped one packet of dried spaghetti, which broke open, the food scattering onto the road.

"Don't bloody worry about it!" said Wayne as Grant stooped to pick up the spaghetti.

Not five minutes passed before every scrap of food had been transferred across to the Hilux. Squeezing in where he could find room, Grant found himself wedged in the middle of the back seat. Wheels squealing, the vehicle turned around and accelerated aggressively away.

As the Hilux's diesel engine slowly subsided into the distance, the normal sounds of Sydney city broke the still night. Distant gunfire recommenced, explosions boomed in quick succession as Indonesian mortars or artillery fired upon a newly found group of "resistance fighters", a term Indonesia was using to describe those Australians who had taken up arms against the invaders. Tracers streaked through the dark sky, disappearing into a thick, low-lying body of smoke. All the while, Sydney burned.

"Australian Air Force believed defeated. Australian Navy obliterated, only 1 ship still in the fight." Los Angeles Times, California.

"Feels like a bloody prison, you know?" spoke Jimmy.

The pair was standing beside one another in the chest deep gun pit, looking out at the forest around them.

"Starting to feel like it," agreed Jase.

A loud, long fart resounded from the gun pit twenty metres away from them.

"Here, you hear that?" asked Jimmy, "that fella's been farting like a bloody elephant for three days!" Jimmy shook his head. "Those Indonesian blokes'd know where we were if they passed inside half a click of this joint, you know?"

Jase nodded, chuckling.

"Watched some fella yesterday running with his hand clenching his bum like it was gonna explode." The incident must have taken place whilst Jase was helping with the daily water resupply. "He couldn't make the latrine, so dropped his dacks and went on a tree over there," the Aboriginal soldier said, wafting his hand in the general direction. "It was like a bloody sprinkler coming out his arse! Went for almost a minute. I said to him, I said, 'Oi fella, you crook? You need medicine?' You know what he did?"

Jase suppressed a smile, shaking his head instead.

"He bloody let rip with the loudest fart I've ever heard in me life, and then shat for another minute! Like a bloody fire extinguisher it was."

Jimmy fell silent, shaking his head, whilst Jase chuckled.

Another fart assertively announced itself, but remained centre stage beyond its welcome, as evidence by the unhappy groan that followed.

Gastroenteritis. The old soldiers called it dysentery, and it had had claimed almost as many lives during both world wars as the battlefields themselves. In this environment, with little to no medical support, no chance of resupply, dwindling food, no clean water, and a determined enemy pushing forward on all fronts, something as simple as diarrhoea would be enough to finish the Australian camp.

"A bloody prison," repeated Jimmy, his dark eyes glaring balefully out at the forest.

Jase knew the soldier was right. The camp was an entrapment.

"You want to leave?" Jase asked softly.

"What I been say'n for almost a week, brother?" snapped Jimmy. "You want me to paint you a bloody picture?" His voice softened slightly. "Yeah, I reckon we should shoot through. We got more chance of survival out there," he said pointing towards the silent, waiting forest, "than we have sitt'n' round 'ere, waiting to get crook like everyone else. The camp's run by some fat joker who doesn't know one end of a rifle from the other. We just wait around wait'n for someth'n' to happen. I dunno about you, mate, but I was always taught to seek out and fight the enemy, not wait while he kills my country." Jimmy fell silent, passing a hand across tired eyes. "And she's dyin'."

Jase finally realised Jimmy was speaking of Australia Herself.

"She's dyin'," Jimmy repeated softly. His eyes hardened and glinted with anger. "We can't just sit 'ere!" he said suddenly, turning to the fighter pilot. "We can't just sit 'ere while our country dies 'round us!"

Jase found the soldier's passion infectious. He simply nodded, remaining silent, mind made up.

"Tonight," whispered Jase. "Tonight we leave."

Jimmy looked relieved. It was easy for the fighter pilot to see that the Aboriginal soldier was more at home walking freely through the forests. At one time, the camp may have seemed a saviour, a safe point for which to aim. However, it became abundantly clear the camp was not motivated, and whilst strength in numbers was true to a point, it was required to actually take the fight to the enemy.

Jase knew Australians were dying out there. Dying in their hundreds while they sat in their camp day upon day, hiding away in some obscure corner of the Cordalba State Forest.

Would the ANZACs have sat by while their country lay in ruin? The answer to that question was a no-brainer.

"The sooner the better," muttered Jase.

"What's that you say?" asked Jimmy.

"Nothing mate. Nothing."

A loud snap of dried branch and crunch of leaf litter brought Jase back to the present.

"It's the Fat Controller," groaned Jimmy, jerking his thumb behind him at the overweight waddling form of Barry, who blundered through the forest to each gun pit, holding a short conversation with each before moving onto the next.

"How you blokes getting on?" asked Barry cheerily.

Before Jase could answer, Jimmy spoke. "Just bloody great boss, thanks for ask'n," the soldier glanced at Barry's gut protruding out over his trousers, "probably not as good as you, though, eh?"

"Why's that?" asked Barry, already starting to move on to the next gun pit.

"Coz you look fit as a mallee bull, boss."

"Hey Barry. Got a quick question mate," said Jase.

Barry chuckled, waved a dismissive hand and continued on towards the next gun pit.

"A mallee bull who's a couple hundred kilos overweight," muttered Jimmy grinning.

"Dunno who put him in charge," said Jase, watching the departing form. "What a dickhead."

"Just another reason to piss off, eh, brother?"

"Too bloody right," whispered Jase.

What was remaining of the day, predictably, passed without incident. The pair waited apprehensively as the sun snuck out of sight in the west, casting a dark grey blanket upon the forest. Nocturnal wildlife began to waken, starting their nightly routine. An owl hooted in the distance, ever watchful for small marsupials upon which it could feast. Much closer, the hissing call of a possum broke the still night air. Fruit bats twittered and bickered between one another as they soared above the forest canopy. Crickets chorused amongst themselves, whilst insects and small animals scuttled through the leaf litter.

The forest was a different world at night. Trees became giant stooping old men with long unkempt hair and gnarled hands. Fallen logs morphed into snickering tricksters, longing to trip up unsuspecting passers-by. The ground seemed to melt, a tiny divot in the ground during the day collapsed into some mighty sink hole once night arrived, ready to snap an ankle, or strain a knee beyond repair.

Noises travelled further. Keeping this in mind, Jimmy and Jase climbed out of their gun pit carefully. The quarter moon was yet to rise, however, and Jimmy wanted to be long gone before its partial light filtered through the forest canopy. They patrolled slowly, weapons held ready, safety catch disengaged, but trigger finger outside the trigger guard. Twice they stopped, taking a knee slowly, until they were sure the scuttling sound they heard was confirmed as a possum scrambling up a tree trunk. The men were heading south towards Brisbane.

Jase knew they would never make the city, but the closer they travelled to Queensland's capital, the more chance they had of crossing paths with Australia's new owners, or more proactive resistance fighters.

Australia's new owners. Jase thought about the phrase and felt uncomfortable with it, but knew it was a realistic way of viewing the situation. He had watched the Australian Defence Force's systematic destruction. Whilst the ADF punched far in excess of their weight, it was nowhere near enough. In his opinion, apart from several small pockets of guerrilla fighters, the Indonesians had been victorious in their bid for the country. Although he hoped to be proven incorrect, he could not shake the thought from his mind.

Stepping on an unseen dry branch, a loud snap reverberated around the forest and crickets in the near vicinity fell silent. Jimmy descended to the prone, gesturing for Jase to do the same. The men lay upon the dark, cold ground for close to ten minutes, the forest's nightlife continuing unabated, blissfully unaware of their presence. Jimmy did not expect enemy to hear the branch snapping, but that was not a reason to allow tactical discipline to slip.

When the Aboriginal soldier was satisfied they were the only humans in the area, he rose smoothly to his feet and signalled for Jase to follow suit. They moved on, slowly, deliberately, and with the exception of Jase, silently.

Dawn caught them resting under a small rocky overhang near the southern edge of the forest. By now, Barry's camp should have realised they were missing. However Jimmy was confident they would not mount a search party. Barry's people were flat out surviving, let alone scouting for missing members.

At midday, a distant, almost inaudible noise woke Jimmy from his sleep. The soldier sat up, concern lining his face, as he reached for his rifle, pulled it to him and cradled it across his chest. That it was an aircraft was obvious. The purposeful, streaking scream of military jet engines disappeared as swiftly as it had arrived. The aircraft was probably more than fifty kilometres away, and moving fast towards the south. It proved that the pair was ever so slowly moving back towards the fight. They may not be able to win against such odds, but it was important to both men that during Australia's darkest hour, as She lay bleeding upon the dry, sun-baked earth, that they at least fought. And if that meant dying, then so be it.

Jimmy rose and wandered carefully through the forest, returning two hours later with a shirt full of berries, roots and fruits. Over his shoulder was slung a large, newly dead goanna.

"Time for a feed," said Jimmy.

Jase continued to sleep deeply.

"Oi," Jimmy dug the Australian pilot in the ribs with his boot. "Time to eat, brother."

Jase groaned and yawned softly, sitting up slowly.

"You're bloody joking?" he said, watching the sun sinking close to the western horizon. "Sunset already?"

"Here, shove that in ya gob," grinned Jimmy, passing a handful of berries to Jase.

While the fighter pilot ate, Jimmy busied himself preparing a fire. Within minutes the flames licked high and bright. Jimmy gutted the goanna and placed the roots inside its abdominal cavity. Once the blaze was established, he placed the animal on hot coals, munching on berries as he waited for it to cook.

"You ever eaten goanna before?" asked Jimmy.

"Nope," replied Jase, sounding apprehensive.

"Don't worry, mate. It's noth'n to worry about. Tastes a bit like oily chicken."

"Smells pretty damn good," admitted Jase.

Jimmy nodded, grabbing another handful of berries.

When the meal was cooked, Jimmy carefully pulled a hind leg clear and passed the joint of meat to Jase.

"You eat that mate. You never tasted noth'n so good!"

Grease dripping down his chin, Jase ate tentatively at first and before he knew it, was peeling what little meat was left from the bone. Chuckling, Jimmy passed him another piece, which was demolished almost as fast.

"Tastes bloody beautiful!" said Jase, licking his fingers.

"Now, you try this 'ere," said Jimmy, pulling the cooked roots from the goanna's belly. "Careful, they're still hot."

Jase found the root tasted not unlike sweet potato with a soft consistency, almost that of half cooked potato. Not crunchy, not soft. By the time the pair had finished eating, their bellies were full.

"'Ere you tell me, Jase, you wanna eat cans of baked beans or this feast?"

"That's a stupid bloody question, mate," replied Jase, reaching for another piece of meat. There was not much left now, but he managed to pull some free.

"Too bloody right eh?" laughed Jimmy.

Darkness swept through the forest faster than anticipated, and before Jase knew it, they were patrolling through the forest once more, heading ever south. Jimmy moved smoothly, well-practised, professional and confident. He swept through the forest like a silent wraith. Jase, however, always seemed to trip on a branch, step in a hole, blunder through an unseen shrub, or walk headlong into a thick spider's web.

Slapping at his face and hair, he imagined a spider the size of his hand crawling across his head. The thought sent shivers down his spine.

"You alright there, brother?" whispered Jimmy.

"Spider's web," replied Jase quietly.

Jimmy stifled a laugh. "Ah, spider's web, eh? Thought you was havin' a fit!"

"Yeah, yeah! Laugh it up," grinned Jase.

Jimmy, trying hard not to burst out with laughter, shook his head and continued on his way. The night passed without event, although Jase's flight boots were not designed for infantry work and he could feel the blisters forming on the balls of his feet. His calf muscles ached and his thighs burned with each stride. However, before he allowed himself to descend into self-pity, he reminded himself of what the rest of Australia was going through right now. A couple of small blisters and some aches and pains paled into insignificance compared to people fighting, dying, and being tortured.

As dawn neared, Jimmy brought them to a halt. Jase wondered what the Aboriginal soldier had seen or heard for him to quietly lay down on the ground, signalling for the pilot to do the same. Then the sound echoed gently through the forest. It was an engine. A truck engine. Within minutes it faded and the pair were on the move again. They were patrolling slowly, deliberately. Jase was learning slowly, though he still felt clumsy. Another engine! Again the pair went quietly to ground. This time the vehicle was closer and was followed by another four trucks. A convoy.

Jimmy pointed ahead of them and silently mouthed, "Road."

Jase gave him the thumbs up to indicate he understood.

When silence once more reigned, they stood and moved on. An hour later, they were within sight of the road. Jimmy signalled a halt.

"We need to get us a vehicle," whispered Jimmy.

"You serious?" asked Jase, incredulous.

"Do I look serious?" grinned Jimmy.

"No."

"Well I bloody am, brother," he chuckled, slapping Jase's arm.

They went prone again as a distant engine came into earshot. Jase landed in an ant's nest and silently cursed as the mongrels began biting his neck and arms. The vehicle grew closer, Jase willing for it to pass so he could pick the ants off him. Trying to rub them from his skin, he almost shouted with surprise as an ant bit him on the end of his nose.

The vehicle, a small Indonesian military four wheel drive, tore past and was gone within moments.

"Gotta be a supply road," whispered Jimmy, his dark, serious eyes, glaring at the road in the near distance.

"What are you planning?" asked the fighter pilot.

Jimmy moved into a crouch and shuffled ever closer until he was within twenty metres of the road. The noise of an approaching vehicle sent him diving back to the ground and rolling behind a thick shrub. The vehicle, what looked to be a small hatchback, hammered past their position well in excess of 100km/h, its engine screaming.

Once the natural quiet of the forest returned, Jimmy indicated for Jase to advance and join him.

"You see that log there, eh?" Jimmy asked pointing at a large, thick log. It was easily as long as the road was wide, and about the thickness of an average man's waist. "We'll drag that out onto the road. It'll force 'em to stop."

The pair strained, cursed, grunted and, in Jase's case, slipped over not once, but twice. Eventually they dragged the heavy log onto the road. Breathless, the men stumbled back into the concealment of the forest, lying down, waiting. Nothing. For over an hour there was no traffic whatsoever. Then as the eastern horizon began to turn a deep, blood red, the sound of a powerful diesel engine drifted towards them. The vehicle was south bound. It was difficult to hear whether it was alone, or whether it travelled as part of a convoy.

If there were more than one truck, Jimmy had stated they would remain hidden. If it was alone, then the truck was fair game.

The noise grew louder, its engine now mingling with the hum of tyres on bitumen, and for a moment they saw a flicker of headlights through the forest. Jase clasped a clammy hand around the pistol grip of his Indonesian assault rifle. A minute later, the lone truck appeared around the distant bend, its headlights turning night into day.

"This is it!" hissed Jimmy. "Wait 'til they're outta the truck. Keep your head screwed on, brother, and shoot straight!"

Jase did not reply. He simply nodded, the mix of adrenalin and fear rendering him silent. A squeak of dusty brakes, down shift of gears and a loud hiss of air brakes saw the vehicle stationary in front of the log. Seconds went by and finally the doors opened. Two Indonesian men walked forward and stood in the headlights of the truck, looking down at the log, hands on hips.

Watching the Indonesian soldiers, Jase realised that Jimmy, in a half crouch had moved almost to the edge of the road. Kneeling, he aimed his rifle and fired four shots in quick succession. One of the soldiers went down clamping a hand to his leg and roaring in pain. Jase aimed at the second soldier and fired a short burst, his ears ringing with the sudden, sharp cracks. The soldier, unharmed, turned and ran back to the vehicle. Before he could reach the truck, Jimmy fired another few shots, one of which slammed into his chest, dropping him. He did not move.

The wounded soldier, however continued to shout and roll around in agony. Jimmy ran forward, and from the standing position silenced the enemy soldier with two loud shots.

"Get over here!" hissed Jimmy.

Jase sprinted to the Aboriginal soldier, slung his weapon and was about to stoop and help move the log off the road, when he felt Jimmy slap him on the back.

"No! We gotta clear the truck," he whispered into Jase's ear. "Dunno if there isn't more of 'em in the back. I'll go right you go left, eh?"

"Righto," replied Jase, his voice shaking with worry.

The men moved briskly down each side of the vehicle, Jimmy quietly pausing at the cabin to ensure there was not a third soldier hiding there. When he was satisfied, he continued to the rear, weapon pulled into his shoulder, finger on the trigger applying gentle pressure, ready to fire. Empty.

Jase relaxed and leaned forward, hands resting on knees as the adrenalin threatened to overwhelm him.

"No time mate! Let's go," said Jimmy running to the front of the truck. He and Jase began hauling the log out the way. Once done, they dragged the dead soldiers from the road and hid them from view behind some thick shrubs. Jase felt sick, making sure to look away from the dead man's face as he carried out the grisly task.

In less than a minute the men were underway, with Jimmy finding it hard to become accustomed to the vehicle's gearbox. The vehicle slowly accelerated south, gears crunching and clutch burning, until the engine faded into the distance, leaving the forest silent.

CHAPTER NINETEEN

"*Prime Minister Hughes confirms British forces have begun mobilising for Australia. Royal Marine Commandos expect to be in combat by week's end.*"
Birmingham Mail, Birmingham.

Ordinarily, a bright sunny morning like this would give way to kids laughing and shrieking as they splashed each other at the beach. However, for Jimmy and Jase, the bright hot sun and cloudless sky was their enemy. Any Indonesians they passed with half a brain could see the vehicle was driven by Australians. They pulled well off the road, hiding the truck in a thicker area of forest and attempted to sleep.

Sleep eventually did arrive, albeit reluctantly, and as the sun kissed the western horizon, they awoke bleary eyed, and feeling almost as tired as they had before they dropped off.

"Mornin'!" Jimmy grinned at Jase, starting the vehicle's engine.

Jase grunted a reply, wiping sleep from his eyes.

As darkness swept across the forest as slow and silent as an assassin, they pulled out onto the road and headed south. An enemy vehicle passing them would now only see the outline of an Indonesian military truck and a set of headlights driving towards them.

"We ain't gonna get far," muttered Jimmy two hours into the journey.

Jase looked at him quizzically.

Jimmy tapped the fuel gauge. "Runnin' low on juice."

"Murphy's law," Jase growled.

"If I ever meet that bloody Murphy," began Jimmy, "I'll knock 'is bloody block off!"

Following a brief rest stop, they discovered one twenty litre jerry can full of diesel, which they poured into the tank.

"Should keep us goin' for a bit," said Jimmy, "but we'll be back on foot tomorrow."

"I thought our luck had changed," said Jase. "Thought we'd finally made the big break."

"Now, 'ere, you listen to me brother," began Jimmy, slapping the fighter pilot on the shoulder. "We ain't doin' too bad. There's mobs of people in worse situations than we are. We ain't dead, we got ammo, and look at that," Jimmy gestured at the forest nearby. "Know what that is?"

Jase shook his head, still feeling depressed and worn out.

"That's one big bloody smorgasbord, that's what! We'll be right!"

They climbed aboard the truck and continued on their way, Jimmy once again crunching through the gears as they slowly accelerated. Jase scanned through the radio stations but was rewarded with static. Only one station worked, and then only very faintly, however, that was in Indonesian and he could not understand what they were saying. Propaganda probably.

Two long convoys of enemy vehicles roared past them at speed, heading north. Jase found himself sinking into his chair as the enemy vehicles swept past. By the time they had gone, he could only just see above the dashboard.

Jimmy looked across at him and burst out laughing. "What you doin' mate?"

Jase grinned and sat up, feeling sheepish.

"Look at this little one," chuckled Jimmy pointing at a vehicle travelling towards them. One headlight worked dimly, the other not at all. As the little vehicle flew past them, Jase was able to glimpse a vehicle that might have once been a Holden Commodore. In the truck's headlights it was possible to briefly see it had been shot to pieces, bullet holes dotting the windscreen and doors.

With midnight nearing, the engine came to a stuttering halt as the fuel tank offered its last drop to the engine. Cursing quietly, the pair climbed down from the cabin, stretching their legs, before rapidly making their way into the protection and concealment of the bush.

"What now?" whispered Jase.

"Noth'n to stop us takin' another truck."

"Suppose not," Jase replied. A flitting memory of having to drag dead bodies off the road assaulted his memory for a moment.

Jimmy slapped the pilot's arm. "Down!" he hissed.

Jase quickly lay down behind a tree as the noise of the approaching vehicle grew closer. The car stopped near the abandoned truck. Voices, Indonesian voices.

Jimmy quietly slid forward on his stomach, gently pushed aside a small shrub and watched. Five enemy soldiers. Too many. Far too many. Allowing the shrub to slowly rebound back to its original position, Jimmy withdrew.

Several car doors slammed, tyres squealed and moments later the enemy vehicle was departing as quickly as it had arrived. Jimmy moved into a crouch and crept forward. At the rear of the truck, near the passenger side tyre lay a large black object which had not been there before.

Jase looked across at the Aboriginal soldier quizzically, although in the light thrown by the quarter-moon, it was difficult to see his reaction. They moved forward cautiously, weapons held ready to fire, eyes and ears alert for the slightest hint of enemy presence.

That it was an ambush was the primary thought in Jimmy's mind. Stopping at the edge of the forest they lay prone for close to ten minutes, watching, listening and waiting. Nothing. Not one sound that should not have been there.

Edging over to Jase, Jimmy whispered into his ear, "You wait 'ere, I'm gunna check it out. You cover me, got it?"

Jase nodded, licked dry lips with an even drier tongue and gripped clammy hands around the weapon. Jimmy advanced carefully until he was kneeling beside the black object. For almost five minutes, Jase watched the dark form of Jimmy appear to rummage through the object at his feet.

"Oi, Jase! Get your arse over 'ere!" hissed Jimmy. "We've hit the bloody jackpot!"

"One of the dopey buggers must've accidentally kicked it out of the car when they climbed out," whispered Jimmy as Jase knelt beside him.

"What is it?" he asked.

"Ah shit!" said Jimmy, bringing out a hand and wiping it on his shirt. "Thought it was a bit o' grub, but it's just empty packets."

Jase saw it was a black plastic garbage bag.

"Fuck'n Murphy strikes again!" grumbled Jase.

"That bloody Murphy, was he Indonesian?" grinned Jimmy.

Neither of them heard the truck until it was too late. The enemy truck came careening around the corner at speed, high beams blinding the pair as they looked up in shock. Skidding tyres, a loud hiss of air brakes and the game was up.

"What was that?" whispered Katie.

"Hmm?" said Ben sleepily.

"I thought I heard something."

"Probably the wind," whispered Ben, rolling over.

A loud crackle of gunfire exploded, followed by shouting.

"Shit!" shrieked Katie, rolling from the bed, quickly dressing, tightening the gun belt around her waist and running towards her daughter's room. "Keep the bloody lights off!" she reminded Ben.

"Oi, Ben," said Craig quietly, appearing in the doorway a moment later. "It's on mate, let's go."

Kane's soldiers were fighting well, regrouping in extended line on the southern side of the house where the main brunt of enemy seemed to be pushing. However, Indonesian soldiers were also advancing from the north.

Matty, Craig, Mick and Ben, lying prone, were spread out along the north-facing veranda.

"Here," whispered Mick, handing Ben a two litre glass bottle half full of chlorine powder.

Ben took the bottle with shaking hands.

"Steady there lad," muttered Mick, noticing Ben's fear.

"I'm right," replied Ben.

Each man held a similar bottle. Once the enemy advanced within range, the bottles would be filled with brake fluid, re-capped and thrown. Shattering on the ground, the deadly concoction mixed, resulting in chlorine gas.

Lying still and silent, the four men watched the Indonesians approaching from the north, emerging from the forest like ghosts. They moved quickly, with a purpose, their weapons ready.

Allowing the enemy to approach within fifty metres, Craig gave the signal. Holding his breath and pouring a small plastic cup of brake fluid into the glass container of chlorine, he recapped the bottle and waited. When the enemy were within thirty metres, the men threw the rudimentary weapons in slightly different directions, ensuring the gas would be distributed in a wide arc. Within twenty seconds of the glass shattering, Indonesian soldiers were halted, bent over double, coughing. One soldier dropped his weapon and fell to his knees in a fit of coughs.

The sound of Craig's weapon initiated the ambush and within seconds all four rifles were barking. Ben fired four shots before the enemy at whom he aimed, crumpled to the ground. The dark, dirty mound continued to move and writhe, so Ben fired another few shots until the movement stopped. Finding another target, his first round found its mark, dropping the Indonesian like a piece of rubbish. When no more enemies were spotted, the firing ceased.

Craig and Matty, however, were astute enough to know that more enemy were hidden within the forest, trying to work out what had happened to their comrades. A thick, white, ghostly cloud of chlorine gas drifted silently into the dark sky in the near distance. Apart from the crackle and pop of fighting on the southern side of the house, the north remained silent and still. Matty slid across to the far side of the veranda and clamped his hand down on the Claymore's initiating device. Seven hundred grams of explosive embedded behind seven hundred steel ball bearings made the Claymore a basic, yet effective anti-personnel mine. The Claymore had been placed as a decoy for an enemy approaching the homestead. It was intended to give the approaching enemy pause, and the inhabitants enough time to withdraw, or effect a counter-offensive.

A second after Matty initiated the device, the Claymore detonated with a loud crump, fifty metres to the east. Immediately following the explosion, Ben heard shouting from the forest in front of him. Until now he had no idea what the Indonesian language sounded like. Brushing a clammy finger against the trigger, Ben jumped as a hand slapped him on the shoulder.

"I want you to go and initiate the drums mate," Craig whispered into Ben's ear. "Go, quiet as you can."

Ben nodded, shuffling backwards on his stomach until he was inside the blacked out house. With the roar of a firefight to the south and the shouting of an unseen enemy to the north, he could not help but feel entrapped, surrounded. Hearing Jade's quiet pleading cries from a nearby room and Katie's equally terrified soft voice trying to comfort her, Ben wanted to go to them. However, he knew he had to complete the task before him.

Cursing silently, he ran to the kitchen, hand sliding along the wall. At the second doorway, he turned left and entered the dark room. Slamming a knee into an open drawer, and stifling a roar of fury and pain, he continued on, kneeling on the floor near the window. He had practised doing this in the dark numerous times before and was confident in what was required.

Dragging the ride-on-mower battery closer to him, he picked up the first two wires and placed them against the battery's terminals. There was a small spark, but no explosion.

"You fuck'n piece of shit," snarled Ben quietly. "Come on!"

He placed the wires against the terminals once more, another spark. Nothing. As he was about to throw the wires aside in anger, there was a thunderous explosion to the west. The drum of fertiliser, mixed with diesel and detonated by a marine safety flare, distributed its rusty shrapnel fifty metres in the air. The detonation hurt no one, but it served to give opposing forces attacking from the north and south the idea that more Australian freedom fighters were in the forest amongst them. Psychological warfare as Mick called it.

Waiting until he heard Craig fire an illumination flare out over the forest, he initiated the second drum. This time the explosion came from the east. Within seconds of the flare popping and throwing illumination down upon the enemy crouching within the forest, Matty, Craig and Mick opened fire.

Ben ran from the room, smashing his leg on the open drawer again.

"Bastard!" he yelled, kicking the drawer.

Moving towards the sound of Jade's whimpering, he found them in the bathroom.

"Come on," he said, picking Jade up in his arms. "It's time to go." Slinging his weapon and holding Katie's hand, he pulled her to her feet and led her out towards the front of the house and the waiting truck. She held the .357 revolver in one hand. Ben wanted to tell them it would be okay, that they would survive to see another day, but he was not certain they would.

Kane's platoon, vastly outnumbered, eventually saw the enemy off. With the loss of two soldiers, his men made their way quickly and quietly to the waiting truck. Matty had already started the engine, waiting, whilst Craig was rounding everyone up. The two dead diggers were loaded first, before everyone else clambered aboard.

"I ain't buryin' 'em here," said Kane harshly as the truck rocked and swayed down the driveway, away from Mick's home.

"What's wrong with here?" asked Mick defensively.

"An unmarked grave? In the middle of nowhere? They're too bloody good for that, mate!"

Mick bit off an angry retort, but could not help admiring the officer's respect for his men.

Although it was pitch black in the rear of the vehicle, Katie cupped Jade's face away from where she knew the dead bodies lay. No child should have to witness the deceased. Swallowing hard, she clasped Ben's hand tightly. When will this end?

Twenty minutes later, the vehicle exited Mick's rough driveway and turned south onto the highway, accelerating towards Brisbane. Matty, driving just above the speed limit, had been selected as driver, because of his fluency with the Indonesian language and as a result of his Indonesian complexion. If they were stopped at any vehicle check points, he should be able to talk them through safely. However, no one bargained on the enemy they encountered at Mick's home giving chase.

Only Kane, sitting at the rear, noticed the headlights in the distance. Within minutes they were closing fast, two vehicles if he was not mistaken.

"Tell him to put his bloody foot down," yelled Kane over the noise of the engine mixed with the heavy tyres rumbling along the road.

"Oi, driving miss daisy! Get on with it!" yelled Spud, seated at the front of the truck. He started slamming his fist against the glass plate, behind which sat Matty, astutely driving.

In the cabin, alerted to the noise, Craig leaned forward and glanced in the side mirror. "Shit mate, we got a follow up."

"Righto," muttered Matty, accelerating. As the headlights in his side mirrors continued to close, he pushed the accelerator down as far as it could go.

The Indonesian vehicles continued to doggedly close the gap until they were within one hundred metres.

"Is it Sunday?" asked Spud loudly.

Somebody nearby shook their head, confused.

"Coz he's driving like it's frigg'n Sunday!" he shouted, thumping his fist against the window again. "Can't this sardine can go any faster?"

Pushing one hundred and fifty kilometres per hour, the vehicle struggled to accelerate any faster, and lost speed dramatically once they drove up an incline. On one particular steep section of road, Matty was forced to change down gear trying to maintain speed. The smaller Indonesian four wheel drives, five of them in total, had no trouble keeping up and within minutes were only metres behind.

Mick dragged out a wooden box from underneath the wooden bench on which he sat. The box was filled with glass bottles gently clinking against one another as the vehicle buffeted along the road. Into the mouth of each bottle was pushed a rag. Inside the bottle was lux flakes mixed with petrol. Once ignited the jelly substance burned much like napalm. Handing them to each soldier, they passed them one to the other until the pair of men sitting at the very rear of the vehicle each held a bottle. Taking out a lighter, they ignited the diesel soaked rag and threw the rudimentary weapons at the trailing enemy vehicles. One of them shattered to the left, failing to ignite. The second smashed directly in front of the first four wheel drive, exploding in a bright ball of orange fire. The enemy vehicles simply drove over it.

More bottles were thrown without success. A dark object appeared at the passenger side of the closest enemy vehicle and Mick knew instinctively that a soldier was leaning out to take a shot.

"Get your head down love!" Mick shouted, pushing Katie forward. Shielding Jade, she curled down as far as possible, her sobbing unheard over the roar of engine and road.

Bright muzzle flashes from the enemy vehicle sent bullets cracking, zipping and buzzing close to the truck, some of them passing through the canvas sides, others speeding off into the forest harmlessly. Another set of bottles were thrown, the first landing on the road uselessly. The second, however, slammed onto the windscreen of the first vehicle igniting in a rage of orange colour. The burning jelly substance distributed messily across the windscreen, preventing the driver seeing where he was travelling. Veering off course, the four wheel drive left the road, ran over two cats eyes and slammed into a tree with a sickening crunch that turned the military four wheel drive into an ugly sports car.

Kane scuttled down the middle of the truck, losing his balance every so often and righting himself against someone's leg or chest. However, after a particularly large pothole in the road, Kane lost his balance, finding half the fingers of his right hand in someone's mouth.

"Sorry mate," shouted Kane, wiping wet hand on his trousers. "Won't happen again," he grinned.

"Could've bought me a fuck'n drink first!" shouted the reply.

Kneeling at the rear, Kane steadied himself against the tailgate, watching another pair of bottles being lit and tossed towards the chasing enemy vehicles. One shattered on the bonnet, the second slamming onto the road, the front tyre driving over it without damage. Kane brought his weapon to bear, pulled it tightly into his shoulder and fired at where he thought one of the front tyres should be. As the rifle bucked into his shoulder for the third time, a loud crump was heard and the next vehicle in line veered sharply to the left, lost control as the rear end slid around, and began to roll. At one hundred and fifty kilometres per hour, a vehicle rolling held not a single guarantee to the lives of the occupants.

Kane immediately started on the next vehicle, a long burst of sporadic, panic stricken return fire erupted from within the Indonesian four wheel drive, shattering the windscreen. The bullets whistled well clear of their target, ricocheting off the road in loud whines. Kane ignored the gunfire and calmly picked his target, rendering another pursuing vehicle useless.

The remaining two Indonesian vehicles slowed down, gradually distancing themselves and eventually disappearing from sight.

"They're gone, mate," said Craig, watching the side mirror. "Keep up the speed, though."

"We've used half a tank of fuel."

"Don't worry about it," Craig replied. "We're probably safer out there in the forest anyway."

Maintaining speed, Matty brought the truck around in a hard right bend, tyres screeching as they began to lose grip on the road. Backing off on the accelerator, the truck, almost at the point of tipping, righted itself, coming around the bend at one hundred and forty kilometres per hour.

"Shit!" shouted Matty, planting his foot on the brake.

THE RECKONING

Skidding to a halt followed by a deafening hiss of airbrakes, Craig and Matty stared at another Indonesian truck parked in the middle of the road. Behind the truck, like a deer caught in headlights stood an Aboriginal soldier and some joker in a flight suit.

"**U**nited States Navy disembarks for Australia. It is believed at least one carrier battle group has so far deployed." (Translation by Jiang Shinan) China Daily, Beijing.

"Mount up!" shouted Craig out the window.

The Aboriginal soldier ran towards the vehicle, disappearing round the back, closely followed by the second man. A loud rap on the glass panel behind Matty's head indicated the pair was aboard.

Slamming the truck into first gear, Matty accelerated aggressively, quickly changing up the gears, the vehicle quickly surpassing the speed limit. Less than ten minutes after they were underway, headlights appeared in Craig's side mirror. Two vehicles, driving side by side.

He leaned back, scratched his beard and swore softly. "They're back," he said.

"Thought they would be," replied Matty, glancing at the rapidly closing enemy vehicles in the mirror. They were smaller, more agile and faster than the large lumbering truck. The Australians had hoped that their enemy might have given up on the chase. However, as the Indonesians closed the distance, it became obvious that they had pulled back and stopped in order to re-configure their vehicles, which now boasted a heavy machinegun mounted above the passenger side.

"Forget that!" shouted Kane to the two soldiers beginning to prepare the home made napalm. "Didn't do much last time, won't do shit now! Start shoot'n!"

The diggers shouldered their weapons and began firing single shots at the enemy vehicles, growing larger by the minute. One swerved slightly, but quickly regained control, continuing to chase the Australians. When the Indonesians were one hundred metres away, the heavy machineguns opened fire, bright orange tracer zipping over and around the truck. Desperately returning fire, Kane watched one headlight shatter. Using the remaining headlight as a gauge, he fired beneath it, hoping the tyre was somewhere there.

Again, tracer snapped and hissed closer to the truck, peppering holes in the canopy. One man screamed in agony, a bullet having passed through his right leg and embedding itself in his left calf. The men either side of him treated the wound as best they could, but given the lack of light, the speed at which they travelled, and the basic first aid supplies they carried, the treatment, whilst stemming most of the bleeding, was insufficient.

Kane fired another few rounds, this time aiming above the headlight at where he thought the driver might be seated. Losing his balance and slamming into the soldier on his right, Kane grabbed hold of the tailgate and used all his strength to keep himself from being ejected from the vehicle. With a loud skid of tyres, the truck narrowly missed a large tree trunk fallen across the road. Matty righted the truck, shouted an apology that no one in the back could hear, and continued driving as fast as the vehicle was capable. Only one of the chasing vehicles safely negotiated the obstacle. The second barely moved the large tree trunk as it impacted at high speed. The Indonesian standing behind the mounted machinegun, however, was sent somersaulting through the air like a rag doll, before hammering onto the bitumen once, twice, three times. Grinding to a halt, he lay bleeding and motionless.

Tracer shrieked past the truck and ricocheted off the road. Several bullets hammered into the rear wheel, which exploded in a deafening cacophony and stench of burned rubber. Matty immediately felt the damage, struggling against the truck as it began wandering towards the side of the road and the deep ditch that threatened to kill them all.

Taking his foot off the accelerator, he steered away from the edge of the road. Heavy braking would ensure he either lost complete control or caused the rear end to slide around making the vehicle roll.

Sensing what had happened, Kane intensified his rate of fire, each muzzle flash illuminating his snarling face a dull orange. One soldier lobbed a grenade, which exploded long after the Indonesian vehicle passed it. Another digger cooked off a grenade, meaning he pulled the pin, allowed the handle to disengage and held the explosive for several seconds before throwing it. The grenade exploded directly in front of the vehicle, causing it to swerve. The shrapnel, however, had seriously wounded the exposed gunner, who was lying face down upon the gun.

Rolling to a stop, Matty and Craig dismounted the vehicle with lightning speed, firing several short bursts before disappearing into the scrub.

Maintaining cover fire, the SASR soldiers ensured a relatively safe exit for those in the rear of the truck. Now with a dead or dying gunner, and beginning to take increasing return fire, some of which hammered home, the enemy vehicle screeched to a stop, before engaging reverse, gear box screaming as the headlights receded into the distance.

Quietly regrouping, they redistributed ammunition and properly dressed the wounded man's leg. Cutting a section of canvas from the rear canopy of the truck, they were able to create a makeshift stretcher onto which they placed the wounded soldier. Bungers, as he was known, was paler than normal, weak and confused. The outcome was not good, knew Kane, although he was the first to help carry the stretcher.

"You'll be right, mate," he said to the softly moaning soldier.

The going was slow and difficult, especially carrying a stretcher across undulating ground that could change from soft soil to ankle snapping, rock hard compact ground within minutes.

"Leave me," spoke the voice. It took moments for the stretcher bearers to realise Bungers had spoken.

"Leave me," he repeated. "Drop me here, you blokes keep goin'."

"Like bloody hell we will!" retorted Spud. "You lie there and shut up!"

Changing out every hundred metres, even Mick pushed his way in to take a turn helping carry the stretcher. The older man was tough as an ox, carrying one corner of the stretcher for almost half a kilometre before being relieved.

When the distant shouting began, Bungers pleaded with them to leave him once more.

"The Indos have got reinforcements. They've found our trail," said Bungers. "You'll travel faster without me!"

Spud, red faced, sweat dripping from his face in rivulets swore harshly. "I thought I told ya to shut up!" he said.

However, it was the hill that made their decision for them. Without any way around, the only way to proceed was straight up the side of the monstrosity. Carrying a stretcher up was possible, but not with an enemy chasing and time against them.

Kane fell back. "Righto, you blokes put him down."

"We can't leave him here alone, mate!" said Spud, breathing heavily. Since the invasion, Kane was no longer referred to as sir, but called a conglomeration of names including mate, Kane, boss, oi, brains trust and now, with the addition of Jimmy to the group, brother.

"We ain't leaving him behind, I'm gonna stay with him!" replied Kane.

"For fuck sake, you can't do that! We'll keep carrying him!" Spud argued.

"Spud, we can't keep carrying him. The Indos will catch us. All of us!

Better to catch a couple than the whole bloody lot!"

Spud shook his head. "You got no intention of being caught," he said, reading Kane's eyes.

Kane nodded. "We'll fight together. We'll probably die together."

"Suits me," said Spud, kneeling behind a nearby tree.

"Fellas, just leave me," muttered Bungers, "I'll be right."

The remainder of Kane's platoon filed through, shaking Bungers' hand, slapping him on the shoulder and ruffling his hair. Saying goodbye to a brother, each in his own way.

"Get goin'," ordered Kane jerking a thumb at the departing group, staring at Spud and ignoring Bungers.

"I ain't leav'n my mate to the likes of those bastards!" Spud pointed at the Indonesian voices steadily growing louder. "I spent long enough as one o' their prisoners, I'm not gonna let Bungers go through the same ordeal."

Kane nodded. "Fair enough."

"Plus, I've got a bloody score to settle with those little bastards!"

Several low flying fighter aircraft screamed across the horizon in the distance. Kane frowned. It had been weeks since he had heard a fighter aircraft, but he thought it odd to hear several together at one time. The noise vanished within seconds.

Silence fell upon the trio. Moving Bunger's stretcher into a safer area behind a medium sized, lichen covered boulder bulging out of the leaf litter like a giant's fist, they helped the soldier move onto his stomach, where he was better able to open fire. Bungers clenched his teeth and remained silent, although agony racked his leg like a red-hot spike. His wound began oozing blood once more, soaking the bandages already in place.

"Take a deep breath, mate," warned Spud. "This ain't gonna tickle."

Spud lifted the injured man's leg, allowing Kane to firmly bandage another thick pad into place. Ideally, Bungers required stitches following a thorough wound scrub and sterilisation, perhaps even surgery, followed by intra venous antibiotics, depending on what damage had been done. However, both men knew that dressing and firm bandaging was the best treatment they could offer their comrade given the circumstances. Kane and Spud crawled into firing positions. Spud hidden within a thick shrub, Kane moving behind the trunk of a large Iron Bark.

The enemy's noise continued to increase, sending chills down Spud's spine. He had no idea what they were saying, but the language haunted him ever since his experience as a prisoner of war. He clenched his jaw, gently touched his index finger to the trigger of his weapon and watched the enemy soldiers walk into view.

Crunching across the forest floor, enemy soldiers walked slowly, confidently, weapons slung, held before them or resting on a shoulder. Some smoked, others chewed gum, but they all talked, laughed and mocked. They were enjoying their new country. It was so much larger than their homeland. A few of them wore unconventional uniforms consisting of a mix of bloodstained Australian Army camouflage and Indonesian jungle greens.

The Australian trio remained hidden, still and silent, hoping their enemy passed them by without notice. Luck, that elusive lady, stuck by them and the Indonesians passed by without incident. As Kane was considering ways in which to safely exfiltrate the area, he saw a second wave of Indonesians approaching from the same direction as the first. Whereas the first wave seemed to consist of soldiers who had probably been in country for months and veterans of many fights, the second wave, with clean, undamaged uniforms, moved with caution. Although they were raw, they did not hold the same blasé attitude as their earlier comrades and Kane knew detection was more likely.

Glancing across at Bungers, he noticed the soldier was paler and more lethargic than before. He swore softly. You're first, thought Kane coldly, staring down the weapon's scope at the tall Indonesian soldier closest to him, confidently picking his way through the forest. Raking his eyes along the extended line of the enemy, he could not see any signallers or obvious commanders who would normally attract the first bullet.

Lying still, silent and calm, all care having departed, Kane was surprised as the second enemy line moved past them, ignorant of their presence. Spud had slowly turned to watch the departing backs of the enemy, ready to open fire at any who happened to turn and spot them. Kane continued facing forward, expecting a third Indonesian line, but none arrived.

Gaining Spud's attention, Kane signalled him to move in.

"We need to get another vehicle. Bungers looks shit house, and getting worse by the hour, we need to get him south and fast."

"What good's that gonna do?" asked Spud. "Brissy's full of enemy. You reckon they'll take a kind heart just coz one of our blokes is wounded? More than likely they'll give us all a third eye."

"There's only one way to find out. We can either stay here and Bungers dies, or we can try and get him help and we either succeed, or we all end up dead."

When Kane explained it as simply as that, Spud nodded. "Fair enough," he muttered.

Heading back towards the road, the going was slow. The pair had to lower the stretcher to the ground often to rest. With weapons slung and no forward, flank or rear protection, they were a soft target, or an easy ambush. Kane knew the risks and with one of his men dying, was willing to try. With more than half his patrol killed since the beginning of the invasion, he knew he had a slim chance to save one man's life. The risks were worth it. They pushed on through the forest, struggling across undulating ground, sliding down steep declines and cursing up hard inclines. Within thirty minutes, and with Bungers no longer responsive, they stumbled upon the road. Several low flying jet aircraft streaked across the sky, followed by the very distant heartbeat of a military helicopter, probably at tree top level, preparing to deploy or retrieve enemy troops from some obscure location.

Kneeling down beside the makeshift stretcher, Kane felt for a carotid pulse and found one, weak but regular. Bungers was bleeding out, no doubt about it, he needed urgent intervention.

"Vehicles inbound!" hissed Spud.

"Righto," Kane responded, running to the opposite side of the road and kneeling behind a tree. "Light the last one up!"

Spud gave a thumbs up to show he understood and pulled the weapon into his shoulder. Although the noise of the fighter jets had long vanished, the noise of the chopper continued to increase. Following several loud crumps and a few shorts bursts from what sounded like a twenty millimetre chain gun, the convoy did not arrive. One truck appeared in the distance, swerving violently, from one side of the road to the other, followed by what appeared to be a low flying United States Cobra attack helicopter.

Kane held his breath as the chopper opened fire, chain gun peppering the Indonesian truck, turning it into a flaming sardine can within seconds. Letting his weapon clatter to the ground, Kane sprinted out into the middle of the road, waving hands above his head. Screaming overhead, light brown fumes escaping the exhaust, blades slapping air, Kane watched one of the pilots look down, see him and acknowledge his presence with a half wave. Thirty seconds later, the Cobra made a second, much slower pass, Kane continuing to wave his arms and jump in the air. Then the chopper banked away from the area, accelerating aggressively.

"Marine Corps," said Spud, smiling. "There's a bloody US aircraft carrier out there somewhere!"

Kane nodded, feeling the elation, but not allowing it to show. "I hope they send support. Bungers ain't gonna last much longer."

The smile disappeared from Spud's face. "I know," he agreed.

Before Kane could speak, the distant crackle of gunfire echoing through the forest cut him off.

Holding Katie's hand tightly and hugging Jade to him, Ben followed Craig and Matty at a fast pace, the group following along in a rough extended line. Trying to control his breathing, legs still burning after negotiating the last hill, Ben jumped at the sudden noise of nearby gunfire. Looking up, he noticed Craig and Matty were lying prone behind trees firing upon an advancing enemy party. Half their number was dead or dying, whilst the second half scattered for cover. Craig shot three in quick succession, Matty dropped another two, and the remaining five disappeared behind long grass where they commenced a volley of return fire.

"Get up 'ere brother!" shouted Jimmy, crawling forward behind the cover of a small boulder.

Jase ran forward from his exposed position and crashed to the ground beside the Aboriginal soldier.

Ben dropped to the ground, being careful to roll on his side so as not to crush Jade. Katie crawled up alongside him, eyes wide with fear. Passing Jade to her, he mouthed, "stay here!"

Crawling forward, Mick not far behind, he took up a firing position twenty metres to Craig's right. Glancing across at Ben, Craig skittered across to him.

"We need to flank 'em. If we get bogged down here, we'll have that Indonesian follow up firing at us from behind as well! Let's go!"

Before Ben could ask a question, Craig was up and sprinting. Pushing himself to his feet with a soft curse, Ben followed, leaves and thin branches whipping his arms and face as he leapt over rotten logs, dodged small boulders and slapped spider's web out of his eyes.

Changing direction, Craig vaulted over a huge fallen tree, landing lightly, whilst Ben tried to jump it, tripped and landed with a loud thump and groan.

"Up, let's go!" hissed Craig. There was no time for sympathy.

Ben pushed himself to his feet and ran on, trying to keep up with the Special Forces soldier darting between trees ahead of him. Careening around what looked almost like a cairn of rocks, Craig brought his weapon up and jogged forward. Knowing they must be close to the enemy's flank, gunshots growing louder again, Ben did the same. Bursting through a thick grevillea shrub, both Craig and Ben opened fire together, killing three unsuspecting Indonesian soldiers in quick succession. Another two knelt up to see from where the new gunfire was coming and died almost as quickly. The first as a result of a well-aimed bullet from Mick's trusty bolt action .303, and the second from a group of bullets, which shattered the rib cage, penetrating lungs and heart.

"Move up!" shouted Craig when he was sure all enemy were dead.

Mick, Katie, Jade, the pilot and Aboriginal soldier, Craig could not remember their names, and the remainder of Kane's platoon moved forward quickly. The group moved on again at a slightly faster pace than before, keen to place as much distance between themselves and the chasing Indonesian group as possible.

Grant, having put weight back on again, was feeling top of the world as he rested under the shade of a tree in the middle of the encampment in the forest on the outskirts of Sydney. Today was unusual as the dull sound of explosive crumps emanating from the city and strangely, from out to sea, seemed more numerous than usual. Sydney always crackled with gunfire most days and nights, but today seemed somehow worse, as if the Indonesians were finally deciding to make an organised push to stamp out Australian resistance once and for all.

It was the fishing group who ignited the spark of excitement in the camp, sprinting waving their arms and shouting, excitement and relief on their faces. They explained what they had seen happening.

"The Indo Navy's being destroyed out there!" they shouted, each talking loudly over the top of each other and gesticulating wildly towards the seaboard hidden behind the forest a kilometre away.

"What?" Grant took a step forward. "By who?"

"Dunno! But they're getting their arses kicked."

Grant and Wayne looked at each other. Hope, something that had been missing from their lives now for months, glimmered, just for a second, in Wayne's eyes.

Moving as one, the entire encampment walked, ran, trotted, limped or were carried to the beach. On that bright, beautiful afternoon, with not a cloud in the sky, they sat on the warm sand and watched in the far distance as plumes of black smoke rose majestically into the sky. Swarms of jet aircraft screamed at sea level flying backwards and forwards all day, although none passed close enough for Grant to identify their country of origin. The group of Australian freedom fighters sat on the beach singing and cheering as the Indonesian Navy was systematically destroyed before their eyes.

"*We condemn the invasion of Australia. All other methods have failed. If peace cannot be kept, it will be made.*" Philippe Perier, President of France. Comments made to media following the departure of aircraft carrier Charles de Gaulle.

USS Ronald Reagan – Nimitz class Supercarrier

Somewhere in the Coral Sea

Captain Jessica Dermont, a young, bright eyed, orange haired Naval pilot, strode along the cramped gangway of the second deck, feeling the gentle pitch and roll of the aircraft carrier beneath her as it ploughed through the ocean at almost sixty kilometres per hour. Her flight suit fit snug, life jacket clasped tight about her chest, helmet clamped under her right arm, excitement and adrenalin thumping around her body. She had been at school when the Second Gulf War erupted, and was still undertaking Navy flight school during the closing years of the Afghanistan war. Today, she realised that this was where the rubber met the road. With hundreds of training hours under her belt, she was about to embark on her first real combat mission over the devastated coast of the Australian Eastern seaboard.

"You alright?" called Cutter over his shoulder.

Cutter, the aircraft captain, would be flying the aircraft, while her responsibility lay with navigation and ground strike capability.

"Sure," she replied, stepping through a doorway and snapping off a crisp salute to a couple of junior sailors who stood to attention, making way for them to pass.

"You seem quiet, is all."

"For once in my life hey?" she grinned nervously.

Cutter chuckled, "Yeah." He turned to look at her, "Stay sharp. You've trained for this. We'll be ok."

She smiled, realising Cutter mistook her silence for fear. No one could blame him for thinking that, especially when he had been knocking enemy aircraft out of the sky since before she started junior high. This was just another walk in the park for Cutter.

Stepping through another doorway, she ascended a long set of narrow steps, becoming aware of the quiet growl of the carrier, as it hammered through the ocean at battle speed. Even with fifteen foot swells, the aircraft carrier rolled softly.

Stopping at a closed door, Cutter turned to her, pulled the flight helmet down onto his head, winked and opened the door, a wall of sound assaulting them both. She stepped through behind him, smelling salt water mixed with aviation gas. She squinted against bright daylight, and revelled in the roar of jet engines above her. Trotting up a long set of metal steps dripping with ocean water, she pulled the helmet down over her head, the roar of aircraft suddenly muffled by the snuggly fitting ear cups.

Then she was home, walking out onto her very own playground. She raked her eyes across the flight deck as an F-18 fighter swept forward under catapult, streaking off the end of the ship and into the sky with a shriek of power. Ground crew had already prepped her aircraft. She and Cutter conducted a rapid before flight inspection, ensuring the jet was serviceable and all ordnance had been attached correctly. Once done, she took the stepladder two steps at a time and lowered herself into the seat, strapping herself in and plugging her helmet communications lead into the aircraft.

"Radio check," spoke Cutter, who was seated in front of her.

"Loud and clear," she replied, firing up her navigation computer, and letting it conduct a self-check.

"Loud and clear," he confirmed. "Canopy closing."

"Neptune two eight, you're third in line," crackled a voice into Jessica's earpiece.

"Neptune two eight, roger that," replied Cutter.

Jessica let the weapon systems spin up and began working through her checklist, oblivious to the deep, reverberating thump that shook the cockpit as another F-18 nearby was catapulted off the deck. She felt more at home as the engines of her aircraft whined into life behind her. As a second F-18 was sent streaking towards the end of the aircraft carrier and sky-borne, Neptune two eight taxied out onto the flight deck, Cutter watching the marshaller carefully, bringing the fighter to a gentle stop and engaging wheel brakes.

There was a blur of activity around the aircraft as ground crew directed and connected catapult to nose wheel. Like a well-oiled machine, they were done within thirty seconds.

"Here we go," Cutter's voice crackled.

Jessica clamped a grip on a small handrail attached to the back of Cutter's ejection seat, rested her head back, and gave the thumbs up. She snapped a salute off at the American flag flying majestically from the bridge.

She enjoyed the sudden, violent acceleration and within three hundred metres Neptune two eight was travelling at just over three hundred kilometres per hour and ascending hard away from USS Ronald Reagan.

"Gear com'n up," spoke Cutter calmly. "Good shot, engines normal, systems good."

Jessica glanced across the port side wing at the carrier battle group below, steaming across the Coral Sea towards Australia, leaving trails of white wash behind them. At the front of the group was HMAS Newcastle, the only Australian Naval vessel to survive the invasion. She had fought long and hard, punching far in excess of Her weight.

Several minutes later they turned lazily back towards the battle group as more aircraft were catapulted airborne. Within fifteen minutes, and all aircraft in their sortie now airborne, Neptune two eight formed the spearhead of nine F-18 fighter/bombers heading for the Australian eastern seaboard.

Ascending to forty thousand feet, the group headed towards the mass of Indonesian Navy anchored off Sydney harbour. USS Ronald Reagan would now be in recovery, meaning the first sortie of aircraft that had departed thirty minutes ago, having completed their strike missions over Sydney, were returning at sea level, and preparing to land, refuel and re-arm. Then they would be airborne again, for another strike. It was this smooth, relentless capability that destroyed the Iraqi Air Force within twenty-four hours.

"Seven aircraft approaching from the North, five miles," said the voice in Jessica's earpiece. "No IFF response. Assume bogies, I say again, assume bogies. Engaging."

She watched five F-18s peel away from the formation. These were the fighter escort, tasked with protecting the remaining four F-18s carrying bombs and air-to-surface missiles. Jessica took a deep breath, heart beating a rapid staccato in her chest.

"Yup, it just got real," said Cutter, as if reading her mind. "Got smoke to the West."

Snapping her head round, she saw the black towers of smoke littering the distant horizon far below, probably the work of the first strike mission.

"Roger that," said Jessica, her voice sounding calmer than she felt.

"Neptune two eight, this is Neptune one three. Enemy shipping lines at two-seven-zero. Hit the carriers and supply ships first, how copy?"

"Good copy, one three," responded Cutter, "roger that."

Neptune one three tasked the remaining aircraft. Jessica blotted his voice out, concentrating on the fast approaching enemy vessels.

"Neptune two eight, two carriers and one fleet replenishment vessel veering to the north at full power. Take 'em out."

"That's a roger," replied Cutter. "You on that Jess?" he asked in the same voice he might ask if offering a cup of coffee.

"Got it," she said, sliding the helmet- mounted sight down over her eyes.

Zooming in, the first Indonesian aircraft carrier took up her entire field of vision. The ship was travelling fast, in an attempt to escape the next strike mission they knew would be inbound. Unbeknown to the Indonesians, the second strike mission had already arrived. She watched an enemy aircraft streak across the carrier deck under catapult. A second enemy aircraft was taxiing out ready for take-off as Jessica launched the AGM-84 Harpoon missile. The warhead took less than one minute to travel twelve kilometres. Slamming mid-ships, the explosion hid the aircraft carrier behind a sudden, bright fireball. In a perfect circle around what had once been an Indonesian ship, the shock wave was visible on the surface of the ocean.

"Good kill," said Cutter clinically.

Jessica focused on the second aircraft carrier, a deep, loud thump shaking the aircraft as the second Harpoon missile streaked away, on target. As she was about to engage the third vessel, a large, ugly supply ship, she became aware of a warning tone.

"Breaking, missile com'n up!" growled Cutter, leaving a string of flares behind, the wing tips streaming vapour as they turned violently away from an anti-aircraft missile twisting and turning as it ascended towards them, launched from an Indonesian destroyer.

Jessica conducted anti-G as Cutter rolled inverted and dived towards the ocean, rapid thudding indicating flares were deploying behind them. Neither of them spoke, each knew what was expected, what was required. This was what she had trained for, even what she hoped for. This mission would make or break her.

Breaking left violently and ascending hard, another string of flares defeated the missile. Jessica concentrated immediately on the third ship, ignoring the concoction of adrenaline, excitement and fear sweeping her system.

"Take him out," Cutter said, that calm voice again, as if he was unaware they had almost been blown out of the sky.

"Roger," breathed Jessica, launching the third Harpoon and watching it explode seconds later against the port side of the supply ship. Less than forty seconds passed before the fleet replenishment vessel disappeared below the surface of the ocean. She counted one small life raft. One.

As for the aircraft carriers, they were listing heavily and spewing thick black smoke. Their time was at an end, and already life rafts were scattered on the ocean around them as the surviving crew abandoned ship.

"Missiles complete," reported Jess.

Within minutes, all four F-18s delivered their deadly payload. Turning away from the sheer hell through which the Indonesian Navy were currently living, they accelerated back towards the USS Ronald Reagan. With the loss of only one aircraft, the fighter escort defeated all seven enemy aircraft.

Jessica felt tired as the adrenaline wore off. She ran through system checks to keep her mind alert. They were flying low, close to the ocean. The third strike mission was somewhere high above them flying back into the fray, having re-fuelled and re-armed. Now, the USS Ronald Reagan was preparing to recover their aircraft, and so on it would go, hour upon hour. The Indonesian Navy would experience an incessant barrage of attack.

She noticed a Seahawk helicopter below them flying full speed, towards the Australian mainland. The chopper must have been almost touching the waves. More than likely, the chopper carried a SEAL Team, who would be tasked with recovering the downed pilots. She silently wished them well, watching as USS Ronald Reagan came into view on the Eastern horizon.

Cutter made two passes, allowing the rest of the strike wing to land. When they had done so, it was their turn to land. Turning hard and descending, Cutter deployed landing gear, reduced speed, extended flaps, and brought the fighter on a bearing aimed directly at the middle of the deck. Jessica had landed aircraft on carriers thousands of times with the simulator, and hundreds of times in real life, however, she still could not carry it out with the confident precision of Cutter. More practise required, she told herself cynically.

"Good bearing, good speed. Neptune has the ball," spoke the marshaller.

Cutter engaged the arrestor hook, which descended down at a forty-five degree angle at the rear of the aircraft. It was this hook that would catch hold of thick, high tensile, steel wires on the deck of USS Ronald Reagan, bringing them to a halt.

Throttling back, they landed with a heavy thud, Jessica bracing herself as they decelerated violently. Disengaging the arrestor hook, Cutter throttled forward, watching the marshaller, as he directed them towards a group of ground crew waiting to refuel and re-arm them. Time was of the essence as the strike mission currently airborne would soon be returning. The ground crew worked with fluid precision born of dogged experience in various oceans around the world.

Jessica was afforded enough time to visit the toilet and down a drink of water before the ground crew had finished. Then they were airborne again, ascending and accelerating away. The Indonesian fleet, once anchored several kilometres from Sydney's shore, was devastation. Jessica stared at the blazing, ruined hulks of destroyers, aircraft carriers, supply ships and oil stained areas of ocean where vessels had slipped beneath the waves, never to return. Life rafts, bodies and debris littered the surface.

"Sweet Mother of Christ," whispered Cutter, as they made a sweep over the eastern edge of Sydney.

Jessica was speechless. Sydney Harbour Bridge lay torn in half, its majesty now replaced by a twisted, steel behemoth. Smoke spewed into the sky from burning vehicles, houses, sky rises and piles of rubbish, one of which looked more like a small pyramid of bodies. It was difficult for Jessica to decipher from altitude.

Rubble, destroyed buildings, demolished homes, long burned out carcasses of vehicles and entire city blocks reduced to ruin, seemed to be everywhere Jessica looked. Sydney seemed to be a defeated city. However, one thing stood out. It was obvious the Australians had battled long and hard against the invaders. They had not gone down without a fight.

Tracer streaking past their port wing brought her mind screaming back to the present moment. Before she had time to react, Cutter was breaking right and deploying flares in case a missile had been fired.

"Come on Jess, you on it?" Cutter barked, as another thick volley of tracer flickered closer to them.

Slamming the helmet mounted sight down over her eyes, she scanned the city, focusing upon the roads and buildings, finding nothing. She cursed silently, allowed her eyes to move over the terrain, pausing and flicking back to an area, had she seen something? There! Muzzle flashes!

It was a Sergey, a Soviet era towed anti-aircraft gun. Old school, not very accurate, but she knew it would fuck their day up if the gunners got it right.

"Missile gone," she said a moment before the harpoon streaked away from the F-18.

"Good work," Cutter said, bringing them around and ascending.

The anti-aircraft gun disappeared behind a mighty explosion as the missile hit, a single, warped barrel somersaulting high into the air.

"Nice kill," said Cutter. That cold, clinical voice again.

With the threat of Indonesian fighter aircraft rendered non-existent, the US strike group split into twos and began hunting over separate areas of Sydney city.

Poorly aimed small arms fire streaked up at them from all quarters, but more often than not missed by up to a kilometre. To be truly accurate, a weapon had to be aimed at least fifteen or twenty aircraft lengths ahead. The small arms did not bother them. It was the anti-aircraft gunners, who were trained in leading aircraft that was of concern. Those foolish enough to fire upon them were targeted quickly and destroyed.

"Armoured convoy, ten o'clock low," reported Cutter, bringing the F-18 around and diving aggressively.

Jessica knew they wanted to definitively identify them as enemy before opening fire. The vehicles were travelling fast, dark fumes blasting from their exhaust pipes as the tanks and armoured personnel carriers rammed long abandoned cars out of their path. Turning the F-18 onto its side, both Jessica and Cutter looked down the right wing at the vehicles below. Then the convoy was gone, drifting into the distance behind them.

Accelerating hard, breaking left and ascending, they ignored the tracer flashes spitting towards them from the convoy.

"All units, Neptune two eight. Enemy convoy bearing two seven zero, tracking along main highway. Engage! Engage! How copy?" Cutter rattled the target indication out like a machine gun.

"Neptune one zero, solid copy. On our way."

"Neptune three six, that's a roj."

Conducting anti-G as Cutter brought the aircraft round, Jessica focused the sights on a main battle tank third from the front.

"Missile gone."

In a terrible, violent split second of disintegrating metal, orange flames and smoke black as sin, the main battle tank became a warped, ruined carcass. The armoured personnel carrier driving in front of the tank, skidded to a halt, one of its tracks destroyed by the nearby explosion. The crew attempted to turn and accelerate off the road, however, the vehicle was as stubborn as a mule and in panic, they began climbing down, one of them cradling his arm.

Coming in low and fast, the aircraft's twenty-millimetre gun thundered, raining death upon the convoy. The gun's song was one long, deep, bark, which sounded muffled from within the cockpit. Jessica knew the noise out on the ground would be heard reverberating from high rises, kilometres away. To those on the ground, trying to survive the main gun of a fighter aircraft was one of the most terrifying experiences on earth. At least that was the testimony of one SEAL whose team had infiltrated deep within Afghanistan and was mistaken for enemy troops by a passing Dutch fighter jet.

"Missiles complete," Jessica confirmed.

"Roger that," responded Cutter, engaging afterburner and ascending near vertical. A second F-18 swept in from the north, vapour trails streaking from wingtips, ready to commence their own gun run. In less than five minutes, the convoy had been destroyed, their speedy escape plan having failed dismally.

Landing to refuel and re-arm, they were airborne again quarter of an hour later, screaming towards Sydney city for another strike mission. Further north, off the coast of Brisbane, the USS George Washington had begun launching strike missions over the Australian city two hours prior to the Ronald Reagan.

Steaming across the Indian ocean, HMS Illustrious saw aircraft striking enemy targets in and around Darwin, whilst USS Abraham Lincoln began striking military targets across Indonesia. Anchored in the Tasman Sea, French aircraft carrier Charles de Gaulle began sending fighter-bombers against enemy locations in Adelaide and Melbourne.

There were, however, thousands of enemy bases scattered across regional Australia, tasked mainly with procuring food and other logistical concerns in support of the main invasion. For the time being, these could wait. Once the enemy had been routed from the cities on the coast, it would be time to strike the remaining Indonesian elements out of Australia.

USS Ronald Reagan continued its relentless strike capacity for forty-eight hours before Marines, SEAL teams and close air support elements made landfall, ready to begin mopping up, as they liked to call it.

Kane, Spud and the quickly deteriorating Bungers, remained hidden amongst the foliage next to the road. Kane knew the attack chopper had seen him and was hoping it was only a matter of time before they would be exfiltrated. Bungers needed urgent attention.

Blood had seeped through the second layer of bandaging, indicating the wound continued to bleed. Using their last bandage, they wound the material around the leg as tightly as possible. If they cut circulation off, so be it, better to lose a leg than a life. Bungers was almost grey in colour, Kane occasionally slapping the wounded man's face to keep him conscious. Each time Kane slapped him, Bunger's eyes fluttered open for a moment and he groaned softly.

Looking at his watch, Kane noticed almost half an hour passed since the attack chopper departed. Beginning to plan what their next course of action should be, he heard the deep heartbeat of a helicopter, growing closer. To a soldier with wounded men and hostile forces scattered throughout the area around him, the unmistakeable noise of a helicopter was a truly beautiful thing.

Kane gave his weapon to Spud and stepped forward onto the road. Disarming himself, he attempted to look less threatening. A blue-on-blue firefight was the last thing he wanted. The Sea Hawk, with two mini guns hanging out each side of the aircraft, suggested it would not be much of a firefight. Kane and his soldiers would be dead in seconds. One of the loadmasters saw Kane, passing the message on to the pilot. Within moments, the helicopter turned and descended, landing neatly in the centre of the highway, throwing leaves, twigs and dust swirling and somersaulting through the air.

The loadmaster held up two fingers and indicated Kane to 'hurry up'.

Looking beyond the loadmaster, he saw the chopper was already near capacity, full of bleary eyed, dirty, frightened Australians. Then he understood. They could take only two more passengers. Sprinting back to the side of the road, he grabbed one end of the stretcher. Without needing prompting, Spud slung both weapons, lifted the rear of the stretcher and they jogged out to the aircraft.

"Gunshot wound to the leg!" he yelled so the loadmaster could hear him. "Lost a lot of blood and needs urgent medical attention!"

Giving a thumbs up and nodding his head, the loadmaster indicated he understood, helping to drag the stretcher aboard.

"No time to argue, get the fuck on board now!" roared Kane over the scream of the helicopter, pushing Spud towards the loadmaster.

Sensing the hesitation, the loadmaster grabbed a hold of Spud's shirt and dragged him aboard. Unslinging both weapons, Spud, his face angry as other passengers held him back, threw them to Kane. The loadmaster gestured Kane to come closer.

Cupping his hands, he yelled into Kane's ear, his accent carrying a thick American drawl. "We saw a bunch of enemy troops moving in from the north. They're about two miles out!" Turning away, he unstrapped a machine gun from inside the chopper and passed it to Kane, followed by three magazines, each containing two hundred rounds. "Stay low, keep your head down, and we'll be back." He slapped Kane on the shoulder. "No matter what, we'll be back!" Then the chopper ascended and turned before accelerating away from the area. He could not hear the loadmaster's last words, but he saw the words formed by his lips. "Good luck!"

Craig led the group of Australians through the forest in a southerly direction, keeping his weapon ready and safety catch off. To their credit, none of the group complained. Some of them slipped and fell, rose again and continued on. Others ploughed through shrubs because it took less energy than deviating around. However, none of them, not one, ever complained.

"My mum's a cowgirl!" Jade told Ben proudly as they stopped to rest.

"I know!" smiled Ben.

Stopping to rest in low ground and using the remainder of Kane's platoon, Craig pushed the soldiers out into all round defence. Using hand signals, he indicated people should drink. No more enemy were heard or seen and those soldiers who had been chasing seemed to have given up. Matty whispered into Craig's ear, before standing and patrolling out of sight. The ever increasing sound of jet aircraft, helicopters and explosions, both near and distant, had raised his interest.

Almost ten minutes passed before Matty crept back into position. Moving to Craig, he quietly went to ground beside him.

"There's a shitload of activity going on out there!" Matty whispered. "The Yanks are here."

Craig glanced at his comrade, uncertainty in his eyes.

"No shit mate," Matty continued, "F-18s and Sea Hawks flying non-stop. There's Indo convoys heading south towards Brisbane, probably reinforcing the Indo Army there."

"Shit," muttered Craig, shaking his head. "Are you sure they're American?"

"We called in enough airstrikes in Afghanistan mate. I'd know a U.S. Marine fighter jet anywhere."

"Let's get the hell outta here!" whispered Craig, climbing to his feet and signalling the rest of the group it was time to move on.

Kane lay hidden amongst foliage, facing north. The M-60 heavy machine gun rested against his shoulder and he stared down the metal sight at an empty road. The smell of gun oil wafted from the metal of the weapon, oddly comforting him. He forced himself to breathe slowly, telling his tense body to relax, but it refused to obey. His thoughts returned to Bungers for the third time in as many minutes, hoping the injured soldier was now in the hands of medical professionals. It was the movement that tore his attention back to the present, and as adrenaline worked its magic around already tense muscles, he watched a large group of enemy walking towards him. Two files, one either side of the road, with one man, obviously the commander, strolling in the centre.

The index finger of his master hand felt cold metal as it touched the weapon's trigger. Taking a deep breath, Kane placed the weapon's sight over the chest of the lone enemy soldier in the middle of the road. He could lie still and hope that he remained unnoticed. However, common sense told him that with enemy filing down both sides of the road, that would be near impossible. Those on his side of the bitumen would be walking almost on top of him. He could either lie still, silent and partially hidden and be killed or captured for his effort, or use surprise to knock down as many enemy as possible. Placing a small amount of pressure on the trigger, Kane made his decision, waiting for the soldiers to move closer.

Checking his watch, he noticed fifteen minutes had passed since the Sea

Hawk flew away. Not too long to wait, surely? The helicopter must be on its way back to his location.

'Hang on, think realistically,' Kane told himself. 'There would be flight time to the US base, possible refuel, and then the flight time back. That's if it isn't shot down.' The realty was the chopper may never return.

"God help me," Kane muttered through clenched teeth, and opened fire.

Bullets slammed into the Indonesian commander, spinning him like a top, leaving him lying on the ground, blood oozing from his mouth and chest. The remaining soldiers reacted well, scattering and finding cover within seconds. Kane managed to drop three or four before return fire hissed and zipped around him.

Within two hours, Craig, Matty and the group they now considered comrades were aboard three Sea Hawk helicopters, flying south, Brisbane bound. Within half an hour, they had been dropped off at Redcliffe Show Grounds, where a small makeshift hospital had been set up. The residential blocks surrounding the grounds had been destroyed, with only blackened remnants of what were once the foundations of homes stood. This gave Craig a clear view out to Moreton Bay, where far to the south, in the very distance, he could see dark plumes of smoke. More than likely, it was what remained of the Indonesian Navy, burning.

Heavy clicking and popping were incessant from Brisbane City itself where large running gun battles were taking place between a combined force of U.S. Marines and Australian freedom fighters. The Indonesian Army was on the back foot, withdrawing from suburb to suburb with heavy losses.

Kane's platoon found Spud and Bungers in the hospital. Bungers was still unconscious, but had regained his normal colour. Two bags of intravenous fluid, one bag of blood and one bag of antibiotics slowly dripped into his veins. Spud explained that surgery had been conducted on his leg, and the doctor saw no reason why the soldier would not make a full recovery.

"Where's Kane?" asked one of the soldiers.

Spud shrugged his shoulders, a dark look descending on his face. "There was no room on the chopper."

Silence descended on the room as the group of soldiers stared at Spud, incredulous.

"We had to leave him behind," explained Spud.

"You had to," began one soldier staring out to sea, his words trailing away. "So where the fuck is he?"

Spud shrugged again, feeling helpless, angry, and responsible. "Out there somewhere. The chopper's going back for him."

Half way through the second magazine, pain racking his body, Kane continued to fire in long bursts. With barrel smoking, it was difficult to see the gun sight, however aiming in the direction of muzzle flashes tended to keep the enemy's head down. With a dull thud, the heavy machine gun fell silent, a testament to the empty magazine. Ripping it out and throwing it aside, he placed the final magazine onto the weapon, cocked the working parts and continued to fire.

Stabbing pain ran up both legs and he assumed he had been shot. A quick feel of the area suggested his legs were still present, which was enough for the Australian officer. An Indonesian soldier rose to his feet and ran forward, however, Kane swivelled the weapon on its bipod and fired two short bursts that tore the man from his feet, leaving him silent and still.

What felt like a red-hot hammer slammed into Kane's left shoulder and he screamed, agony wracking him. Losing the strength of his left hand, he let the arm lie uselessly on the ground, blood oozing out a large hole at the top of his bicep. Again, the M-60 fell silent, this time permanently. Kane pushed the weapon aside and took up his rifle, which was awkward with only one functioning arm. Continuing to fire, he killed another two soldiers and wounded a third before the weapon was empty. Throwing it aside, he reached for the last functioning weapon, Spud's assault rifle.

A dull thud and pain emanated from the centre of his chest, eventually reaching every area of his body. Unable to scream, he groaned as agony assaulted him, bright red bubbles dripping from his mouth. His vision blurry, pain throbbing through every fibre of his being, Kane continued to return fire, wounding at least one more enemy soldier.

Spud's weapon fell silent, its last bullet sent down range. Kane rested his cheek against the rifle, exhausted. Rounds continuing to ricochet, snap, whizz or crack near him. He did not hear the helicopter arrive, nor did he witness the sheer devastation of the mini gun as it tore apart the Indonesian platoon, leaving all enemy dead.

He groaned softly as rough hands grabbed his shoulders and feet, running for the helicopter. The aircrew lay Kane on the floor, quickly dressing his wounds as best they could, before take-off. Sitting him on a seat and strapping him in, they requested the pilot fly immediately to USS George Washington, anchored east of Brisbane city. Aboard the aircraft carrier was a complete hospital, trauma surgeons in attendance. The pilot did not hesitate, pushing the chopper to its limits, trees and roads zipping beneath them in a blur.

Kane's body continued to throb with agony, each breath a nightmare, each blood bubbling cough sheer hell itself. However, it was the vision of Brisbane that seemed to take the pain away. He saw the distant city burning, but more importantly, he saw the Indonesian Navy laid to waste. Flicking his concentration back to the city he knew that somewhere in there, amongst the rubble and ruin, were his men, his platoon, now safe, secure and ready to find their families.

"Come on, stay with me buddy!" yelled the loadmaster, slapping Kane's face.

Australia. His country. His people. Safe. Finally, they were safe again.

He smiled, and as the chopper slammed down onto the deck of the aircraft carrier, medics sprinting out to meet them, Kane died.

EPILOGUE

"'Ere, there's that fat joker again!" spoke Jimmy, prodding Jase in the ribs.

He pointed at Barry, the fat man standing at the far edge of Redcliffe Show Grounds being interviewed by an American journalist. The pair walked closer to listen, and sure enough, Barry was talking about how his group of freedom fighters, led by himself of course, had systematically destroyed one Indonesian platoon after another. Fat, useless, lazy, arrogant Barry had done nothing of the sort, and both Jimmy and Jase knew it. Unable to run more than twenty metres before being severely winded, there was no way Barry could take on an Indonesian child, let alone an entire platoon.

Jimmy chuckled, shook his head and walked away.

"What, you're just gonna let him get away with that?" asked Jase, angry. "We know bloody well he just lay low during the entire invasion!"

"Let 'im have his moment of fame, brother. It'll all come out in the wash. Besides, it's your word against 'is. What's important is we know what we done. We know we fought," Jimmy said, prodding his chest. "And that's all that counts. We know. It's enough."

Jase nodded. "Yeah, you're right," he replied.

Grant stood with the rest of his group on the eastern side of the Sydney show grounds, where thousands of people had been gathered. Some families had been reunited, while others were still looking. A few were utterly devastated, having received news from others that their families had been killed during the invasion. He could not believe the sheer destruction that swept Sydney. The harbour bridge lay in ruin, the Opera House no longer existed, and half the sky rises were either burned shells, or still burning. Hundreds of thousands had died in Sydney alone. It would take years to rebuild the city, let alone the country.

"Got me side arm, Granto?" asked a voice.

Grant turned to see the grinning face of Boomer.

"I owe you a bloody beer!" Grant said, shaking the Navy Diver's hand.

Jade lay in Katie's arms, fast asleep, exhaustion having claimed her hours before. Katie leaned against Ben, who wrapped his arms around her, hugging her to him. Mick, quietly dismantling his old .303 rifle, sat nearby.

"Where to from here?" asked Ben quietly, watching the sun descending into the west.

There was no reply, and he realised Katie, like her daughter, was asleep.

"Where to from 'ere?" asked Mick, glancing at the younger man. "Waddaya mean Ben? It's back to Bent Wood Cullen Bone and the farm. I tell you one thing," Mick pointed a cleaning cloth at Ben. "If those bastards have touched the frozen beef in my freezer, I'm gonna be bloody pissed off!"

Ben chuckled, deciding farm life would not be so bad after all.

"How you blokes getting on?" asked Craig quietly, squatting down between Ben and Mick.

"Bloody good now it's all over!"

Craig nodded. "That's good. Just letting you know, Kane didn't make it." The SASR soldier patted Ben on the shoulder, stood and moved away, leaving the pair silent. Mick cursed, Ben tightened his grip on Katie and pushed his face into her hair, closing his eyes.

As for Craig and Matty, they cleaned their weapons, enjoyed a quick meal and fresh water, before restocking their ammunition and deploying with the next SEAL Team into the centre of Brisbane.

The Australian Prime Minister John Casey and his cabinet had been killed during the first week of the invasion, following an airstrike on Parliament House. Although the ADF were defeated as a cohesive force, dotted around Australia were small groups of soldiers. They might have been cut off and isolated, but they managed to take the fight to Indonesian forces. Over the span of the invasion, almost 20,000 Indonesian soldiers were killed by the Australian guerrilla fighters.

Recruiting civilian members, the few remaining ADF members taught them skills needed to take the fight to the enemy. New Zealand's Special Air Service was on the ground the day the invasion took place. Alongside their Australian counterparts they dealt devastating damage to the Indonesian rank and file, killing almost 600 enemy for the loss of one of their own.

HMAS Newcastle, the only Royal Australian Navy vessel to survive the invasion, sank 7 Indonesian destroyers and badly damaged an Indonesian aircraft carrier. The carrier could not be repaired and was later scuttled in the ocean off the coast of Indonesia.

In fact, Robert O'Garretty, a young Irish history buff and later to become an academic on the conflict, wrote the following in his controversial book, entitled, "Australasia: The Beginning of the End"

"Had the allies not intervened, Australia and New Zealand would more than likely have defeated the Indonesians by themselves. It might have taken another 10 years, yet their sheer dogged determination will to succeed and resourceful nature would have won the day."

Within the week following Australia's liberation, an urgent government was formed until such time as a proper election could be held.

Compulsory national service was introduced causing a divide in public opinion. However, the majority of Australians were in favour of the move.

It took close to 7 years for Australia to be rebuilt, although Her people would never properly heal. A dark chapter in Her history had been written. Only future generations would be able to talk about the invasion without pausing as dark memories, or deep pain washed over them. Those generations did not yet exist.

Mick was relieved to see the graveyard lay untouched by the invasion. Walking through the neat rows, he spotted the familiar grave. It remained untouched by decades of time.

"Brother," he spoke quietly, kneeling before the headstone.

46310 CORPORAL

J. S. Hargraves

6th BATTALION ROYAL AUSTRALIAN REGIMENT

2nd FEBRUARY 1967 AGE 25

A SOLDIER'S SOLDIER DEARLY LOVED AND SADLY MISSED BY BETH

Passing a hand over the letters etched into the concrete, his mind returned to that fateful day. So much blood. They had tried their best. Closing his eyes,

Mick bowed his head, hand resting on the headstone. The bullet had done too much damage.

"I'll always miss ya mate," Mick spoke, patting the headstone, before standing. Walking away, he glanced back at the grave he knew so well.

Inside one month, outnumbered and outgunned, Indonesia agrees to a peace treaty and officially withdraws from Australian soil. But a group of stoic Indonesian soldiers refuse, believing it is possible to win and claim Australia and her precious resources. They continue to fight, even if their country has tucked tail and run. They own the forests and high ground of inland Australia and if intelligence reports are accurate, number more than 10,000 strong.

Turn the page to read the preview of book two in, The Unforeseen Series... **Aftermath.**

Mick and his family have returned home to the farm following Indonesia's withdrawal. But thousands of battle-hardened enemy soldiers remain hidden in the forests and hills, ready to strike when they are least expected. This fight will take Mick to the limit, and protecting his family will require all his strength and determination.

Jimmy and Spud lead a platoon through the Australian scrub on relentless guerrilla strikes. But when they find themselves outnumbered and outgunned, it might have all been for nothing.

A new Australia will rise again…or will it?

"**R**eports suggest 40 Commando supported by the Royal Navy have driven Indonesian invaders away from the coast in Queensland. The war in Australia is all but won." – *Yorkshire Post (UK)*

The half-rotten corpse that had once been an Indonesian soldier lay prone, riddled with maggots. SGT Craig Linacre knelt slowly beside the stinking mess, rifle cradled across his chest. The large exit wound at the back of its skull showed the fatal wound. Craig could see what was left of the decomposing brain beyond. But what interested him more was the soldier's webbing. The pouches appeared full and might hold valuable information. Wary of booby-traps, Craig tied a rope to its belt buckle and moved back, feeding the rope out as he went.

Taking cover behind a nearby boulder, the special-forces soldier looked across at Matty in the near distance and nodded. CPL Matty Nasution gave thumbs up, before returning his attention down the barrel of his weapon, giving cover. Taking a breath, Craig pulled hard on the rope. He felt the weight at the other end shift and knew the corpse had rolled over. Good, no booby-traps so far. Bringing the rifle into his shoulder, Craig was stepping out from behind the boulder when the corpse exploded. He was thrown to the ground, winded. In a few seconds he climbed back to his feet, dazed, yet instinctively scuttling behind the boulder. The charge had obviously been rigged with some kind of delayed detonator.

Shaking the fogginess from his brain, Craig peered around the boulder and saw a pair of half rotten legs – from the knees down – lying beside a crater. Nothing else remained of the corpse. Gaining Matty's attention, he signalled they were moving out. The explosion would have been heard from kilometres around, and if there were any Indonesian soldiers still in the area, they would be moving towards the explosion.

As the pair of SAS soldiers slowly made their way through the brown, dry, waist-high grass, several dull thumps could be heard in the distance. The men paused, taking a knee to listen.

Silence.

Soft wind teased the surface of the grass for acres in every direction.

210

Then a high-pitched shriek, growing in volume, shattered the peaceful deathly quiet.

"Cover!" roared Craig, diving to the ground as artillery rounds exploded nearby.

An Indonesian artillery battery had zeroed its guns in on the corpse, waiting for the booby trap to be triggered. If they fired fast enough, they'd be able to take out an entire platoon. Maybe more.

Pushing himself into a crouch, Craig was deafened by a ringing screech in his ears. He looked across at Matty, who was shouting something. No sound reached Craig.

"Go!" Matty's lips formed the word. "Go!"

As the ringing in his ears began to dissipate, he heard more thumps in the distance.

"Go!" he heard Matty screaming loud and clear. "Go!"

Sprinting through the grass, the pair heard a familiar high-pitched shriek as artillery rounds streaked down onto their position. The rounds slammed into the ground exploding between the two men with devastating effect.

Pain wracked Craig's body. It felt like he'd been in a cage fight. Groaning, he pushed himself off the ground, spitting dirt from his mouth as he moved into a crouch. Patting down his arms and legs, he checked for injury, but nothing seemed broken or bleeding. Spotting his M-4 nearby, he reached for it, checked it over before cradling it across his chest.

Matty lay prone nearby, motionless. With a grunt, Craig moved to him, squatted beside him and checked for a carotid pulse. With relief he felt a strong pulse and patted Matty's cheek.

"Hey mate," Craig muttered. Patting the skin of Matty's face Craig spoke again. "Oi! Matty, time to move mate."

There was no response.

"For fuck sake," Craig said, knowing time was of the essence. He was strong enough to drag Matty perhaps five hundred metres before being forced to rest and find concealment. That distance was not enough to clear the current area which would more than likely be crawling with Indonesian soldiers within the next hour.

Craig slapped Matty's face hard. "Oi, dickhead!"

This time there was a groan and slight movement in one leg.

Unceremoniously rolling Matty over, Craig slapped him again. "Wakey wakey," Craig said, casting a glance over Matty's body checking for obvious injury or haemorrhage.

More dull thumps reverberated in the distance.

"You're fuck'n joking!" snarled Craig.

Picking up Matty's weapon, he tucked the rifle into the unconscious man's chest webbing. Grabbing Matty under the arms, he dragged him as far as possible before the distant shriek indicated artillery rounds were inbound. Dumping Matty, Craig dived to ground, buried his face into the dirt and hoped for the best. The barrage fell slightly short of their position, exploding on and around where the Indonesian corpse had been.

When the last shell exploded, Craig slowly climbed to his feet, body still aching. Keeping as low a profile as possible, he dragged Matty away from the area. Three more artillery barrages hit, some close, others not so much, showing the enemy gunners were making small elevation changes to ensure maximum coverage. By the time night began to fall, Craig, now exhausted, had dragged Matty close to a kilometre out of the area and had found a small depression in the ground where he had chosen to lay low for the night.

Setting up a Claymore anti-personnel mine facing towards the most likely enemy approach, he kept the clacker, the device used to detonate the explosive, tied to his right hand. Inadvertent detonation was near impossible, as the clacker had a safety catch of sorts. The safety catch was easy enough to disengage with a single hand, meaning the mine could be fired within two seconds. Filled with seven hundred steel ball bearings embedded in composition explosive, the weapon was designed to injure and maim rather than kill. One wounded man required two others to carry him, effectively taking three soldiers out of the fight.

Should enemy stumble upon their position, seven hundred ball bearings would whistle through their ranks at knee height, before Craig opened fire. If the Indonesians did find his position, more than likely, Craig would be overrun and killed along with the unconscious Matty. But at least it would be a bittersweet victory for the Indonesians.

Eventually the artillery fire stopped. Before long, the sun slid below the horizon and dusk arrived, the light beginning to fade. Craig checked Matty every five minutes. He felt for a pulse, listened for breath sounds and while light remained, continued checking for any obvious sign of blood seeping through his clothes. He placed Matty in a lateral position so that if he vomited, at least it wouldn't compromise his airway.

He slung Matty's weapon across his back and shoved the unconscious man's spare ammunition into his own half full pouches, so that if a fire fight started, at least he'd have plenty of ammunition. Craig was conscious of the fact that he and Matty had been inserted on the understanding that they were to patrol out of the area themselves. No friendlies were looking for them. The Australian Blackhawks were no longer operational. They had been decimated within the opening weeks of the invasion. The Royal Marine choppers that had inserted the SASR patrol would be busy on other taskings, infilling, exfilling, resupplying or providing air support for Royal Marine Commandos or Special Boat Service (SBS) soldiers on the ground.

Craig found the first few hours easy to remain alert. The majority of the time, he stared through the night vision goggles, ever watchful for enemy movement. Every fifteen minutes he pushed the goggles up, away from his eyes, allowing a minute or two for his vision to rest, before lowering them back into place. Apart from the chirping crickets, the night was silent. A far cry from what Craig expected. No Indonesian soldiers had arrived to investigate.

Slowly crawling to the opposite side of the small depression, Craig watched. Every hour he changed position, moving between the four compass points around the circular depression in the ground. It was past midnight when he began rubber necking, exhaustion attempting to claim him. He had not experienced a decent night's sleep in more than three weeks. Craig lost the fight, cheek resting on his weapon, breathing softly as sleep embraced him. He did not hear the vehicles approach. Did not see the headlights in the near distance. It was the slamming of the car doors that broke Craig's slumber. He was immediately alert, adrenalin responsible for his fast response. He pushed the night vision goggles up and away from his eyes, instead using the night vision capability of his weapon mounted scope. He watched the Indonesian soldiers exiting a number of four wheel drives to swarm the area where the booby trapped corpse had been lying earlier in the day. No problem, he was close to one kilometre away, and at night it would be near impossible for them to track him.

His heart sank a second later when he heard dogs. A series of aggressive barks broke the still night. German Shepherd, he thought. A goddamn military dog.

"Fuck," he muttered to himself.

He hoped his track had gone cold by now and the dog was incapable of finding his scent, but anything was possible. Flicking the night vision goggles away from his eyes, Craig stared down the infrared scope of his weapon and settled the target reticule over the dog's body.

For close to ten minutes, he watched the animal seeking his scent without success. Happy that the dog was no longer a threat, Craig slowly swept the weapon's infrared scope across the gathering of Indonesian soldiers. They were all armed with military grade automatic weapons; most with their native SS1, which was the standard assault rifle of the Indonesian Army. Some, however, held the Steyr, used by the Australian Army. No doubt taken from dead Australian soldiers. A wave of anger warmed Craig. He counted the vehicles, seven in total, all four wheel drives, one of them a Land Rover. Thirty enemy soldiers in total, and one clueless dog. Craig smiled, allowing the target reticule to settle over the animal once more. It was not particularly well-trained. Over such a short distance, and regardless of the hours which had passed, any tracking dog worth its salt would have found his scent, faint as it may have been, and worked towards him .

The scent of a human was given by dead skin cells drifting from the body, and a good scent trail in perfect conditions with little wind, rain or snow, could remain in place for more than a week. If tracked by dogs, the most secure place was on high ground, particularly on the peak of a mountain, where the wind was more likely to change directions easily, move in obscure patterns and scatter a person's scent in random, un-trackable arrangements.

Craig had no such luxury. If the animal were testament to any true formal training, it would have made a bee-line straight to him. Thankfully, although it had obviously been given some informal instruction, the German Shepherd still had a long way to go before it would join the ranks of the true tracking dogs.

Sweeping the infrared scope across the Indonesians once more, Craig settled the target reticule over the chest of a man wearing a bandana and holding an SS1 across his chest, with a pistol holstered on his hip. He was the only man with a pistol, and was also the only soldier talking and gesticulating angrily at the others gathered around him in a half moon. The leader; the leader of any group of soldiers, whether it be a corporal or a general, was always discouraged from advertising their status, particularly out-bush, as they would always become the first target of a sniper team or a deliberate ambush.

There was a loud groan beside Craig and Matty rolled over.

"Fuck me dead," Matty said, holding his head.

Craig shot a glance at the soldier, "Welcome back, now shut the fuck up," he hissed.

Matty crawled up beside Craig. "What's goin' on?" he asked, still nursing his head.

Craig did not answer, instead returning his attention to the night vision scope attached to the top of his weapon. Staring down the scope he saw that the Indonesians, to a man, were all staring in his direction. The dog was barking and carrying on like it had rabies. Then a torch was turned on, and several enemy soldiers began walking towards them.

"Shit," whispered Craig. "It's on, mate."

It was at that point he realised Matty had slid down onto his back, holding his head and groaning.

"You right, mate?" Craig whispered, tapping Matty's shoulder.

"Yeah," he managed between groans. "Gotta killer headache."

Returning his attention to the weapon's night vision scope, Craig saw that the enemy had halted whilst the dog handler took a knee, wrestled with the barking animal for a moment and then released it from the leash.

The German Shepherd now had no need of scent trails. The dog was intelligent enough to marry up the sound of Matty's voice with the scent trail it was unable to find so recently. It zeroed in on the Australians' position, sprinting towards them.

Ignoring Matty as he rolled around groaning and muttering meaningless phrases, Craig settled the weapon's target reticule upon the dog's chest. The sooner he killed the animal, the greater the area the Indonesians would have to search in order to find the Australians. He knew from previous reconnaissance that none of the enemy were using night vision goggles, and if they had them, were probably now out of usable batteries.

Lying silent, continuing to ignore Matty, Craig waited and watched as the German Shepherd sprinted towards them. He willed the animal to veer away, to become confused and return to its master. He tried to avoid killing dogs where possible. But the animal made a bee-line straight towards him. Tongue lolling from the side of its mouth, the animal began barking in a staccato of noise, which was Craig's cue to fire the shot. There was no squeal or howl of pain. The dog simply dropped to the ground like a used doll. The dog's barking had hidden Craig's silenced weapon, and with the animal now dead, the Indonesians still had no idea exactly where their enemy lay.

Craig had no idea what the Indonesians were shouting, and thought better of asking Matty, who was now lying prone, still holding his head and snoring softly. Something was wrong, Craig knew instinctively. He had worked with Matty through operations in Kosovo, East Timor, The Sudan, Iraq and Afghanistan. Never had he seen him act like this.

AFTERMATH

The Indonesians retreated to the vehicle as more orders were shouted. A mortar tube and base plate were unloaded from the rear tray of the vehicle and setup within a matter of minutes. Then a mortar round was fired with a dull thunk, heading almost vertical. A loud pop was followed by daylight in a square kilometre area as the illumination round activated. Craig pushed his head closer to the ground and clenched his right eye firmly closed. If the night vision from his master eye was destroyed, he would be unable to use the night vision scope attached to his weapon.

"Happy new year!" roared Matty, now lying on his back, arms splayed out beside him. "What a light show! Give me a beer ya jack prick!"

Craig dived on top of him and pushed his hand over Matty's mouth.

"Shut the fuck up!" snarled Craig. "You wanna get us bloody killed?"

Matty muttered something, but the noise was rendered into a slurred mash of sound beneath the palm of Craig's hand.

Within minutes, Matty had rolled onto his side and deteriorated back into sleep, snoring softly. Craig knew something was very wrong. Ensuring the Indonesians were still confused as to their exact location, Craig took the time to send a text burst transmission via the PRC-112, a radio slightly larger than the size of a man's hand, requesting an immediate medical evac and air support. Almost three minutes passed before a secure text appeared on the radio's LCD display:

"Exfil your loc 5 mikes."

Five minutes until exfiltration. Craig silently berated himself for not requesting exfil hours before. However, in his defence, he had been told the British choppers were flying to the limit in support of Royal Marines and SBS troops on the ground in the area. Any requests, he had been instructed, would either be refused flatly or could take up to two hours to fulfil.

Five minutes to exfil. It did not sound long, but in current circumstances it would feel like an eternity. Craig still clamped his master eye shut against the bright illumination round fired by the mortar. He remained silent and still, praying that Matty continued to sleep. Now with the dog neutralised, apart from the faint splutter of the flare as it drifted towards earth, there was silence. One sound, one word uttered too loud would alert the Indonesians to their whereabouts.

He could hear them muttering amongst themselves. Peering through the blades of grass into which he had buried his face, Craig saw the Indonesians looking in all directions, still oblivious to his whereabouts. The dog handler was distraught, he noticed, feeling sorry for the soldier. Craig loved dogs, and hated killing them. Tonight had been the second time in his career he was forced to kill a dog in order to protect his patrol. The illumination round slowly faded out, the dark night once again closing in around them.

Matty was now lying supine, breathing loudly. Craig moved to him.

"Wake up, mate." He patted the man's face. "Matty, wake the fuck up!"

"You got that beer bro?" asked Matty, his speech slurred.

"No, mate, no beer," whispered Craig. "We're in the shit, we've been compromised. Air support and exfil are inbound. They're a few minutes out.

How you feeling?"

"Exfil?" Matty roared with laughter." What the fuck? What, are we playing Call of Duty? Wanker!" He laughed again. "Bring me a bloody beer!" he shouted.

The Indonesians were hissing amongst themselves and looking in Craig's direction. He left Matty giggling and muttering to himself on the far side of the depression. Lying prone and staring down the night vision scope attached to his weapon, Craig watched the enemy soldiers push out into extended line and advance toward his position. In the background, he saw the mortar team, consisting of two soldiers, preparing another round, more than likely a second illumination round. Now they knew the general direction in which the Australians were hidden, a second illumination round would kill all hope for Craig and Matty. They would be found and overrun in less than a minute.

Two dull thumps from Craig's silenced weapon and the two man mortar team were no more. The Indonesians, apart from three, went to ground and returned fire. Bullets hissed and cracked less than a metre above Craig's head. Ignoring the return fire, he settled the target reticule over the chest of the first of the three men still standing, firing un-aimed shots from the hip. Squeezing the trigger, Craig watched the man fall from sight. With the number of organs and vital arteries in the chest and upper abdomen, one bullet in or around the chest area could do so much damage. The second man dropped as fast as the first. The third soldier dived to the ground before Craig took a sight picture, although he released several shots into the long grass where he thought the soldier had landed.

Rounds slashed through thigh-length grass metres from Craig, or snapped above their position. He remained prone, holding his fire, allowing the enemy to deplete their ammunition. One Indonesian stood and ran forward. Reacting in less than a second, Craig took a sight picture and fired, the bullet passing through the man's intestines and exited his back in a bloody swath. He fell to the ground howling in agony.

Feeling the PRC-112 buzz in his trouser pocket, Craig pulled the device out and read the infrared screen.

"Spectre 3 inbound, 1 mike out, mark friendlies."

The AC-130, or affectionately known as the Spectre gunship, was a heavily modified C-130 Hercules, a heavy-lift aircraft operated by the United States Air Force. Along the left side of the aircraft were two 20mm cannons, one 40mm cannon and one 105mm Howitzer artillery gun. The pilot wanted Craig's position marked so that his crew would not inadvertently fire upon him.

Opening a pouch and keeping his head down as enemy fire continued to rip through the air metres above him, Craig pulled out an infrared strobe, activated it and tied it to the back of his webbing. Thus, lying prone, the strobe would be facing skyward, flashing an infrared pulse twice per second.

"Friendlies marked."

AFTERMATH

A moment later, the infrared LCD of the PRC-112 displayed the pilot's response, which consisted of two words. Two words which brought relief to any patrol in the middle of nowhere, outnumbered and in the shit:

"Danger close."

Although the enemy fire was loud, Craig still heard the soft rumble of the Spectre gunship high above him. The pilot would begin a left pylon turn, bringing all the aircraft's guns to bear upon the Indonesian position.

Trace seemed to streak out of thin air 5,000ft above him, followed closely by the roar of the 40mm cannon, sounding like the deep howl of some enraged dinosaur. The rounds hammered into the Indonesians. Craig felt the thump of massive bullets smashing into the ground.

"What a bloody light show!" Matty roared with laughter, splayed out on his back again, watching another long stream of trace rounds pouring from the AC-130 towards the enemy position below.

The Indonesian fire had mostly stopped, although some must still have been alive as the Spectre gunship continued its destruction. A bright flash from the sky destroyed Craig's night vision. The boom of the 105mm gun followed a second later but was quickly overshadowed by the ever increasing screech as the artillery round descended towards earth, on target for the enemy position. Exploding with deadly efficiency, chunks of earth rained down around the Australians.

Apart from the distant hum of the AC-130 high above them, the area was silent. Craig ensured the infrared strobe was still securely fastened to his back before crawling forward. Staring through his weapon's night vision scope, all he saw was the empty enemy vehicles parked several hundred metres away. Knowing that their engines would now be cool, he was not sure the gun crew of the AC-130 would be able to see the four wheel drives.

Attached to the barrel of Craig's weapon was a small rectangular infrared laser pointer. The device was used for indicating an enemy position to close air support assets that may have overlooked a particular area.

Lying still, he lased the middle vehicle and waited. Close to ten seconds later, the mighty 40mm gun spoke again, explosive rounds hammering through the vehicle and turning it into a piece of scrap metal. Flicking the laser off, Craig allowed his night vision to recover. Minutes later, he stared down the scope. Two vehicles were destroyed completely; the remaining pair seemed relatively unscathed. Lasing the furthest vehicle, Craig waited half as long before the 40mm opened up again, rounds slamming through the remaining vehicles with violent ferocity, rendering them useless.

Matty was breathing noisily, although not quite snoring. It sounded more like his tongue had relaxed back in his throat. Craig moved to him and rolled him onto his side, which seemed to help. Something was wrong and the more time passed, the greater confidence he felt calling for a medivac was the correct decision. Craig crawled back to the rim of the depression in the ground and stared down the night vision scope towards the former enemy position. Nothing moved. The vehicles were decimated; one of them was alight, the hiss and pop of melting paint, upholstery and rubber echoed gently out over the silent plain.

His concentration was so deep that Craig barely heard the helicopter approach until it was slowing and descending less than twenty metres from his position. Even before the chopper touched the ground, a medic and two soldiers were running towards him carrying a stretcher between them. Noise, time and situation precluded any thorough questioning as to the events which had occurred. Matty was simply lifted onto the stretcher, the medic tapped Craig's shoulder and then they were running back towards the helicopter.

"Fuck me!" shouted Craig as he climbed aboard, the scream of the chopper's engine deafening him.

A headset was pushed into his hand. Taking off his combat helmet, he promptly placed the headset over his ears, inhaling a breath of relief as the noise was dampened. With the helicopter on strict blackout, Craig used his weapon's night vision scope to look for, find and ensure that Matty too was wearing a headset. He was. Unconscious or not, the last thing he needed was permanent hearing damage. The stretcher was strapped to the floor of the helicopter with Matty buckled to the stretcher.

Noticing a cord attached to the headset, Craig followed it with his fingers until he found a communication plug. All he needed to find was the comms jack into which to plug it. A firm hand grasped his shoulder, probably one of the loadmasters, who had night vision goggles attached to their helmets. The load master grabbed the jack out of Craig's hand and following a half second burst of high pitched sound, he was listening to the crew's conversation.

"—I hear you, just not sure," said the American voice. "That dude got comms yet?"

"Roger that," said another voice. "Hey pal," said the same voice. A hand tapped Craig's shoulder. "Pal, you gonna need to fold the boom mic down in front of your mouth. "

Craig found the mic and pulled it down to his lips. Following the comms cord with one hand, he found the small box. Pressing the transmit button, Craig said, "Thanks for the exfil."

"You're welcome, guy," the broad American voice said, which was probably the aircraft captain. "I'm in contact with the Spectre. They've spotted an artillery battery off to the west. That one of yours?"

"No, mate, not ours," replied Craig. "They're the fuckers responsible for this whole mess!"

"Roger," said the pilot.

Feeling the seat straps dig into his shoulders and belly, the chopper banked hard away from the exfiltration area. In the far distance, Craig saw the faint, flickering outline of the AC-130 Spectre gunship as every gun on board opened fire upon the Indonesian artillery battery below. The Indonesians had no chance of survival. They had nowhere to run and nowhere to hide. He almost felt sorry for them. Almost.

"How's Matty doin'?" he asked.

"Is that his name, hun?" it was a woman's voice.

"Yeah."

"Matty's not in a good way," she sounded distracted or busy and probably was, he realised.

AFTERMATH

"Okay," Craig replied, trying to sound calm. "Will he be alright?"

There was no reply. Craig felt anger and fear welling in his chest, although he remained silent. The chopper descended violently and turned hard to the left, before levelling out. Craig brought his weapon to bear and looked through the night vision scope to see treetops whipping by close beneath them.

Christ, don't hit a power line, he thought.

"Will he be alright or not?" Craig asked.

"Look hun, I don't know. He's got a dilated right pupil and weak grips on his left hand. He has diminished consciousness. I'm suspecting he's haemorrhaging on the right side of his brain. He'll need a CT scan and possibly burr holes drilled into his skull. I won't lie to you. He can survive this, but it's gonna be a close call."

Craig didn't say anything. He knew it had the potential of being serious, but he now realised the situation was critical. He might lose a brother tonight. He felt numb, unaware of the seat belts digging into his body as the chopper turned. He was oblivious to the door gunners calling out fast approaching structures, trees or power lines over the intercom and was clueless as those same obstacles whipped by only metres beneath them. Everything seemed to be a blur.

The dull impact as the chopper touched down upon the deck of USS Ronald Reagan brought Craig out of his reverie. To the east, the sky glowed a faint gunmetal grey, silhouetting the mighty aircraft carrier. Before the pilot began the shutdown procedure, the medics had carried Matty's stretcher clear of the aircraft and were running. Unstrapping, Craig unplugged his headset, pushed himself clear of the chopper and sprinted after them. One of the door gunners tried to stop him, but he broke free of the grip.